Contents

To Bill

Washing the Dead

Washing the Dead – 1921

In the unheated house, Ellen screws up paper and stuffs it into the black range. Her candle flickers and the world shifts, metamorphic and chancy. Some mornings, when it is less cold, she might pause in her lighting of the fire, arrested by a headline or paragraph that she skim-reads, mouthing words she will scrumple and burn: *unemployment rises*, *child drowns in the docks*, *double life of a bigamist*. In it goes: the city's history; poor and rich, weak and strong, all jammed together.

Inevitably, the stories she does not fully read are those that most haunt, the ones she wishes she'd kept. Today, Ellen balances twigs on the unread newspaper – beech wood with a dusting of moss. In the garden, more branches are stacked, and logs too, carried home from country walks. She is lucky to have coal this month, a present from a man she works for, an engineer in the Kinsgswood mine.

The boys have told their mother that they've hacked the coal into manageable lumps, but this batch could do with being hammered again; they are not as willing to help as they once were, especially when it's coal from the engineer. Ellen frowns, chooses the smaller pieces, balancing the shiny blackness over crumpled paper and wood. She likes that this is the shored-up past, a compacted energy she will never quite understand.

If she doesn't exactly enjoy these early risings, Ellen doesn't hate them either. Between night and day lies a stillness where the worst of life, its troublesome hauntings, can be shaken out, as a tablecloth of crumbs. In the gloom, Ellen imagines her embroidered cloth fluttering and thinks of tall ships and paddle steamers in the river, some from Ireland, all of them navigating hidden channels, creeping up with the tide, then listing as the water flows back. Beneath that narrow gorge, the coal seam probably stretches: from Ireland, across to Wales, slipping back into Bristol and deep into Somerset – an invisible line.

It is 6.00 am. Later, Ellen's three healthy sons will stumble down for water heated on the stove; they'll peck her cheek and go back up to wash. She is grateful for small things: that the boys were too young to fight; that by the time Lawrence had enlisted it was all over. She is grateful too, that, unlike their father, the boys don't drink away their earnings. And most of all, she is thankful that out of the eight births, only one child is dead. She crosses herself and hopes that God doesn't enquire too deeply of her piety.

Sometimes Ellen squints into the city sky and sees death everywhere – the ravens fluttering back, their spread of black wings like a cloud of war and illness. She has heard that in the Dings the measles is spreading. Pressed close in damp rooms, it is not surprising people get sick. Once or twice she has been asked to work in the slums, but she always refuses. Tells herself the place is not quite safe but, in reality, she is afraid of glimpsing a mirror life, the self she yet could be.

After she has lit the paper, has held her hands before the yellow flickering, has taken in the music of cracking wood and shifting coal, Ellen wipes herself on a cloth. Outside, the darkness thins and a pale moon dances over the warped windowpane. The shadows flutter and follow across the floor as she opens the scullery door onto crisp coldness, an earthy smell, as if someone has been digging through the thick, long night. Ice, as usual, has frozen on the inside of the window, forming its lace tracery, an architectural puzzle. If she could better draw or write, she would mimic the filigree patterns, the light shifting over the spider's web of ice. But she has no skills to get down what lives in her head; she cannot hold ideas from one day to the next. How is it that she is newly surprised when, in autumn, along with the ice, the damp smell reappears – as regular and as unsettling as those visits of Connor?

Last time her husband turned up, he told her how he had missed the neat kitchen: the flagged floor, painted shelves, the hissing tap and stone sink. He stood on a chair and carefully replaced the floral teapot on the top shelf, next to the fragile bone china. The teapot had been their wedding present and Ellen's half sister had taken it when she'd left: *She'd steal anything*, Ellen said as Connor climbed down.

Perhaps it's no more than a borrowing, Connor replied, not turning to look, but offering some sort of veiled promise.

Below the best porcelain sits the dowdy brown teapot and the white china Ellen now prefers. She takes the plates and lays them on the side-table next to the butter in its glass dish, the loaf squatting on the carved board. The bread is brown and homemade; the baker lets her use his oven, and for this favour she washes and starches his thick apron and, because he is kind, he loops her into more favours she must repay – sends back white bread, sometimes cake.

Last time Connor came courting his children, bringing shoes from the factory in Cork. One week spread into two and three and Ellen's life re-formed, shaping itself into something it had once been. And then the telegram; his scramble of clothes into a leather bag, the dash for the ferry. And Ellen has not glimpsed him these last four years, although he once visited her father. Even the telegram she recently sent has not brought him back – and hers was not packed with lies.

Once the kettle has been filled and placed on the living room stove, she returns to the copper, thinking about the incompatible, the melt of its touch. She is careful not to douse herself with the water fizzing from the brass tap while she pours bucket after bucket into the copper vessel.

9

After each libation she makes a wish, just as she instructs the children to do as they stir and mix the Christmas pudding. Surely it cannot hurt to dream of Connor?

For a while, when Ellen was young, and after her mother had died, she was sent to Sunday School. While the sermon rumbled on in the church where her father sat, she was dispatched to the drafty hall, where the teacher, troubled by nerves, read stories in a wistful voice: Noah and the flood, people drowning, the Red Sea parting. And many times the teacher told of Abraham and Sarah and how the servant girl, Hagar, was sent into the wilderness, carrying her child – banished there by the jealous wife. Once, as the children took their break and the teacher poured elderflower cordial, letting it fill to the glass brim and flow over the top, she asked Ellen if it was wrong these days, to take an eye for an eye? The Old Testament, she confided, seemed more straightforward than the New. Ellen remembers how she pressed her own hands to her face, as if to stem the drowning talk, while the liquid flooded across the table, cascaded over the sides and puddled onto the quarry-tiled floor.

Later, after others had cleared up the mess and given the teacher sweet, whisky smelling tea, the children sat again cross-legged, each with a homemade biscuit. The teacher stared at the twelve of them, as if surprised they were eating her biscuits and then fluttered on, into stories of Greek myths, flights to heaven and back, telling of too many dead children. She told of *The Mabinogion* and jealousy and punishment, swans and improbable couplings, gods no better than men. Ellen thinks that if she could shape her own religion, it would be of the teacher's strange faith, stirred up with sad blue eyes, pretty dresses and a curl of crochet that the woman went at, as if stitching and stories were a cure for death.

Yet for all their importance, Ellen now struggles to

disentangle the half-remembered tales; there is a jumbled bag of words, a residue of ghosts and spells that she shakes out and offers to her own children. She is certain that this is why most of them: Lawrence, Lilly – even James – can read so well, why the youngest girl, Anne, is quick at Board School, why Lil talks of the Central Library and the books she will borrow.

When the copper is finally full, and the tin bucket back on its hook, the vat is ready to have its fire lit. But this will happen later. Meanwhile, Ellen wipes the large table, flicks over a tablecloth and watches the whiteness and starched cleanliness unfurl and settle. She is humming a wispy tune, but cuts the ragged noise short. Why was she not more attentive? She could have set about a music hall song, and instead she has bumbled into this hymn that conjures her child's death. She stands a moment, takes a deep breath and pushes away the face that comes to her, smiling and laughing, clouded when impatient. *Keep working*, she tells herself. *Don't think. Keep your mouth closed against the hurt.*

She has filled the copper, not because she needs to – the boys would do it – rather because it seams her into a day of activity. Wheeling the pram with its squeaky brake, piled with people's white sheets, with bundles of clothes that she will wash and starch, is a thing to keep her sane. Making the world clean and newborn – this is medicine. What else is there to do, but forge the day, thin life's pain?

Lil is already tiptoeing around upstairs, leaving the younger ones, Martha, Anne and little Fanny, to sleep. Lil will soon be down to make porridge and slice bread for her brothers' sandwiches before she sets off for the factory. A few weeks ago she had come home, dumping the shopping on the table and said she'd had enough of looking after children; she couldn't take it any more. Then she had walked up to Fry's, where her friend already worked. She has delicate hands and is clean, they've told her, and her work is careful. In a year, Lil might go into the hand-made

11

section, where the nicer sort of girls work.

Martha, as the second daughter, might be expected to help, but Martha is the princess. The family carries her story; their own strange and tangled myth. The long labour, the cord wrapped around her throat. Then, when she'd fought off death for the first time, him paying her back with coughs and fits, fevers and disease, so that, even when she was seven months – and Connor had once again packed his bags – the blonde scrap was more bronchitis than baby, coughing and coughing, yet laughing too, as if she liked this game with black-cloaked death. *Don't be so cock-sure*, Ellen whispered. *My mother was like you, and Death got her when her back was turned; fording the icy river, he sucked her down in a second.*

Later, when the child got influenza, Ellen nursed her; and Lil, though only seven, was mother to the boys. There was no affording a doctor and no family to help. Ellen's half sister had been living in Bristol, but the two had argued and Eve had disappeared, in the same predictable way as Connor. When the baby finally went limp – just when they'd thought she was safe – Ellen went on with the nursing and the rocking, the dripping of milk between cracked lips, the breathing of breath into the collapsed lungs.

The wind howled like the music to Ellen's grief, and the curtains lifted and fell as death rushed in and out, impatient for his child. And then Martha's pulse faded to nothing and Ellen laid her before the stove – its doors wide open, flames licking – constantly checking the bundle had not turned grey; for she knew the look of flu death. She burned more coal than they could spare, refused to believe she'd lost her curly-haired favourite. What was it all for, she asked herself: the effort and the love? And if God did this to her precious child, wasn't she better off worshipping the moon and stars, the gods of revenge and metamorphosis?

She sat until dark, aware of the children doing

something in the scullery: bringing her bread, lighting the lamp, putting coal on the fire, whispering. It was raining outside, the pattering on the scullery roof tapping strange syncopated rhythms while the darkness pressed in. Still no sign of life, no breath from the baby's dry lips, no pulse from throat or wrist. It was then that Ellen heard the voice: *It is time.* It meant, for sure, that she should lay out the body, tend it as she did those other corpses she was paid to prepare: warm water, scented herbs, soap. She placed the baby on the low nursing chair – wooden with a stick back and deep cushion – and poured water from the kettle into the tin bath she had fetched. She picked the bundle up, its skin as white as the knitted woollen outfit, undid the buttons and slipped the clothes off, sponging the cool white flesh and laying the slack torso on a cloth between her legs. At her back the younger boys squashed in at the scullery doorway, crying. Along two of the walls, racks of clothes were hung over the airer; she had brought all the laundry in, so the warmth of the fire was not wasted. The children should have been in bed, but they knew what the smell meant; they had accompanied her plenty of times, huddled in a corner in the homes of the bereaved.

Ellen does not know if the heat of the fire roused the lifeless baby or her rambling prayers, or perhaps it was the jolt the corpse was given. For at that moment Lil came barging across, crying that she must not wash the baby and make it dead. And that was when their world cracked open and Ellen felt a fragile trembling from the pulse at the naked baby's neck. A butterfly flutter. In one movement, she had pushed Lil away, swept a shawl from her shoulders and bound the baby in warmth, bringing the bundle to her mouth to huff and breathe the thing to life. And this is the miracle, the charm that coats the second daughter. The story they all re-tell, like she is their own Snow White.

But there is, of course, more than one type of 'special'. And Ellen sometimes wonders if she has paid for cheating death by being given her last child, special in that other way, born when she was too old, before her husband left for the third and final time; special Bonnie with his almond eyes and simple ways, their other unintelligible myth.

'Are you taking washing in today, Ma?' Lil stands at the door, buttoning up her boots, hair draped over her shoulder.

'I'm going out to clean, and there's a body to do, too. A note left in the night – one of the houses on City Road, the place your father did work for – made those pretty laced shoes, the children's ones.' She sees Lil's expression. 'It's all right – it's not a child that's dead: the note says the governess; the old spinster they kept, that was half deaf and did the garden.'

'So you'll need something, too?'

'If there's enough bread. Do the rest of you first. They'll probably give me a glass of milk.'

'Remember how I took those shoes? How Pa danced me around the kitchen when I came back saying they wanted a second pair?'

'He was drunk, and only two in the afternoon.'

'They brought a glass of milk on a tray; let me sit in the cool and drink, and the place echoed, like everything there was important.'

'What our Martha wants. That's the sort of grand house she might get some day, if she keeps her looks and voice – or if Connor sends her money.'

'She'll get the house, all right – only she'll be on her hands and knees cleaning it, and if she daydreams, it'll be a cuff around the ear.'

'Have some bread while you do the porridge, and don't be mean. She'll face the world soon enough. Let Martha dream.'

*

14

It takes courage to face the day. As the darkness thins, outlines emerge: earth, bricks, chimneys, dirt and hurt. But also, in her pocket-handkerchief garden: rosemary, thyme, lovage and buckler leaf sorrel. And against the redbrick wall, sweet peas in summer. Runner beans often scramble beside them, and in pots are the rhubarb, raspberry and currant bushes. All this growing keeps at bay the words and sometimes even the thoughts.

Sussex Place may be respectable: grand houses down the road, country-side, neat terraces, rooms rented out, but whoever you are – in Bristol, or elsewhere – people unpick you with gossip, and if not with that, then with the pity. The talk rattled on long after her husband left the first time, filling up the decent silence, whoring away in the shadows. Ellen still pulls her head up high and acts dignified – wears gloves and a smart hat with an expensive hat pin – just as though she hasn't been deceived, didn't walk in on her husband and half sister. She'd only let Evie stay so the girl could get work; but whatever mess had happened in Frome happened here too and she wishes her stepmother hadn't asked the favour. She wonders why she feels such shame when the guilt belongs elsewhere. And her deformed baby sent like a sign: too old to be having sex; too old to keep her man.

Turning into a busy street, after Ellen has seen Anne and Fanny to school, Martha appears. The child's figure is curvy, her face like her father's: elfin charm and green, sharp eyes. She has his sing-song voice, his delicate way of moving.

'Shall I walk with you, Ma?'

'You're late, girl. They'll give you the strap at school.'

'Not me, Ma. They know about our trouble. And, anyway, Old Crusty likes me.' Martha links her arm with her mother's, squeezes it and gives a wave to the woman in the vegetable shop, a place where she sometimes helps.

15

They both look across the street at the slight woman hauling sacks out to the front of a shop where carrots, turnips and potatoes are piled in a cheerless display. Ellen sighs. In her mind, like the Day of Judgement, she resurrects the men dead from the war and slots them back in their rightful places, manning the trams, hauling coal, carrying the heavy potatoes. When she brings her mother to life, she is unsure whether to kiss her or push her back under the water.

Ellen turns to her daughter. 'It's hard work for the women – with so many husbands and sons dead. So little money.'

'Sometimes it's hard whether they're dead or not.'

Ellen releases her daughter's arm. 'For me or for you?'

'For us both. He's wrote me a note. Sent it next door again. Says he's sorry about the death and might I go over to Cork and help Evie with baby Susan – now there isn't a child here to mind. Says he could find me places to sing.'

Ellen walks on, adjusting the cuffs of her jacket, holding her head high. Martha follows as Ellen turns down to the bigger houses on City Road.

'And will you leave me, too?' Ellen whispers at the carriages and carts rumbling down the street, the people rushing, cloche hats pulled down, coats buttoned up. There is no point in words sometimes. Better to keep things hidden, use words for the practical. She turns as her daughter catches up. 'On the way home, hang around by the Co-operative. They'll give you butter again, if you smile right.'

At the corner of the street a group of men lounge, some smoking. Each day, labour is hired on the docks and those who do not get work spill back into the city streets and pubs. It is good that the boys have apprenticeships but she worries that no employment is certain and even spring is late coming. Martha kisses her mother's cheek and slips down the alleyway to the school, running across the empty playground. For some reason, Ellen remembers that telegram from Ireland and Connor's face as he read it: *Evie dying. Come immediately.* There are some fictions that are pure evil, she thinks. Mostly, you can make life happen by imagining, can make it dignified by working, but sometimes, the devil stains the effort. These days, she frequently thinks of Sarah and Abraham; she has sent Eve off to the wilderness so often she is bored of retribution.

The house is three-storied and grand, a detached affair, built early in Victoria's reign. Ellen would have liked a peek inside the hallway, where chandeliers glow out whenever she walks past late. But she knows better than to knock at the stately front door with its columned porch and instead follows a meandering path past flowerbeds, trees and urns. She gives a quick look around, then snaps off one or two twigs from the camellia. The wrong time for cuttings, but just as death is unpredictable, so is life. She slides around to the back entrance, tapping quietly because it is early and the family may not be up. Within seconds, the door opens, as if someone had been watching, and a woman she vaguely recognises ushers her in. The accent is Irish, a soft patterning of sound that reminds her of her husband.

'Come in, my dear; she's in the back room, up on the table, ready. We were hoping that you'd get here before she was all stiffed up.'

'I came as soon as I could.'

'They spoke well of you in the Post Office; said you'd do a good job, and not cost much. She's no folks that we can find.'

Ellen follows the servant down a corridor, past a warren of rooms: store rooms, small sitting rooms, then a large kitchen, with a young girl chopping and stirring spicy things. Ellen nods her head and is surprised when the girl gives her a curtsey, like she is Somebody.

'I'm sorry for your loss, Missis.' For a moment Ellen

thinks there is some confusion, and is about to explain that she is no relative to this governess, when the girl casts a quick look at the other servant, and this woman also speaks to Ellen.

'It's hard to lose a child.'

Ellen stands there, in the large kitchen with the smell of mixed spice stirring up her despair and, for the first time in two weeks, she cannot manage the pretence. For two unbearable weeks she has found proper words to speak to her children, to the neighbours and to the priest; she has described how the measles made Bonnie weaker, how she sat with him on her lap and sang to shush his moods. And now, here in this kitchen she's been ambushed and undone. Her mind swells with images of her last child, his floppy fringe and shy smile and big head, his slow understanding. And Lily playing with him. Lily who did not blame the child, as she did, for being the last betrayal of a husband who came back and stayed only three weeks. She feels herself lightheaded and grips the side of the table, knowing that the sense and air and colour have utterly drained from her.

'Here, have a seat, love. Clara, get the lady a glass of cooking sherry and a piece of the best cake.'

They sit her down at the scrubbed pine table and make her drink and eat, though she feels sick and wants to work, wants to allay the stiffening of that dead body and along with it, her own self.

'But it won't hurt to rest a while, Missus. Sit and I'll warm up the water, get some flannels and lay out Florrie's clothes. She wanted her best – but told me I could have the garnet; it's still on her finger.'

Ellen nods, used to these accommodations and bits of opportunism. She grips the table and downs the only alcohol she's ever taken, drinking in something of the house with it – its silences and hierarchies; its calm.

*

Later, shut in with the body, that has more sense than the other servants and does nothing to vex her, she remembers how the owners (who she can hear moving in other parts of the creaking house) are Quakers. Decent people who give to the school. Ellen wonders if the cook tells them they take sherry in the cake. She looks around the simple staff living room, dimmed by the shut curtains – low green armchairs, small bookcase and table in the corner with a baize cover. This is where the live-in servants spend their time. On a side-table lies some crochet and knitting, a bundle of stitching that perhaps belonged to the governess. Maybe someone else will finish this work and the pale coloured purl will be stitched into the fabric of another life.

The body waits on a table pushed along one wall. She is not young, and this Ellen expects, but she is taller than most. Ellen's fingers are shaky as she sets about her work, hoping she can forget Bonnie, forget her child. She catches hold of the long, grey hair dangling around the woman's shoulders and twists it out of the way so it pools, then flows over the table's smooth edge. The body is lying on a blanket, clothed and covered with a white sheet. When she carefully undresses it, the limbs resistant, she exposes a long neck, slack breasts, old stretch marks across the woman's stomach. Sometimes Ellen is upset by her job; other times she sees it as a calling, an act of decency and respect that she, who communes so well with the dead, is well-placed to do. When the woman is naked and lying on her back, Ellen gently closes the startled blue eyes.

'You do not have to watch me, Florrie: I will guard your secret.'

The governess has loose skin, except for the arms, where muscles pad them out. At the woman's throat and across her forearms are bands of darkened skin, weathered from working in the garden, the acre that spills some of its flowers and seeds into the street, into other lives.

Ellen feels the dead woman's distress and hushes her as

she might a baby, telling the body that she is used to nakedness, that there is no shame in being washed for death. Whatever the illness has been, it must have been gnawing a while, for the body is hollowed and easy to move. Ellen has no need to call for help when it is time to turn Florrie over and then turn her back again.

Resting a cushion under the woman's chin to keep the jaw shut and stop the facial muscles stretching, Ellen dabs Vaseline on the drying lips. With the grease still on her fingers, she rubs at the swollen finger joints, then slides the pretty ring off and places it in a glass bowl on the sideboard. She looks at it lying there, wondering if it was a present from someone dead in the war and whether it matters that the cook will inherit. There are too many widows and too many spinsters now: plenty of spare wedding and engagement rings in the pawnshops. A bad time for a nice-looking man like her husband, who had never been good at saying no, even before her half sister came along. At least the war has made Ellen's situation normal – single women flock the city like starlings.

The first job is to plug the orifices, then she settles into the business of washing with the scented cloths. Ellen massages the body with a tenderness she hopes the spirit feels and accepts. As her hands trace bones and muscle and knots in the body's frame, she intuits the stories embedded and the stories yet to be told. Holding the dead, Ellen feels their potential and has a sense of lives being offered up, as if she is the receptacle for everything people have been and still might be.

Sometimes it is a burden, she thinks, as she silently smoothes and tends the skin, that the dead must insist on speaking. But when she tried to explain to Father O'Ryan, after Mass one day, she could tell that he thought it witchcraft and told her that perhaps she should stay away from bodies for a while and come to church more often. She knew he thought her an imperfect sort of Catholic, converting because of marriage, and she did not bother to say that there was no other time to come but Sunday Mass, that she had a large family, took in washing and saw to the blind woman who lived two doors down. Bring everyone with you, the stupid man would have said, but she forgave him his ignorance for he was young and unhappy – she could see that – and so far away from the fields of Ireland.

Ellen sits by the side of the body longer than normal, although she knows there is laundry to collect and sheets to get on the line for a blow. But she feels that the governess has something to tell, so Ellen presses her ear close to the bones of the woman's neck, running like tracks down to her breast-bone. All these stories, the woman says. Who will tell them, if not you? Could you not learn to write more than a list, for what will happen when you die and we die again? Ellen considers this, as she threads a flyaway strand of the woman's hair around and around her finger.

'And what of Bonnie?' Ellen whispers back. Her poor dead child that she has washed and buried only weeks before. Who would tell the truth – that he was more than a husband's poisoned gift?

And so it is here, sitting by the governess that Ellen decides how the stories will come about. She speaks softly so the people in the kitchen do not think her odd.

'It's true,' she tells the dead woman. 'True that the dead can live again. But when they visit, the story gets jumbled. Is it my version, or theirs, you want? Or perhaps I must learn to lie.'

In the kitchen, the voices grow louder and breakfast dishes are washed with a clattering and splashing of water. The women shout to one another over the noise as they open and close cupboard doors, chop vegetables.

'It should be a modest lunch,' says one. 'Given the circumstances.'

'Do we feed the woman washing Florrie?' the other

21

asks in a more hushed voice.

'She won't stay. Not when she's been touching the dead.'

Ellen thinks of Connor, Sarah and Abraham – all our vexed and troubled lives. The greasy smell of frying sausages creeps under the door and the weighing scales make a *clunk, clunking*.

'You're spilling the flour,' a voice snaps and the strained words hold all the disorder of the day, its adjustment and grief.

Ellen imagines eggs cracking, perfect yolks gliding into the basin, milk poured from a jug to beat into yellow batter. And inside her, held in suspension, are all those fractured stories; her own tumour eating away. She thinks of the garden outside: a rich mulch of leaves piled beneath the laurel, caterpillars cocooned in sticky pockets and amongst the curled leaves of the cyclamen, ladybirds biding their time. When spring finally breaks, someone else will tend Florrie's garden and Martha may be across in Cork. Who knows what will grow and what wither? Ellen imagines her unspilled words flying from the garden, a release of moths, burning past the magnolia, bypassing the church and fluttering up to the waxy moon. Once they were gone, would there be ease, and was that, anyway, what the world wanted?

When the body is neat and clean, dressed in an unfashionable tight-waisted dress that covers the weathered skin and birth marks, Ellen pats the woman's hand.

'Who am I to judge? We are all scarred in our ways.'

She takes the pennies from her pocket and places them on the woman's closed lids, a strange sort of benediction. Then she picks up the crochet, the colour of moon-light, and places it in her own bag, not sure if this is theft, or a gift from beyond the grave.

Holes – 1951

Early evenings, sitting with a beer and newspaper in the lean-to, the tacked-on affair beyond the kitchen, Sam had become good at ignoring the cold. He sipped his stout and read of landslides, floods in Kansas, casualties in Korea. He didn't want to know that Clement Atlee, whom he'd voted for, was the reason the economy floundered. Life was problematic enough. Whenever he glanced up, he could see out of the rounded windows his manicured – and slightly distorted – garden, and also that of his neighbour. Sometimes her unkempt trees and bushes annoyed him; other times they seemed an enviable wilderness – a world that demanded nothing of him. He folded the paper and rested it on the stool, then stared into the dark liquid.

When he looked up again, it wasn't a surprise to see a shadowy figure. The person's arms rested on the dividing stone wall, gazing into his garden, as if assessing the neat summer crop: runner beans, peas, broad beans, carrots, potatoes, strawberries and rhubarb. He handed his neighbour the surplus, so perhaps it was in her interest to monitor growth, to watch out for the slugs, the feral cats. What was less easy to gauge, was the damage that lay hidden: the slow erosion of eel-worm, club-root beneath the surface, the tight regrets and secrets. Chemicals controlled the weeds, but he could think of nothing forensic enough to uncover what Beth might choose to hide.

There were many nights Sam thought of her, when he wasn't worrying about his wife, rationing, paying bills, reflecting on the troubling miracle of four young children. Sometimes he imagined digging his fertile loam, only to discover that everything good had gone. Often he dreamed of deserts and dry fields, of cataclysmic climate change, himself alone and hungry, and Beth a phantom of his imagination.

When he came out into the dusk, where bats flitted and veered like drunken birds, he carried a brown cardigan so that Beth could drape it around her. The dog followed, nosing into the bushes and long grass.

'Thanks, Sam. What would I do without you?' She dragged hard on a cigarette. Perhaps the cigarette was the reason she'd come out, or perhaps she was there knowing he'd join her. The next minute she'd tossed the half-smoked thing to the ground, grinding the stub with her toe. He wondered if she was wearing her black or red heels. 'It always tastes bitter. A useful sort of reminder.'

'What does he think you do out here, if not smoke?'

'He doesn't think. Anyway, he's off to the Conservative club. Didn't much like the supper I made – an onion tart from my new Mediterranean book.'

'I'm not surprised.' Sam waved away the cigarette she offered. 'Doesn't he find the stubs?'

'I say they're yours.'

'I don't smoke.'

'I say you have secrets.'

She was his cousin and had married the man he worked for in the garage. Once Sam had thought Arthur was someone you could admire, aspire to be like. He was older and good with money. Saving for a house in the country. But now that Sam lived next door and viewed Arthur through Beth's eyes, he had re-assessed; he thought the man narrow and selfish, someone who lacked ambition. If Sam had pushed further, he might have said that Arthur was conventional and cared too much about appearances. But then Sam would have had to conclude that this was his own limitation. If he had thought less about gossip and other people, everything might be different. He often wondered if it still could be.

They were resting on the dividing stone wall that, with

its pennant stones, came to chest height. This was where they talked, he by his vegetable patch, she under one of the stunted apple trees that had once belonged to an orchard or farm. If you dug deep, the land would turn up Roman pots and Medieval tiles, but he doubted that, in the future, anyone would know of these cousins co-joined, the wall their boundary. In his own house, the lights splashed out in a wasteful sort of way. When Fanny, his wife, moved from room to room, folding the washing, clearing up after the boys, polishing the furniture, it was as if she chased away shadow, but to him, who had also grown up with candles and gas lights, hers seemed a cold sort of brightness, brittle and contourless.

'How's Fanny?' His cousin followed his gaze, looking back at the joined houses, one in darkness, the other spilling light.

'Much the same. The boys exhaust her. She takes to bed. Says she wishes she'd never left that job in Somerset. I suppose that means she wishes she'd never met me. I'm lucky to get any dinner.'

Sam knew he sounded peevish, that in a minute his cousin would tell him to be kinder to his wife and that he was too much of a bully, too strong a character for the slight and delicate girl he'd got himself. So he added, hoping to risk something and soften things between them, 'She says I should have married you. When you and I are together, I'm a different person.'

He looked up into Beth's hazel eyes, evasive and shadowy in the evening light. She was not beautiful, but she was strong and self-possessed. When they had been children, because she was a year or two older, she had dominated. But once he was into adolescence, he had gained the upper hand. If it had not been growing dark, he would have hazarded that she was looking back tenderly, expectant. The next moment she had slung off the cardigan and thrust it back.

'You made your choice.'

She was off then, back to her house where she would tidy in a careless sort of way, or perhaps read all evening. When her husband came in, they'd go to bed late, and next morning, she'd be up and out to work, even before he was. Hers was an energy other people might pay for. It was strange, Sam thought, that Arthur had let her go on working, staying in the police force after they'd married. Sam would have stopped that – he had no interest in living with a woman who made a fool of you. Beth had laughed when he'd once said this to her.

'That's why I'd never have married you, even if you'd asked.'

That was the day she had looked down at him wiping his hands on the oily rag as he lay under his fancy car. He had dragged himself out from underneath, where he had been fixing the exhaust. She stared for a long time and then fiddled with the garden bits he had in boxes on the shelf, examining the stored seeds in packets and pots.

'How do you know one from another? They all look the same to me.'

'Some, like the runner beans, you just know. The smaller seeds I sometimes label. That packet rubbed off. I'll just have to guess, have a surprise when the things come up.' He was not really paying attention. Women's talk ran on. Sometimes clear, sometimes secretive, full of underwater routes. When Beth started talking again, the subject seemed utterly disconnected.

'Our family have strong genes. A tough lot. No disability, no illness.'

He ignored her. The car needed a good clean. He should check the differential oil levels and gearbox, adjust the carburettor. She shoved the seed packets back, and the sound of the lid sliding over was not right, he'd have to tidy up after her. Her voice drifted down to him from where, back under the car, he could see two red shoes moving around, as she spied on his neat labels, the tools in rows, the pickled cabbage.

'And as for you saying that cousins shouldn't have each other's children, it looks like I've got yours anyway.' She called through the open back door of his house for John, William and Jesse. 'I'm home from work, Fanny. Send them over the wall when you're ready. Tell them I made an apple pie last night. A weekend treat. I'll take the baby too, if you want.'

Three years earlier, when Beth had told him that the house next door to her was for sale, he had wondered what she wanted. He had nevertheless gone to look, taking his wife – and the three children. They had tramped in the muggy heat all the way from Fishponds, and Beth, smiling, had met them at the gate, flicking off her red apron and draping it over the dividing wall. Sam carried Jesse, the curly, blond baby, while his eldest, John, who had walked all the way without complaining, took his Aunt Beth's hand, smiling up as if they were allied. William, the middle child, who was three and a whinger, clung to Fanny. Fanny was plumper now she'd had the children, but her face was round and pretty – much prettier than Beth's. Her blue eyes had a far-away look, but that was because she was short-sighted and wouldn't wear her plastic-rimmed glasses.

They traipsed into the house, like some bizarre extended family, up the stairs and into the three bedrooms and around the bathroom, the women ignoring the damp smell, the rotten window ledges, the stench of alcohol and piss.

'Renting was good enough for your parents and mine,' he said to Fanny as the man showing them around talked of mortgages and ground rent. 'Our house in Fishponds is fine.'

'Please Sam,' Fanny pleaded, and she turned to Beth for help. 'The garden makes a difference. Having children here

27

will be easier.' The baby started to cry, smelling milk under Fanny's camouflage of rose perfume.

The cousins pretended, as the two toured the 1930's house, that there hadn't once been something between them. In public, Beth was more often rude than civil, and even here, in this house that they were later to buy – a house that shouldn't have had so much wrong with it – she mocked him, saying he had no imagination and failed to seize the day. Not always, he had thought. Not always. Did she want him to remind her how he had kissed her under the mistletoe the Christmas before, even though they'd both been married? It was at the works 'do', in the empty entrance, with the sound of shouts and singing coming from the rooms beyond. When someone had knocked on the outer door, they had sprung apart and she'd pulled a strange face – as if he were insulting or just plain ludicrous. After that, she had scarcely spoken, but whenever she visited the garage, she'd curl herself around Arthur and ignore her cousin.

Once Sam and Fanny had settled into Downend Road, it was his wife who sought out Beth, as if trying to undo the cousins' strange rivalry. How could Fanny have known how things were, when even their own family had no clue? Or perhaps she had guessed and thought it easier to keep an eye on her rival. Sam would not put it past his wife to have taken one look at Beth's way with the children and to have known that, enemy or not, this spare pair of hands – with her own mother unwell – would ensure the couple's survival.

And now, three years on, nine years into their marriage, this was what life amounted to – survival. Too many children and too little money. The evening was mild and Sam could smell something heady, maybe the broad bean flowers, maybe something in a neighbour's garden. The dog clambered onto the back wall and Sam called him down, not wanting another set-to with the man over the back. The old man's bitch should have been seen to, not kept in an outhouse; it was hardly Sam's fault there were puppies.

But it wasn't just animals multiplying; there were prams everywhere: children and babies on every street, prams squashed into houses, into pre-fabs and flats. After the first war, and now all over again – babies to re-stock the ruins. He supposed he and Fanny were a statistic: the logic of post-war history. When you stepped back from the press of things, you could sometimes glimpse the future's reckoning. He imagined telling someone how he had married his wife because there was a war and her fragility had touched him.

After they had moved in, a fourth child was soon on the way. Fanny shifted herself downstairs and made the front room into a bedroom, as if to stop more babies. She said the stairs made her chest hurt and after she'd given birth to Morris, she got pills from the doctor. It was wonderful, they agreed, that pills were free; if she'd had to pay, she might have gone without. Might be dead.

In her new room, Fanny asked for pretty curtains, curtains her sister, Lil, hemmed and he stood on a stepladder to hang. It took him and Lil a day to make the place nice; by the time they had finished, it was dusk. He poured two tumblers of whisky and they clinked glasses, surveying the painted shelves, rugs, curtains, the second-hand dressing table that Sam had turned into a desk. Through the open windows came the screech of swallows and the high, light laugh of a girl.

'It's all right,' Lil said. 'Fanny hasn't gone far. At least you didn't marry our sister, Martha. Leaving you to go downstairs is one thing, swanning off to London to go on the stage is quite another thing.'

He had never told anyone, least of all Lil, that for Fanny, upstairs might as well be London.

*

29

Now, as he stood out in his garden and identified the scent of honeysuckle and mulberry, he called again for the dog, thinking about chance and fate and how one day others would dig this garden, live in his house. He shone the torch on the leaves of flowers and vegetables, illuminating sections so he could pluck off multiplying snails and caterpillars, then drop them into the bucket of salt water. In her house, Beth's shadowy outline moved from room to room as she turned on small lamps; she knew he watched: equally, he knew she spied on him. He rummaged in the stone hole where she had hidden her cigarettes, fumbling at the packet until it opened, then delicately put his finger inside, teasing one out that he could steal.

By now, his cousin would be pulling out books – myths and legends, perhaps a romance. He remembered how, when he'd had first moved in, he'd got Beth a puppy – a thank you for finding the house – and, before it had even arrived, she'd named it Thisbe. He had not known the name was female; she had not grasped the dog would be male. *Who cares?* she'd said, as she took the wriggling, licking bundle into her arms. *People are stupid. They'll never know the difference.* After a month, she handed the bundle back over the wall: *It's a mistake*, she said; *Having a puppy's a mistake*. He was used to dogs: the loyal type, the ones that bit, the ones that strayed, those that really belonged elsewhere; he was not used to this mongrel. It seemed to obey no one, and crawled through the hole in the stone wall, partly Beth's, partly his.

Once the war came, Sam had stopped his reading: the world itself was story, urgent and vivid. He'd got a job as a mechanic in the docks and was an air-raid warden. Sometimes he met his cousin out in town – and other girls too – but they were bossy, so full of themselves now men were absent and they had the jobs. The long days and nights, the air raids, the fires in homes and the city centre, made the days surreal and thickened. He thinks he mightn't have married if not for war, if Fanny's visits from Somerset hadn't seemed so light, so charmed.

And now he is thirty-eight and the war has been finished six years, and yet it hasn't quite ended. It is not just the visible scars: the bombed-out churches and bull-dozed buildings, the stories of near misses, dead friends and missing family – it is the dreams. Always the same interminable evening: he a warden, driving on a road that is sinking beneath him. Overhead the sky erupts and splits. Each time, when he arrives at the smoking, crumpled house, he pulls the red-haired girl from the rubble; each time he hopes she will be alive.

On the weekend, as if drawn by the dream, he went down into the Anderson shelter and re-examined the things he had stacked there. In the subterranean space lay a garden roller, deck chairs, compost, old letters, orange boxes, ancient tools and chemicals locked in a box. The boys sometimes played there, though he'd told them not to. He shouted whenever he saw bodies erupting from the ground, his children breaking out from a crypt. He wondered if he should demolish the shelter, but knew that if he did, it would be sod's law and soon there'd be another war.

This particular Saturday, when he climbed out from the hole, his clothes holding mustiness and decay, Beth was in her garden picking blowsy roses. The older boys were already clambering over the wall, invading her territory, guns held aloft. Sam strolled over, hoisting up curly-haired Jesse, who couldn't climb. Beth appraised her cousin's work clothes, his tanned arms, the sleeves of his shirt rolled up.

'Overalls suit you – better than they do Arthur.'

'He doesn't much wear them. Anyway, you didn't always favour the working man. Remember that letter from

London; you were going to marry some rich so 'n' so in a suit.'

'You can be mistaken.' That was the most she had ever given him. With the flowers across one arm, she fumbled at the hole where she had hidden the Players. It was a place she sometimes left messages: practical directives that she might just as well have slid through the letterbox: *Send boys over tonight. Any spare carrots?*

When Sam finally drifted back inside, he opened the paper; his friend was stuck in Korea. Fanny watched him. She had been cooking dinner in the lean-to kitchen: meat, cabbage and potato, all in the troublesome pressure cooker. The pressure often built so fast and unexpectedly that she had to run at the pan with a spoon, lashing out until she released the catch and the steam came hissing out. The glass room filled with a dense, white cloud. If the children were there, they cheered when she came diving into the cover of the living room, followed by the stewy smells of meat and cabbage.

Sam wondered what she thought as she perpetually assessed him – sometimes her scrutiny led to affection, other times argument. He was tired from working nine days in a row and had his hands folded on the table, trying to read the paper; he would have nodded off if he'd closed his eyes.

'Beth charms those boys, like she's a princess and they're her suitors. If she had one of her own, she'd not find it so easy. She's like my sister Martha – lady of the manor.'

Sam was staring off blankly into the distance and could see the children out in the garden picking strawberries, some to take over to Beth, some for the boys' own dessert. John, as the oldest, was up the quince tree, directing operations. William and Jesse had filled their bowls, eating as they went along, offering some to the dog. The youngest, Morris, was already tired, so Sam had brought him in. The child played at his feet, a crumpled *Beano* spread across the floor. The child talked at the pictures, making up the improbable stories he couldn't yet read.

As he sat there, aware of his wife's perfume, of her hips and breasts, he recalled how, after the first baby, they'd moved to a place of their own, away from Fanny's mother, who was waking in the night, coming into their bedroom to say her dead husband wanted the floral tea-pot. When his mother-in-law went to live with her daughter, Lil, he rented a house not far away, down a lonely lane near Snuff Mills.

In that pretty rented house, surrounded by trees that moaned when the wind blew, he remembered an evening when Fanny was ripping at a tin of cream with a sharp opener – she'd never been much good at cooking – and she had gouged the sharp, curved end into her hand. Immediately, the blood gushed, as if she was emptying the tin of a strange red liquid. Blood splashed over his work shirt, over the lino and across the pine table. Fanny whimpered yet did not cry; she stared at the hand as if it belonged to someone else. And it was then that Beth burst in. Like an apparition, she was suddenly there, as if she'd been waiting, or calculating. Beth knew to hold Fanny's arm up, put pressure on the wound, make her lie still.

Sam looked out of the kitchen window and marvelled at the sturdy boys slinging and spilling the precious fruit, who might not exist, if not for Beth, who had saved Fanny's life.

'Our sons are good boys,' he offered; an opening he hoped would appease.

'Good-looking boys,' she retorted. 'A bit like you, perhaps less like me.' She moved her food around the plate; she was on a diet again and said it was easier if she ate earlier than everyone else.

'If you ate more, you'd have some energy.'

'And I'd be huge. You'd stop loving me.'

He could not work out if this was a joke or not; they'd not been to bed together for months. He couldn't bring himself to say what she was waiting for – that he would love her whatever.

Sam pushed his beer aside and went to shout out of the window. The fight had escalated and the boys were flinging their strawberries at one another, squashy missiles in a perpetual war. He was not as cross as he might have been – there was enough fruit to have already made jam and endless puddings – but the boys jumped apart, assuming he'd get the stick. When he turned, Fanny was smiling. Her head was arched to one side and her fair hair curled prettily from the heat and steam of the kitchen.

'Those boys do as you tell them. It's as well someone's in charge.'

'Is it? I'm not so sure. I do as my father did – and I didn't much like him.'

'And am I like my mother?' He looked at her, with her soft arms and legs that he wanted to stroke. 'What are you thinking, Sammie? A penny for them!'

He could not tell her the things he really thought. And she would not want to hear that he'd just decided he should rotate the crops, keep the plants strong and disease resistant, so he said instead,

'We should have a picnic this weekend, like we used to with your mother. The car's purring along. I've a tank full of petrol.'

'I'd like that. Could we get as far as the moor?' She looked wistful, no doubt wanting Exmoor, but probably thinking any moor would do.

'Not the moor, but a heath or some fields on the way?'

She came across and kissed him on the cheek, perhaps hoping to persuade him to take her back to where she'd been happy, working as a companion in a house that didn't just have a gardener, but a cook and cleaner too. He slid his arm around her pliant waist.

*

On Saturday it was dry and hot. He told the boys, as they bundled into the back seats that they were lucky having a car when many did not, when rationing had only just stopped. If he hadn't been such a good mechanic, with access to fuel, he wouldn't have been able to keep the thing going. When they drove out through the city and then into the dusty roads that led south, he liked how people stared at the Lanchester, admiring the running board, leather seats and wooden dash. He wore his hat at a jaunty angle, as if he was important, and the children must have felt he was, for they waved regally as people pressed into the country hedges to let the car pass.

Beth and Arthur were meeting them at a place he'd carefully marked on the map; he did not say that he used to bike there with girls, in the days when he'd been carefree and people thought him a catch. Fanny had insisted that Beth should come too: *The children will be a handful,* she'd said. *Beth will bake cakes,* she added, and, *Beth will bring corned beef sandwiches, just like mother did.*

Once this was settled, Fanny looked for flasks and the blankets to sit on. Lil, Fanny's sister, and her husband, George, were also invited, but at the last minute, a message arrived to say Lil's husband was unwell; the cough he'd picked up in the war was serious.

If Lil and her husband had been there, things might have been different. Lil would never have let her nephew climb along the tree that edged out across the shallow lake. Lil had helped to bring up her siblings and would have guessed the child might slide on the mossy wood and topple in. But Lil was not there, and Beth was picking wild flowers with Morris, making a daisy chain to put around his neck, as if he were a Roman lord – Pyramus, she called him, because it was a character in a book. *Mus,* the three year old repeated, demanding his crown.

35

It is just as Fanny has poured the last tea from a thermos, and is packing up that a strange yelp cuts through the quiet talk. Sam has been completing a crossword and Beth calling over answers. The splash comes a second later. By this time Sam is sprinting towards the lake, jolting over the uneven ground so that the grazing cows, poppies and cornflowers dance up and down as he runs. He leaps over a cowpat and small ditch and gets to the lake as ripples are spreading in concentric circles at the place the child has plunged in. The child's head comes up and bobs under for maybe the second or third time and Sam slides and pirouettes along the damp trunk, gripping overhanging branches, getting to a place he can lean in and grab at the surfacing wet hair. The spluttering child rises in his hand, as if Sam has plucked out of this liquid pool a mythical being, born of the moment. The father lets go for a second and grabs instead at the shirt as the boy goes down, and this time he has a better grip and heaves the saturated and awkward body up onto the branch that dips dangerously in the water. Sam's feet and clothes are soaked, but not like his child's, and he knows that if he goes in too, they will both drown, for he never learned to swim. The others have come thundering behind and Beth, quicker and more agile than her husband, is balancing just behind Sam on the trunk that is sticking out, like a pirate's plank, into the restless water.

Fanny, at the shore, is whimpering, *I told them to keep away, I told them to keep away,* even as Beth and Sam haul the boy back onto land and Beth flips the child over, putting his arms up so she can press rhythmically on his back, getting the dirty water out of his lungs. The child coughs and chokes and cries at the same time, his body heaving and shaking. Fanny stands all the while, squinting at them, her hands plucking at her face, as if insects run across, while William, holding onto her skirt, cries, *I didn't do it,*

Dad, it wasn't my fault, it wasn't my fault.

Beth works calmly and croons reassurance, yet Sam hears how her voice shakes. 'He's fine, he's fine. You didn't swallow much. You're lucky. You're fine now.'

Sam sits with his knees up, recovering, taking gulps of air, turning over his wet sleeves and watching Beth's movements. Arthur fusses around Morris and Jesse, taking them by the hand, as if left to themselves, they too might take lemming plunges into the still lake, with its mirrored clouds and dragonflies hovering.

Later, after they have bundled everything into the cars and John, who is ten and should have known better, has been wrapped in the blankets, a precious parcel, and has been made to sit shivering and waiting in the Lanchester, his mother and brothers finally come and cram in next to him, and Fanny makes clear, with all the adults as witness, that Sam is not to beat John when they get home, that she doesn't want the child running away on top of everything. And it is after this, feeling that things are somehow always his fault, that Sam realises the Lanchester will not start. It is one thing after another, he thinks: his child nearly drowning, Fanny blaming him, Beth being rude as they do the crossword and now this. He gives another heave on the starter handle, his wet sleeves sticking to his skin, and Arthur stands beside him, making useless suggestions. Sam knows already that he should have checked the spark plugs, that the battery water level may be low. And not for the first time, he is amazed by how the most inept get to be the bosses. Arthur is speaking to him as if he is slow-witted, as if he cannot see what is in front of his nose.

'Look, Sam,' he insists, 'You missed a plug.'

'I was about to do it.'

'That child'll get pneumonia. We need to drive him home – forthwith.'

'You're in my light. Could you just move.'

'I can pop him in the Ford and come back with a rope.'

The Lanchester bonnet is up and flapped over, and Sam has already checked four sparkplugs, wiping each one on a rag as his eyes flick over the engine. *Forthwith*, he thinks. *What sort of man says forthwith?*

But Arthur keeps droning on. 'We can get everyone in our car. Take everyone back. Why are you so touchy?'

'The dog's gone. Thisbe has gone.' It is Beth. They look around at the low hedges, cut fields in the distance, the heat haze, expecting to see the dog's tail wagging above mole hills and rabbit burrows. Beth sighs. 'You go home with the boys, Arthur; there's French bean soup on the stove – give it to Johnny and anyone else who wants it. I'll stay and look for the dog.' She leans through the open car door to reassure the children. 'He won't be missing for long; I'm a policewoman, remember.'

They smile back nervously and clamber out of their own car, John leaving wet patches on the leather where he's been sitting.

'Can I stay?' Jesse is smiling up at Beth.

'It's fine by me, Fanny. I won't take my eyes off him.'

'It's too dangerous. You turn your back and bad things happen.'

As they are about to drive off, Arthur winds his car window down fully. 'If I don't pass you on the way back, I'll be here in an hour and a half. Don't kill each other.'

The car bumps off down the lane and Sam and Beth look away. Goldfinches flit along the hedge, flying up to feed on the alder. On the far side of the lane, lambs bleat. Just ahead, bullocks are grazing with the milk cows and beyond, there is a tethered bull.

'It's going to rain,' Sam says, to break the silence. 'The cows are lying down.'

'Are you going to help me look for the dog or stay here?' She looks him up and down quizzically. She has a Roman nose, much like his and her face is long, her eyes shrewd and intelligent.

'At your service.' He offers his hand, trying to be the gentleman.

They trudge up the hill arm in arm. He feels her movements within him, the slight pressure of her arm, a lemon scent he hasn't noticed before. She isn't wearing her heels now, but the light shoes give no support. For someone who works in a uniform, it amazes him how impractical she is the rest of the time. At the top of the field, where Jesse had spotted the dog, they find a stile and stony lane that winds up steeply. They are both puffing by the time they scramble to the top and push through the overhanging greenery. They emerge out of dank shadow into a bright opening where a ruined house sits in a cobbled yard. Its whitewash has faded, nettles thrust from its base and brambles clamber through the open doors and windows. It's a suntrap, hidden and protected, with butterflies sunning themselves on the weeds and tall flowers. There are Large Coppers, Purple Hairstreaks, a Red Admiral. On a black water pump, a Peacock sits with its wings outstretched. Beth turns and smiles.

'Is this real? Or have we stepped back in time?'

'I've picnicked in the field – never knew this existed. A Hansel and Gretel cottage.'

'Well, beware the wicked witch, then.' She flicks him on the arm, playfully. 'The blackberries are really early. Do you think they're ripe? Shall we pick them?' She is fingering plump berries. 'But we've nothing to put them in, Sam.'

She stares around, as if looking for a solution, taking in the isolation of the place, the steepness of the climb to the car and back. Although there are no clouds in the still, blue sky, as she parts the brambles once more, a misty rain begins to envelop, and everything is stuffy and still, the smells of leaves and earth intense, the air muggy.

'We'd better take shelter.' He is not sure if he says it or she does. The barn, by the side of the house, has been

39

filled with sweet hay and from a hole, that had perhaps once been a huge knot of wood, they look down the sweeping field to the blue lake, with its puckered surface and the black car waiting patiently in the lay-by.

What happens next is a dream and yet, with the electrical storm brewing, perfectly natural. They talk while the rain gets heavier, pattering on the roof, and then he offers his jacket, shuffling it around her shoulders, trying not to touch her sallow skin. She is staring at the lake and the fallen trunk that is a black slash in darkening water.

'How close life and death are,' she whispers.

And then, perhaps so she does not have to talk more, she offers a cigarette from a packet in her pocket. It is years since he has smoked openly, but he takes it and moves to the barn's entrance and she follows with the lighter. They are careful that no sparks drop to the dusty, dry floor, that there are no unforeseen consequences. When he offers her a drag, she takes the cigarette and sucks at the place he has sucked, drawing the smoke in and expertly blowing it out. When he takes it back, their fingers briefly touch, and the nicotine and her skin are drugs; the clandestine taste of youth: games of hide-and-seek, races at the park, bodies pressed close. In the sun it had been pleasantly mild, but here in the shade he is shivering.

'I need to get warm,' he says and stubs out the cigarette, then moves deep into the barn. Or perhaps she says this, and even pulls him by the arm. He is not sure who says what, who touches first.

And they are sitting on the hay-bales and he has his arm around her and she has leaned into him and, from somewhere, there is a flash and the low grumble of thunder. She says barely a word, and he is not sure what, exactly, he grunts back, but he knows, for sure, that this thing is mutual. He would like to tell her, as he courts more slowly, that he does not just want her body – although, if he is honest, it is the thing he has most often thought of;

he wants the closeness they have shared before, the magical thing he glimpsed wandering up the lane with her and, here in this sealed up world, the thinning of irony and the loose feel of trust. And hidden in the hay, beneath the hole that gives out onto the rest of the world, even these thoughts dissolve when she kisses him, her breath in his. Something tumbles her into his arms and lips and skin. Even as he presses deeper and she sinks with him, he understands that this is a drowning and that the salvaging of it will change things forever.

They brush off the itchy hay and dust down their clothes, make their slippery way along the paths and back over the field – the dog following. The cows are still lying down, but far away in the lake a man fishes, sitting alone in his small rowing boat, close to the reeds. At one point, looking across, Beth slips on the wet grass and Sam reaches out and steadies her. But irrevocably, their steps take them back to where a woman stands dismissively at the garden wall and a man has a posse of boys, each a handful. He is Sam and she is Beth, his cousin.

As the days pass and nothing changes and not a word is said, he accepts that this is how things will be. Sometimes he is sad, other times relieved. Beth is stony, watchful; he stays at work more than usual. When he tries to unravel the complexity of that alchemical day, he wonders if he was duped. Did Beth's husband, who picked them up in too careless and cheerful a way, know how everything would pan out? But how could they have planned such an operation: make his child fall in the lake, stop his car from working? How could they have known about the barn at the top of the hill, the dog sleeping in the hay?

'Life is all about risk,' she whispered as she'd had him in her arms. Or this is what his faulty memory tells him. 'There are homes for children who don't come out right.'

He isn't sure if he heard this or if he read her thoughts, or perhaps this is his own logic as days stretch into months.

A year later, Sam is fixing a fence; he says it is to keep out the kitten that Arthur has bought his wife, a present now she no longer works. With his shirtsleeves rolled up, Sam mixes cement, plugging the gaps and holes in the wall. His own boys are making a go-cart out of pram wheels and later, he will help fix a break, maybe find some red paint. Beth is over in her garden, holding the baby, while Arthur sits smiling, showing off his son, Benedict, to visitors who have come to take tea. Sam is glad his cousin has finally got herself a child, though he thinks it a strange looking creature, one you'd be hard pressed to call handsome.

He is getting used to the way that holes open up when least expected. Fixing the wall is easy; the subsidence inside is more problematic. It is Beth's rudeness he wants, but she only smiles and sometimes stares oddly, as if he is some kind of relic. The scrape of the trowel, the gentle sounds of his boys' voices in the heat of the afternoon fills the air. Inside the house, in her own room, Fanny will be doing accounts: the builder's, the garage's; jobs that makes her happy and help them save. When her sister, Lil, arrives, everyone will go in for tea.

Such days are pleasant enough, and the evenings too, now he does not yearn for dusk, or the offhand messages shoved in a hole between stones. With the boys asleep and Fanny quietly flicking through magazines, cutting out dresses that her widowed sister will eventually come and take away, time passes in a measured sort of way. Lil will adjust the uneven patterns, cut the rough edges and sew things back together. Then everything will be decent, the dresses presentable, and the world will never guess how once things were utterly botched, and seemed like they could never mend.

Bob-a-Job – 1952

He was small for his age in 1952, so was used to finding ways to placate, to avoid being bullied. He would ingratiate by making people laugh and had learned to cope when no one claimed him for football. He was also, despite his asthma and size, a good runner. So when he was partnered with John Hawke for Bob-a-Job, a boy already at high school and renowned for toughness, for being in scrapes, he'd known he might need special skills, especially flight. Other years, even when he'd been paired with some older child, his mother trailed around too, saying he was too young to be out on the streets, knocking on doors, offering work in return for a shilling. But Bob-a-Job was something the Cubs and Scouts organised every Easter, and children of all ages scuttled around the streets in uniforms, working in pairs or groups: carrying shopping, polishing silver, sweeping paths, or just hiding up lanes and ambushing each other with peltings of water bombs. For Andrew, though, with his mother in tow, the week was torture; at the end he'd stack his shillings on the mantelpiece, next to a neatly filled-in card (in his mother's writing) indicating names and addresses of the people he'd worked for, jobs accomplished and the adults' signatures.

This year would be different; he'd made a stand. Said he'd hint about her and the scout master if she insisted on coming. When John Hawke turned up on the Saturday morning, they peered out at the stocky lad on the front path. The boy was pale and tall, dark hair slicked back with the brylcreem Andrew's mother wouldn't let him use. He looked confident, as if he were used to finding his way around.

'He's old enough to make sure you're safe,' she whispered, pushing a sandwich wrapped in greaseproof into Andrew's hands. John was lolling outside, appraising the Victorian house, looking up at the flaking green paint. He knocked again, more insistently. Andrew's mother opened the heavy door an inch, then pushed it shut. She turned back to her son. 'Are you sure you don't want me to come?' Andrew shook his head. 'Well, I suppose he's big, so no one will take advantage.' Didn't his mother know that this was part of the excitement, the risk – working out who was the loony, which house to avoid? Everyone knew the story of Brian Wilkes who'd been given an axe by the blind man and asked to chop wood, but then got a splinter in his head.

It was not polite to leave John standing so long in the porch, especially since he could see Andrew's mother peering through the coloured glass of the door.

When she finally opened it wide, she brushed down her spotty apron and smiled, holding out her hand. 'How do you do?' The boy wiped his hand and then let it be claimed. 'Aren't you Fanny Leach's son? I worked with your aunt Lil: tragic, it was – her husband dying, too.'

John looked uneasy, as if conversation wasn't a part of the deal. He muttered, 'Fanny Hawke, my mum is now. I'm staying at Aunt Lil's; Mum sent me – to do gardening and stuff.'

'How sweet.'

The boy frowned.

'Remember now; you should knock on doors where gardens are tidy and houses nicely painted.'

John, whose scout uniform was already muddy, stared at the auburn bouffant hair, the red nails and high heels of Andrew's mother. He thrust his hands deep into his pockets and chewed his lip, nodding at the instructions, agreeing that they wouldn't cross the main road, wouldn't tackle jobs that involved blades, would be back by four and not go inside the houses of strangers.

'They never solved those murders in the park.

Remember that.'

All she ever talked about was death, Andrew thought. Concentrating on it so much, she was likely to conjure it.

'And remember what else I told you, Andrew?' Here, she turned on her son, rattling off the specific people and places they should avoid; she mentioned the builder's name twice.

'But he's not drinking now,' Andrew said. 'And you used to say he was a saint.'

His mother launched into a story that Andrew hoped John could not follow – and would not repeat. While she spoke, Andrew looked away, staring at the sky, or at his own feet and then at the holes in the front lawn. He did not want to see on the face of the goliath boy, a recognition of how smothered he had been.

They were about to set off when his mother looked startled, as if she'd had a premonition of yet another danger.

'Wait. Stay here. How stupid of me.' She rushed back inside the cool hallway. John, who was taller than Andrew, pressed his face to the stained glass window and peered into the interior of Andrew and his mother's life, a world Andrew knew to be palest yellow and sometimes dusty pink. John would have observed a coloured version of Andrew's mother racing away and a minute or so later, he would see the other worldly figure return. She would probably have snatched off her apron, may even have added make up; there was a pot of cold cream on a ledge in the scullery and a powder puff that smelt faded and flowery.

When she did return, the two boys jumped as the door swung open: overhead a flock of pigeons circled, and from next door came the wailing of the new baby. Andrews's mother pulled a face and he didn't know if she would complain about the noise of the child or the mess from the neighbour's birds. She thrust two parcels at them, brushing away the strands of hair that had fallen over her face.

'I've made a quick salmon paste sandwich for you John, so you won't be hungry, and there's two slices of cake from last night.' John grunted and took charge of the food, and Andrew tried to work out if the boy was grimacing or smiling. Andrew followed out of the gate, ignoring whatever his mother was hissing; he pulled at the wooden contraption that never shut properly, and he knew that it would swing open again after the two had gone. Since his father had died and the builder no longer visited, nothing seemed to work properly.

The two boys walked down the street in silence. They turned left along the back lane, away from prying eyes. It was then that John stopped.

'Your mum's okay. She's like this woman in a film my dad took me to. It had Cary Grant and the actress was like your mum, only she had different colour hair.' In the lanes, it smelt of dog's piss and petrol from a car someone was revving in a garage. 'Do you get much chocolate and sweet stuff at Easter?'

Andrew didn't know what to say. If he admitted he did, John might demand it; if he said he didn't he might look like a loser. 'Sometimes.'

'Listen,' John said. 'I'm only doing this Bob-a-Job lark because mum says I have to; she does the Scouts' books and it looks bad when I never turn up for stuff. She does it for free,' he added – perhaps because he didn't want Andrew to think his family rich. 'Look, once we've names on the list, I'm off. You can do what you like, but I'm saying people said to come back another day.'

At the first house – a shabby two up, two down that smelt musty – the old lady took the Bob-a-Job card and peered at their names, written in capitals.

'Are you Connie, the widow's son?' she asked Andrew, looking him up and down, as if summing up identikits of his mother and dead father.

'I am,' he said, feeling John's stare and the contamination that came from being pitiable.

'Then you can stand inside while I get a shopping list. Keep your dirty feet on the mat.' They stood in the hallway, with the ticking clock and hat stand, exchanging glances that felt conspiratorial. The old lady gave them a silly basket, a list neatly written in pencil on a scrap of cardboard and a half a crown. 'Ask the shopkeeper to write down what each thing costs. And don't lose the change.'

Trudging up the hill towards the small row of shops: barber, bread shop, corner shop, haberdasher's and the launderette run by the Chinese people, John thrust the list at Andrew.

'It's not that I can't read; it's just her stupid writing. I'm better at sums.'

Andrew took hold of the delicate loops that reminded him of his crazy mother's writing, the letters she'd sent after his dad had been killed by the motorbike. The spiritualist said that if she wrote her apology down, it would clear the air and the dead mightn't haunt her. For his part, Andrew quite fancied seeing a ghost, especially if it was his dad.

Andrew read the old lady's lacy words out to John, mimicking her voice, saying that they should buy nice lean ham, mind, and eight pounds of waxy potatoes, not too much earth: *I don't want to be paying for what I can't eat.* John grinned and pulled cigarettes from his pocket, then beckoned down the side alley with the dead end.

'I'll sit on the wall in the corner and hold the card. You go get the shopping.' The older boy had taken command of the shortbread biscuits the old lady had also given them.

'I'm hungry,' Andrew tried.

'Buy an ice-cream with the old biddy's change.' John had a cigarette behind his ear and was fiddling with some strips of metal. 'It's a part of my steam engine – works on

47

meths. School's for losers; building stuff is better.'

The pleasurable feeling of solitude Andrew experienced, trudging up the hill, was marred only by the basket he was forced to carry, with its patched bits and ridiculous moth-eaten flowers. He held his arm down straight, the basket hidden behind his shorts and decided that if he saw another scout, he would drop it. He whistled a tune his dad had liked and wasn't fearful, as his mother was, that the motor-bike which had veered across the road and killed him would still be lurking.

Later, after he had brought back the shopping and after he and John had garnered the old lady's spidery writing, fixing it on their Bob-a-Job card, after she had rummaged in tins and pots until she found a shilling, they went on to the doctor's house to harvest that old man's illegible scrawl. He asked them to carry boxes full of forms from one large room to another, which they did. But he seemed unsure of why he was re-organising and they suspected, if they lingered too long, they might have to carry all the boxes, paper and files back again – and all for one shilling. People said how he was forgetting things, forgetting who his patients were and which ones were private and which National Health. In the room they were emptying, a girl, who might have been his grandchild or the cleaner's girl, was throwing a dice across the floor, then adding up the numbers on a sheet of paper. *It's hot*, she announced, each time they came back in. *Why won't anyone play?* When they got outside, the sun made them even hotter in their stupid uniforms with the yellow cravats tied in a knot around their throats. John turned to Andrew.

'You should go on the stage; you could be as funny as Laurel and Hardy some day. You got the old lady and the doctor, too. Do me, now.' Andrew grinned, was about to mimic the lumpish walk, the vacant expression, then stopped himself.

'I can only do old people; when we get old, I'll do you.'

Andrew fixed on the card and considered the two lines of writing. John looked over his shoulder and groaned.

'This is taking too long.' He kicked at a wall until a stone came away, then looked at Andrew as if he should find the solution.

'I suppose we could split up, get it done faster.'

'So I've got to do my fair share of work?' And John laughed out loud. 'They said you were a mummy's boy, but you're okay.' He kicked the stone sideways at Andrew who failed to kick it back. 'Okay, Andy. Let's meet in two hours. And mind out for the mad axe man!'

Not long after, Andrew saw John in the distance taking a dog for a walk. Andrew hollered across in a Scottish accent that he was doing a wee bit a shopping and had been asked to take a wee dram when he got back. John waved, pointing at the dog and then held his nose. Later, in a house with flaking paint worse than his own, Andrew was told to wash dishes. He often helped his mum, but in this house there was a scullery with soap that made his hands sting and a washboard and Wringer pushed into one corner. All the time he was there, a woman kept demanding of him, wasn't he finished yet, and a child whined that she was hungry. The house felt bad, and his own home and his mother patiently waiting, seemed a better place. When the woman asked him to cut the lawn next, he said that he was only allowed to do one job and she said she'd see about that and paid him the shilling begrudgingly.

'What do the scouts do with all this money, I'd like to know? I wouldn't skivvy for nothing, I can tell you that.'

At the next house, a street away, he stood on the doorstep with the sour smell of the unhappy house pursuing him. This neat place was not one he knew anything about, but he was gaining in confidence and

49

rapped on the red front door, thinking about his mum's crying and whether it was to do with his dad or the scout master. The person who opened the door stared, probably taking in Andrew's fair hair, girlish eyelashes and uniform. It was a man smartly dressed, with a shirt and tie on and a brown pullover over the top. Andrew wondered why he didn't feel hot.

'What school are you at?' he asked Andrew. When Andrew told him Dr Bells, he nodded, as if he approved; he was holding a newspaper as if he'd just been reading. 'Could you sort out jigsaws and playing cards?' Andrew nodded. 'Do you like chocolate?' Andrew nodded. The man opened the door more fully, gave a quick look up and down the road and invited him in. 'You've a nice face,' the man said. 'You look kind. Are you kind?' Andrew nodded again, but felt strange. This house was turning out worse than the other. It was as if the real purpose of Bob-A-Job was to make you realise how safe and privileged your own life was. 'Wait here,' the man said, and went up the stairs, which, strangely, had no carpet. Andrew could hear the person moving around a room upstairs, opening drawers and bumping things around. A heavy piece of furniture was dragged across the floor. Even before the voice had finished calling out,

'I'm up in the back room, come on up,' Andrew had lifted the latch and was gone, back down the steps, along the street and down a side lane; away from the house that smelt of the man's sweat.

When they met by the lane to the grove, Andrew didn't tell about the house he'd been afraid in, but detailed the other: the dog trying to push its nose up his crutch, the fat dad with his high-pitched voice, saying, *Do you play the piano, boy? Can you play me a tune?* John squatted behind the low wall that led to the stream and overgrown meadow and offered Andrew a cigarette.

'If I tell you the addresses I've been to: you can go

50

back and get their signatures on that card, and I'll look after the money we've taken.' John had a habit of staring hard and flicking his greased fringe back. 'Listen,' he said, sucking on the cigarette and then blowing out smoke as he squinted. 'I'll tell you what I'll do. I'll see you're okay when you get to high school. But you've got to get the rest of that card filled up. It's boring and I've stuff to do.'

Andrew felt the weight of this. If he had to do it alone, there might be more men – or even women – calling him upstairs. If he didn't get the lines done, John might make things difficult. That was, if Andrew didn't pass the Eleven Plus or go to Grammar School. He wasn't so clever in school this year, what with his mum and things, and his friends were growing taller, but he wasn't. Perhaps he was going to end up stunted and stupid, too.

As they crouched behind the wall and talked, some of John Hawke's words came out high pitched; Andrew watched the dark hairs along the boy's upper lip move, a shadowy line articulating as he puffed at his cigarette. Andrew looked at the smooth paper stick in his own hand and knew he had to pretend he didn't notice John's voice breaking and that he would have to smoke too. His mother went through a packet a day, but she'd said she'd whip him if she ever caught him at it or on the drink – she only did it herself because of nerves.

'Stick it in your mouth, stupid.' John brought out a silver lighter. 'My other aunt's,' he explained. 'She gave up when she got the cough. Said I was to wait until I was fourteen, like her brothers.'

Andrew gave a hesitant pull on the cigarette, taking the smoke inside his mouth, then huffing it out quick. It tasted like he'd eaten a bonfire, but the stream of smoke curled out beautifully. He was in the mafia or something, closing a deal, being in on the hard scene. He puffed again and this time the smoke didn't get out quick enough and invaded his nose and throat. It caught in his chest and hurt, then he took a gulp and coughed and spluttered out pain and dust, bending double like he'd be sick. John laughed, not unkindly, slapping him on the back, telling him he'd show him how to smoke properly if he wanted.

'But not today; I'll be off in a second.' He puckered up his handsome face and squinted into the sun, only he didn't move, as if he was reluctant to go, as though he too liked being with someone who was different. They were crouched down by the old house that guarded the lane to the grove and muddy stream.

'When I'm gone, don't go in there,' he said, nodding at the lonely place with its wild hedge and drawn blinds, 'She's mad.'

Perhaps he was remembering his promises to Andrew's mother. Remembering how good her homemade cake was and that somewhere in this town was the person who had killed two girls.

'She's a witch,' Andrew agreed. 'She's bent and wears black and gives you the evil eye.'

His mother, who liked history, had told him how this house was old, part of the original village, also that it had subsided and this was because they lived on fault lines. He was used to her pretension. Whatever she read came spilling out and he was full of the same jagged knowledge.

For now, he was pleased he had John's attention. He embellished. 'She has a cat that spies on you. Her daughter is the one at our primary school what cooks and has the girl with callipers.'

The boys stared into the ragged interior of the garden, tying to connect the neat woman who dished out potatoes and smiled in primary school, with the old woman in black who shuffled along the street and shooed away children.

'Okay then, if she's not so bad, I dare you to go.' John laughed and punched Andrew in the arm until he yelped in pain. Andrew didn't quite know how to respond, but knew to act like this was friendship.

'Come round my house later,' Andrew shouted, throwing aside the lit cigarette and running, holding the card tight, his money stuffed down his sock, slipping under his heel so it hurt. He guessed John wouldn't follow to get the Bob-a-Job shillings: down the smelly lane, past the stream and broken shed, over the fence that led into the garden of the big, lonely house that had once been a farm. There was a goat in this garden and Andrew hoped John would be as afraid of it, as he was.

John hadn't followed, but Andrew climbed into the garden anyway. There was a swing in the hedged corner. He was half way over the lawn when a noise made him turn. The goat was there, standing quietly in the long grass and blocking his way back. No longer on a chain, it stared at the interloper, perhaps as surprised to see a boy, as Andrew was to see it. Then the animal bent its head and buckled the two curved and sharp horns under, as if to charge. Andrew turned, bounded over the lawn and felt the goat follow. He could hear the swish of grass, and his back prickled as if any minute it would feel those vicious horns. Over the grass Andrew skittered, down a brick path where the pattering of hooves echoed behind, past a swimming pool with water gleaming and brown leaves floating, then straight up to some grand French doors. He had not once looked behind, and he yanked at the smooth brass knobs, his breath coming in short, asthmatic bursts. Miraculously, the doors swung open and he was in. Outside, the goat stopped and calmly set about the grass.

Andrew found himself in a large sitting room with two settees and a grand piano. On the mantelpiece, a clock ticked and he could see himself, looking bedraggled and shocked in the ornate, gold mirror. The goat came and stared in at the window, its yellow eyes malevolent, then it dropped its head and tugged at the flowers growing in pots on the patio. This was not the first time Andrew had been in Anvil House. Once before, his mother had brought him there because, just after his father had died, there'd been kittens for sale, and they had stood in the grand hallway and a woman had cast around for the kittens, but had not found any and then had said she supposed they were all gone. If Andrew could find his way to the hallway, he might be able to creep out the front door and no one would know he had ever been there. He could slip down the drive the other side of the fence from the goat.

'You'd better come with me,' said a voice, and he wheeled around to see a thin, elderly man sitting at a desk in a darkened alcove, papers spread everywhere.

'I didn't mean…' began Andrew.

'Heather's friends always come in the wrong doors.'

'I'm not…' But the grey haired man, surprisingly agile, had jumped up and was leading him through a door and down first one passage and then another. When they went through another small door, they found themselves in a barn, where a horse munched behind a wooden partition.

'Have you come to ride?' the man asked, shouting up into the loft area for someone called Heather. 'My daughter's too preoccupied with boys these days – gets all and sundry to ride the blessed thing. Although you look a bit young – for her or the horse.' The animal made a blowing sound and put its large head over the wooden stall, nudging at the man's arm. He patted it in a way that suggested he didn't much like animals. 'We've just got this one from Abergavenny – the yearly sale there; it's near where I was brought up. The other animal's tamer.'

The man assessed Andrew. 'You're not really dressed for riding; your legs will get sore in those shorts.'

'I can't…' The man frowned.

'So she just asks anyone in the house for any reason?' Andrew was not sure if it was a question or an assertion. 'Why are you here, then?' The man, who was wiry, with cropped hair peered down. The boy had the Bob-a-Job card in his pocket, so he pulled it out. It was crumpled and

54

the few lines of writing looked scruffy and inadequate.

'Do you want anything done? Jobs?'

'Ah, I see. You're here for that.' He didn't think to wonder why a scout had barged into his living room rather than knock at the front door. 'You must think I'm mad, then. Don't worry, I won't ask you to clean out this thing, although you could take it for a ride, I suppose?'

'I can't…haven't ever … except the donkeys at Weston.'

The man laughed. 'This one would give you a bit more of a ride than the donkeys at Weston. You'd think you were in the Wild West.'

He was leading the way up some wooden steps in the barn, up to where hay and bits of tack were stored. Andrew hesitated at the bottom, but when he looked out into a cobbled yard, all he could see were the closed doors of more barns and a high, panelled wooden fence with a great padlock keeping it shut. Halfway up the steps, the man looked around and followed Andrew's gaze.

'We have to keep it like Fort Knox, otherwise in this area, someone would steal the horses. Come on; I'm not going to eat you.'

Andrew climbed the wooden rungs, keeping well behind, remembering the house and the other man who had wanted him to follow.

At the top, the thin man waited for Andrew and then showed him the leather bridles and saddles, the brushes and buckets as if they were something to marvel at.

'It costs so much – the tack, the feeding, the vet's bills. She has no idea. If I weren't a dentist, if her mother hadn't been rich, we couldn't afford it – but she doesn't seem to appreciate that.'

The dimly lit barn smelt of unguents, leather and hay – a pleasantly medicinal cocktail which, at that moment made Andrew feel sick.

The man gestured at a small trap door. 'You first. Shortcut. Back into the house. Into my study. I've thought of something you can do.'

Andrew shifted toward the brown painted doorway, wishing that he'd let his mother come after all. The latched door creaked open and beyond was a large room decorated candy pink, a frieze of unicorns at ceiling height. There was a table shoved across a door and another door led into a small bathroom. A desk was in the middle of the room and a standard lamp was balanced over a battered armchair, on which lay an open book. He read the title as he climbed down from the trap door: *Social Anthropology*.

'Go on, go on. Just go and sit down. Use the bathroom if you want. I'll be in, in a sec.'

Andrew would have liked to use the bathroom, but was scared that the man would come in while he was peeing. He sat on the edge of a camp bed, holding the Bob-a-job card, which he twisted into a funnel. When the man also pushed himself through the tiny trap door, he was holding something in each hand – a thin wooden board, folded over, and a box that rattled.

'If you can't play chess, I'll teach you. If you can, I'll beat you and then show you how to win. Is that worth a shilling of anybody's time?'

The room had once been his daughter's, he said, but because she kept escaping through the barn to meet boys who climbed over the fences and because she needed, at the very least, to pass some exams – he had moved her out. He had given her an even bigger room upstairs and had taken this as his study. It was here that he read, here that he sometimes slept or escaped a household of women: three daughters, a mother-in-law and a wife who barely spoke. All this he told Andrew as if the boy understood, and also grasped the other things the man merely implied. He set up the chess board, pleased that Andrew already knew the game.

While they played chess, they ate sweets and talked about books and the welfare state; he told Andrew that families were an artificial construction and that some societies managed them better.

'You see, Andrew,' he said, taking the knight threatening his queen, 'my wife comes from a different class. Just because I think money should be spread out more fairly, it doesn't mean she does.'

They had three games in a row and when Andrew heard the clock chime four, he asked if the man – Mr Evans – would let him go.

'I hope you don't think I've kept you locked up? You're a clever boy. You'll do well. Get a free place to a good school, or something, go on to university. I wish my daughter had your quickness. Your game's improving no end.'

He sighed and hauled the desk away from the door, then led them both down a passage. From a glass jar, standing on an antique table, he pulled out a pound note and offered it to Andrew. 'I'll enter my relatives' names in your card; I'm sorry, I've probably used up lots of people's time.' He took a pen and filled up all the remaining lines.

As Andrew was about to leave, the man looked up and down the huge hallway with the paintings on the wall, the rugs on the polished floor, the seven doors opening off.

'Did you say your mother was a widow?'

Andrew nodded, but wanted to say that it was all right; he didn't need pity because he couldn't really remember his father, who had worked a lot. Mr Evans led the way through into the back kitchen where a housekeeper was chopping potatoes and peeling carrots and where two fridges hummed.

'Where is everyone?' he asked. 'It's like a morgue.'

The woman turned, her lips set. 'Isn't it usually, with no-one speaking, and everyone blaming me for something?'

'Ah, it's you that rules us, Margery. And it's you that will tell me off when the boy, here, goes.'

The short, middle-aged looking woman eyed Andrew,

as if she had the measure of him, suspecting him of coming there to get what he could, knowing that Mr Evans was a soft touch. 'They've all gone shopping. If you've forgotten, your oldest daughter is getting married in a week; everyone else is flat out, organising.'

From the freezer, the man took a large block of vanilla ice cream. 'But perhaps you prefer strawberry?' he asked. Andrew mutely nodded. 'But, nevertheless, I expect your poor mother would like vanilla.' He pulled out two more bricks, one strawberry, one chocolate. 'Here you are. Hurry back so you get them in the freezer. When you want to learn some more chess, come and see me again.'

The dentist ushered Andrew into the hall, then out through the front door and onto the gravel drive, as if he'd found a stray kitten that might be better off elsewhere. He stood waving for a long time as Andrew hurried away, down his winding driveway, past the goat in the fenced garden, away from the grove with its fetid stream and back up the long scrubby lane to Fishponds. At one point, Andrew put the cold blocks down, and as he pissed, long and satisfyingly into the hedge, his cold hand was warmed by his own skin.

When Andrew reached the road of neat Victorian houses it was empty, and the witch's house was exactly as he had left it: brambles reaching out to catch you, ash trees, bushes, flowers and shadows – simmering and kaleidoscopic. He felt as if he had popped down an extraordinary rabbit hole and was reappearing only seconds later; he half expected to see John still waiting. Just like Alice, he was not sure what he had discovered, except that the world was full of tectonic plates, lives stacked on lives, and in some places discussion, oddity and fracture were normal. A curtain twitched and he hurried away up the steep road, the blocks wrapped in the jumper that he had taken from around his waist. Somehow he felt that if he let the precious ice-cream melt, a new way of thinking might melt with it. His mother didn't even own a fridge, let alone a freezer, and he wasn't sure what they would do with these three large slabs. But the bricks of ice cream didn't just say *eat me – I taste of luxury.* They said: *You, Andrew, are clever; it's alright that you're a thinker.*

When he saw John Hawke straddled across a wall half way up the Road, he almost believed that the power of thought must have conjured him.

'I knew you'd have to come back this way, Andy,' John said. 'I went to yours to pick up the card and money. Your mum's gone looking for you, to the scout hut.'

As if this was of no consequence, Andrew placed the bulky jumper on the wall between them.

'Do you like ice cream? Strawberry or chocolate?'

John's eyes widened.

'Where'd you get that? All I got was a gobstopper.'

Andrew was already unwrapping the chocolate slab and passing it over.

'But I expect your poor aunt would like vanilla?'

And he took that slab too and placed it on top of the other, as if this were bullion and he, Andrew, were finally cutting the deal.

Drowning – 1961

Matt and I made a rough camp on the empty beach, so Thomas could dig with the new spade and bucket and I could nurse the baby, tucking her down beside the windbreak. Behind us towered grey limestone, and at my feet lay stones threaded with quartz and dolerite: I collected the sparkling ones as treasure and discarded those with impurities. In the throwaway pile were ones of geological interest: compacted skeletons and long dead organisms, fractured surfaces sharp to the touch, colours that didn't somehow please. At that point in my life, I believed too much in perfection.

We ate our sandwiches at once, although it wasn't long past breakfast: corned beef and cheese, apples and crisps. Then Matt and I tried to read the paper. We took turns feigning interest in the tunnels, sandcastles and molluscs that Tom insisted we play with; I smoothed stones and white, fragile shells, even licking one, to see if it tasted as salty as in my childhood. Tom laughed and licked one himself, grinning at me under his flop of fringe. Then he grimaced at a mouthful of grit and spat out gobs of saliva onto the drying sand. He toed at the wetness, eyeing me to see if I would stop him. When I didn't, but instead held my hand across the baby's face, sheltering her from the sun, he jerked my fingers away.

'Come to the sea, Mummy. Put Chloe down.' He was dragging me up to follow, to chase him again to the water's fizzing edge.

I was worn out with the sleepless nights, wishing we had stayed at home that summer so Chloe would finally settle. I was cross, too, that my husband took more chances than me to close his eyes, to turn his back, or to read scientific papers – articles on war-time brainwashing, on how the truth is complex and ever changing, like patterns left by a tide pulling sand this way and that. He was a pharmacist, but would have liked to be something different. Whenever Tom went careering off to the headland, it was I who scuttled in pursuit, the baby once more dumped on a blanket. If I had been more awake I might have complained – or perhaps I would have enjoyed standing at the sea's brink, watching ferries chug into the harbour, the people waving. There was a time I might have explored, or squatted to poke in weedy rock pools, telling Tom the names I'd once learned myself: Hermit Crab, Gribble, Dead Men's Fingers. But that day I was all lethargy. The world, despite its canopy sky, the expanse of dipping water, seemed a boxed-in and finished affair. In London, people partied and wrote racy books, women claimed their independence. But here was I, living the life of my aunt and widowed mother.

I gave Tom his toys and sat on the damp sand, changing Chloe's nappy. I imagined Matt's face as I told him: *you're selfish, a bully, you're a flirt – we've nothing in common.* I was thinking I should maybe get divorced, and I savoured the word, feeling its heft and legality – although in reality, I had no idea how you made it happen, and, in any case, both his family and mine would have been appalled. And there was the baby now, as well as Tom. As if sensing the mutiny, Matt came and propped himself beside me.

'Hey, Tabs. We're on holiday, you know – our only holiday. Why are you always scowling? Anyone would think I'd press-ganged you into all this.'

I snorted, stuffing bits of pooey cotton wool into a plastic bag along with Chloe's sodden nappy. Crossly, I pulled the new one tight, tucking it under first one side, then the other, inserting the safety pin, hand protective against the baby's hot skin. I barely noticed how Chloe wriggled at the tightness and turned her blueberry eyes to her beloved Tom.

61

Matt smiled at Chloe, then crouched down beside me, sliding his arm around my waist and nuzzling into my neck. He was pecking at my skin, as if any minute he might eat me up. He smelled as ever of something vaguely musky, a hidden sort of scent that you wanted to possess by digging yourself deep inside it. He ran his fingers up and down, half tickling, half fondling, his hands caressing my full breasts, unusually womanly now I was feeding.

'Not here, Matt! People will see. Tom will!'

'People?' He looked incredulous. And it was true. Barely anyone was there – just an old couple setting up collapsible stools under the barrier and two others standing near the darker rocks. He whispered to me, brushing against my cheek as he did so. 'Let's have an early night.' I could hear his breath, the swooshing echo of lust in my ear, like the sound of shells, promising they held the ocean. 'I'll make the supper,' he said. 'We could buy fish from the boats, even get a bottle of wine.'

'Perhaps…'

'What would you like, then, if not that? What do you really want?'

He was exasperated, but curious, too. Perhaps he needed to see if I could surprise him. I stared up into his pale blue eyes and suddenly knew. It did not matter, for once, if my actions impressed or bored him.

'I want to swim. I haven't swum for months, haven't been alive since I was a child.'

Saying this – surprising myself, if not him – it was as if I had found something that I'd lost. And I saw, too, how words have power. You say something and make it happen.

'Go on, then. Take as long as you like. I'll mind the children.' He kissed me on the lips and his skin was hot, tasting of butter-closeness, the lust that had bound us both.

I picked up my towel, left my husband and children by the overhanging rocks. Our beach was to one side of a harbour that jutted into the bay. As I walked away from Matt, Chloe in his arms and Tom singing songs, I squinted out past the moored boats and saw a different shore on the other side of the harbour, a sandier one where our parallel life might have played out, had we gone to sit there and not here. Behind the quaint harbour, white houses spread along the hillside as if they were glued on and might at any moment landslide away. Our own holiday cottage was somewhere up there, with its claustrophobic rooms and impossibly dangerous garden. It had been raining earlier, so the beach was still fairly empty, no one trusting that the clouds wouldn't open again. Matt and I had thought getting wet was better than having another argument in that pokey kitchen.

We had wanted to wear out the children, and pretend to them and to ourselves that we'd never been happier. And here I was, miserable and finally alone, standing at the shoreline with a towel around my waist, no more contented than I had been back at our camp. Shuddering each time the sea washed my feet and ankles, I couldn't imagine immersing myself in the greeny-blue stretch of water, though that was what I had wanted only minutes before. I stared across to an isthmus half a mile away, where I could make out large boats and a rough, stone jetty. I had thought I might escape to that lonely jetty, but now I'd changed my mind, knew it was further than I could manage – though once I might have dared. In my childhood I had swum in lidos, in lakes too.

People were picking their way now down the steep steps from the road, then setting up camps at discreet distances from one another, deckchairs and bits of canvas pegged down. For the first time that week, the watery sun looked set to last. A dark skinned child came shrieking down the beach, followed by a lithe grandmother. They charged at the waves, sending white sprays up in a perfect arch; even before the foam had landed they were ploughing into the deeper stuff, throwing themselves in and beneath the coldness. Soon they were just blobs, seal heads sleek and swimming. That was a good way to go at life, I thought.

I edged in further. The water was so cold it hurt, but I knew if I could survive the first bit – getting my waist cold and then my chest and shoulders – it would become easier, even pleasurable. I cautiously moved into the green, lapping sea, dipping myself up and down as it became deeper, getting gradually colder, practising for what lay ahead. I might not be able to make that other shore, but I could swim out as far as the pair having races, diving under like bold sea creatures. If I were downstream, they wouldn't know I was following, was too cowardly to make my own way without a guide. I was scared of risking the darker water that lay just beyond. In the middle of the bay, half way to the distant jetty, there was a platform belonging to one of the fancy hotels. I'd seen people diving off or sitting sunbathing, recovering from the long haul.

I lay on my back and drifted, rising and falling with the swell, the ocean below, the sky above, and I hoped, should I need to put my foot down, I'd feel the reassurance of sharp stones or the bite of sand. I'd always needed an anchor, something to weight me, or tug against. I could hear the chug, chug of a boat and faint voices on the beach. My other life was waiting on the shore – the blueberry baby, the fretful little boy, my handsome husband.

It was then, as I curved back into the chill sea, twisting with the waves, drifting back to shore, that I caught sight of the woman. She was standing at the sea's edge and the man beside her held a soft cream towel, as if he were her valet. It was obvious she wanted to swim, but the shock of the cold had halted her. She was too thin, too vulnerable to iciness, perhaps. I thought her beautiful, like the Italian woman I'd known in my exchange year and been half in love with. I was normally shy, but I swam towards her.

'It's really good. It gets warmer, I promise.'

She squinted out at me. Then smiled, a slow smile that was almost a grimace. I thought I heard her say, *Ecco, Allora* as she threaded her way through the same stony route I had followed not long before. She waded closer and I saw how she was olive skinned, as I had once desired to be, and that she, too, shuddered as she splashed water over her arms and torso. She was wearing a fashionable two-piece and I felt dowdy in my navy costume.

'Oh, oh,' she called out, and turned back to the man who stood there, waiting with the towel. 'It's cold,' she shouted and he smiled, peering into the sun and shading his eyes with one hand. I realised she was Irish, not Italian and, despite this, I wanted to take her from him, and was thinking of something clever to say. But she plunged in anyway and came swimming towards me, head high, so that her piled dark hair would not get wet.

'Thank you. I would have turned back if you'd not called out.' Her voice was accented and the soft words puffed out as she pulled an elegant breaststroke. As she swam close, her wide mouth stretched into that strange smile, her head arched regally out of the waves. 'Ah, if one could always swim away.' This she sighed out. She was older than I had first thought, maybe in her thirties or forties, but there was something poised in her – something reckless, too. We swam silently together, moving out to where the grandmother and child raced back and forth. Then the silence grew too much.

'They look like locals – like it's their sea. I followed them out before you came.'

She turned her head and appraised me.

'Well, I'm just borrowing their sea for the day; I have to go back to Ireland tomorrow. Perhaps I should swim back home right now. Do you fancy a paddle across the Irish sea?'

I imagined the swell and loneliness, how I would sink and drown and see her delicate stroke forging ahead. I laughed, holding back the fears that were always ready to tumble out.

'My children are on the shore. I don't think I should let you abduct me today.'

'Well – it's the children I'd probably far rather abduct. I should have liked children. It's too late now. You're lucky. *Blessed*, my mother would say.'

I told her it didn't always feel like that. We huffed out our words, shuddering at the cold, while we floated and crested, drifting, then pulling a few strokes.

'I think very little of life feels blessed, unless you are looking back – or forward. We perhaps have to invent our blessings.' She told me how neither she, nor her sisters had children. 'A family curse,' she announced it as if this were myth. 'My father ran off with his wife's half-sister. We're not quite legitimate, you see, so the good Lord has dried up our wombs. Well, that's what Auntie Mary says.'

The man on the shore was still there, like her fixed marker, her buoy. She noticed me staring at him with his towel and then at my own dots: Matt, Tom, the baby.

'He will stay there all day. If we go to Ireland and back, he'll be waiting when we get washed up at dawn.' He had looked older than her, sixty perhaps, but I didn't want to ask questions. Between us, we were prising something apart and I dared not spoil it, snap life shut again with the usual dowdy chatter. She held one arm out of the water and waved, as if she were drowning or needed saving. He waved back and I thought it sweet how fond she seemed. Even if I didn't know of her wildness then, I must have sensed it, felt its toxicity.

'Why don't we swim out to the platform. I wasn't quite brave enough on my own.'

She measured the distance, assessed how much better a swimmer I was than her. 'Are you good at life-saving, too?'

'I will if you will.' I was in love with her green-pebble eyes, her olive skin and aquiline nose. We turned to face the open sea, the white waves breaking at the distant entrance to the bay. 'I won't swim my crawl; I'll do breast stroke with you.' I pretended I was being gallant, so I wouldn't outstrip her, but in reality, I was scared of getting breathless, of the slap of cold water-salt knocking out my last bits of strength.

We set off sedately, past the child and old lady, past the great rock that jutted to our left. I guessed that the woman was as aware as I was that we were moving out of our depth, that the sea was already tugging beneath us, indifferent and cold. Neither of us spoke. She was frowning slightly, concentrating. Our arms, cleaving the waves, made a mesmerising and soothing sound.

Half way there, the platform began to recede, as if someone hauled at it with a great chain, heaving it across the restless sea, all the way back to Ireland. I told myself to stay calm, not to panic. I had seen others on the platform, so it was manageable – although I hadn't, until now, taken into consideration the tide and how that might change the distance and difficulty. Did someone up on the terrace of the hotel watch our foolish, audacious splashings, murmuring to the waitress that they would not have risked it at this time of day? I imagined the current carrying us both away, the unknown Irish stranger dying alongside me. I put on a spurt, pulling at the oily water that was getting colder second by second. Even as I launched onward, all my instincts screamed, *go back, turn around for Matt*, my beloved Matt.

There was more of a swell here, too, a keener sense of the sea's indifference, its power to use or toss you aside. I was aware of fish and other shadowy creatures moving along beneath us, and thought how something might stretch up and grab my ankle, pulling me mercilessly down, while I gulped and whimpered for salvation. I swam faster, trying to catch up with my panicky whoosh of breath, not wanting to be limestone and the sea-bed's silt. My stroke grew awkward. More used to crawl than breaststroke, I was timing things badly, water sloshing in my eyes and open mouth. I thought of my fragile baby, whose name I did not like, of my son who was comic – but I did not consider my husband again, nor this woman whom I'd tempted into my broken life. Everything is a lie, I suddenly thought, but perhaps you can choose the better lies, edit yourself, re-package the version you think is the truth. If you leave your husband, it is one broken thing; if you stay, a different sort of fracture.

I did not once look back. Could not look back, in case the foolish woman needed saving. I wondered if she knew this, if she could read the truth of me as I darted away. Soon, I could hear the slosh and slap of sea against the raft-like platform, a lonely sound, full of the hollow darkness that lay beneath me and ahead. I wanted to cease this cold business of moving arms and legs in heavy water and having the salty slop of sea in my mouth and face. Three or four strokes from the raft, I slowed, acted casual, pretended it had all been easy, no doubt that we'd both make it. Despite its bleakness, the water cresting the sides of blackened wood was beautiful, the raft a sacred thing.

When I tried to haul myself up the metal ladder, water cascading from my body, streaming from the heavy costume and from my shaking arms, the sea took hold, tugging me down, sucking me deep into itself. I felt a new swell of coldness, the raft creaking and shifting like a living thing, telling me that each dark night cuts you; that loneliness presses deep. I was only flotsam, my hands clinging to cold metal rungs and my breath coming in short gasps. *If I let go, it would be easy, somehow, this gentle sinking forever.* I rested a second and heaved again. A huge weariness and heaviness was spreading from my head to my wrinkled feet as I climbed the stiff, shiny rungs.

Up on the shifting raft, the wood was warm and soft as a bed, the heat of the sun pressed into the greying planks. A wet patch stained the wood dark wherever I moved and when I sat down, legs over the side, I noticed how a strange shadow like a creature circled my wet costume, as if the wood had taken parts of me into itself. I checked for the woman and she was there, lumbering along, metres away, treading water, a quizzical expression on her beautiful face. She came towards me, not tired at all, as if she was used to swimming, used to the testing of self, and used to people multiplying, metamorphosing into strangeness. I hoped she did not know she had been abandoned, left to drown in my wake. She gave no sign and was instead calling out, 'Wonderful. Wonderful. An adventure.'

She swam to the side, rested a second, then hauled herself easily up the steps, coming to flop down beside me, her sharp, tugging breath matching my own. I could see that her olive skin had gone pimply and blue and she wrapped her arms around herself hugging in the scant warmth. I wanted to put my own arms around her and feel the shock of skin-touching coldness. She looked me up and down, as if she could guess my thoughts, then sighed. We were companionably silent, taking satisfying, shuddering breaths, gazing back at the smudged beach, the coloured flap of canvass, the small figures dotted, the beach flags fluttering their red and yellow warning: like adventurers of old, we were foolhardy and magnificent.

'But at least it's ours now, we've gained something,' she asserted, knowing what I was thinking, peering back at the posh hotel on the rocks, with its deckchairs and lunching area outdoors. She put up two delicate fingers. 'That's to the rich kids. If some holy Joe wants to turn us off, they'll have to swim a damn long way to do it.'

'You make me feel like a pirate. Like a child playing.'

She laughed. 'Be a pirate! That's what I am. A pirate who steals people's lives.'

When I asked her what she meant, she brushed the question away and touched the lapping sea with her delicate toes, the nails painted palest, pastel blue. Down in the water a silvery shoal darted from her strangely refracted foot. Clare – for that was her name – shook her head, as if theirs was a predictable pattern. She pulled her foot up and twisted to stare at the isthmus with its hidden cove, simple jetty and three moored boats.

That morning Matt and I had walked out of our cottage and climbed high, threading along the cobbled streets until we could touch the petrel sky. We trained our binoculars on this far peninsular, spotting the huge house behind beech trees, then focused on wedding guests, surging in and out of the harbour cafes, the women clutching wide-brimmed hats as they climbed aboard the rocking boats to take them across to the Isthmus wedding. A man had given his hand to a girl balanced on high heels, one foot extending into the shifting boat, the other on land. I told Matt this was how my life was: poised on one unsteady foot, a second before pitching into deep water. When I repeated these things to Clare she looked at me with interest.

'What did your husband say?'

'He said that I was ever the drama queen, and we should go and get some lunch.' I was intending to stop there, but added – 'I think Matt should have married my sister.'

I did not tell Clare how that morning I had decided to leave him, before he got more chances to leave me.

Clare nodded, as if what I'd said or what Matt did was what might have been expected. She pointed out a smudge of whiteness on the isthmus that must have been a marquee; band music had started up and was tossed across to us in discordant gusts.

'I'm meant to be there,' she suddenly said. 'It's my god-daughter's wedding. But I couldn't bear it. Simply couldn't bear the idea. I bailed out. I'll turn up for the party tonight, perhaps.' She scrutinised me, as if to assess what she could risk. 'It's complicated. I went out with the man she's marrying.'

She had turned to sit cross-legged and stared across the bay towards the distant grand house, with its fluttering flags and banners. She may have been over forty, I decided, but could have passed for thirty, perhaps less. I wanted her to talk more, but felt that she had dismissed the subject.

Later, I would think about her, embellishing her story and imagining what I would have done if I'd been her. She told me the man still loved her, but that her god-daughter was pregnant. We sat a while longer, talking about men, about our desire for chocolate and saltiness, about the places we had swum when we were children: quarries, lakes and rivers, the sea. She had shuffled closer and our arms touched as we sat side by side. Then we noticed that the gap between the shore and the raft was growing. The tide was coming in; it had covered the big black rock that we had set off from and was reaching its way back up the stony shore, probably about to snatch my jelly shoes and abandoned towel. Her dot of a man was still standing just as she'd said he would be.

'I suppose that means the tide will help us back, if we're lucky? I'm a bit whacked.' I did not mind letting her know that I was not as confident as I'd first pretended, although perhaps she'd known this all along.

'Do you know, I believe in luck, in four-leaved clover and such nonsense. I think it was fate that you were there for me today, to make this horrible event better; it's fate that we'll get back.'

'Do you really believe in fate?'

'Mostly. Other times I think life is how you make it.'

'And how would you make it, if you could choose?'

'Like now. Moments like this.' She smiled and I smiled back. I was stupidly in love. Before we once more slid into the sea, a sea colder than ever, she turned to me and said, 'You're lucky to have a husband and children. Hang on to them. Don't be like me, only wanting what you can't have.'

It was easier going back. Even those moments when it seemed as if the shore wasn't getting closer, we knew that each stroke, each pull, was gliding us to safety, back to the thing we thought we hadn't wanted. When at last our legs and knees scraped on the stony shore, we stumbled to stand upright. Clare clasped me and we toppled forward, supporting each other as we made our way up the wobbly beach, waves pushing our legs this way and that. I could feel the cold sheen of her skin against mine, the muscles on her shoulders and then, as I slipped my hand down, could feel her delicate ribs. Her arm circled my waist and I didn't care if she thought me fat.

'Wonderful,' Clare exclaimed as we waded towards the man. Our feet kicked up a fine spray of water and we splashed our way out, picking a route through the sharp stones and gritty sand. She gave me a last squeeze and the world turned back in on itself and the sounds of the sea receded to a hushing moan, far at my back.

The man gave an ironic bow, then threw the towel around Clare's shoulders who snuggled against it and pressed her damp body into his. She smiled coquettishly and I didn't know if I was being dismissed or if she was communicating something new and secret.

'Good luck with things. Thanks for the adventure.' And she turned, like a queen with her attendant, while I trudged alone up the beach.

When I stubbed my toe on a stone and cried out briefly, Clare didn't look back. So I glanced up to see if Matt was coming, but it was Tom, not Matt, who was bounding towards me, dragging another towel across the sand, then dropping it half way so he could run faster.

*

My mermaid friend turned up again, just once and years later. It was after Matt had left me – not for my sister, but for my best friend. I was living with the four children in my mother's holiday home in the south west, waiting for the London house to be sold. Rummaging in a village jumble sale in a marquee, I was looking idly for a salt cellar, turning over mounds of clothes, a feather boa, books, a box of crystals and coloured rocks. An older elegant woman, serving behind the stall, was also ploughing through the pile, head bent, pulling out bits and pieces of clothing that she placed decoratively across the top. Perhaps thinking she was doing a good job at assessing my style, she hauled out a floral blouse with a large bow at the neck, then held it up against herself, turning her head at an arch angle, perhaps in imitation of me. When she gave me that strange smile, I stared back, sure she would recognise me and say something. Her hair was grey. She hauled out orange trousers and a bright green old lady hat with a ribbon and artificial flower sewn in, and I felt the lick of contempt as she took in my cropped hair, my dowdy T-shirt and brown cords.

'Now this is what I call an outfit. Are up for an adventure?'

'Mummy, can I?' asked Ruby, one of the twins, taking the hat and plonking it on her ten year old head. When I paid over the money, my fingers touched Clare's cool palm and I almost spoke, almost said, *I love you.*

Then Ruby clutched hold of my hand, her shock of ginger hair covered by the old lady's hat. Outside, I breathed in cold air and bright sunlight and saw things for what they were: what the mermaid had told me that day on the beach was deceit, or it was something she'd felt for a moment and which for a moment had been a partial truth. *Hang on to the man,* she'd told me – when she might have said something else, might have set me free, or even taken me with her.

And now I had four children, not two. Over by the candyfloss store the others lounged, picking bits of the pale pink stuff off with their fingers, stuffing it into their open mouths. Tom was minding the younger ones; when he saw me he raised his hand, casual and assured. It had been stuffy inside the jumble sale marquee. Depressing: all that abandoned stuff, as if all our stories only led to the same dull place. Out here, I could feel the the space of my life: the estuary with its constant flux, the crazy village I'd come to live in, the large house my mother and aunt said they'd one day sell me, and I'd be a fool to buy.

'Shall we get the ferry home?' I asked.

'Too expensive?' queried Tom, for I'd trained him well.

'Ferry home, look for seals, buy fish for supper.' They looked at me as if I'd gone mad – and that's how it felt. 'Have a barbecue: eat nuts, cakes, wine, then abduct the neighbours.'

'I don't like fish, said Ruby. 'Or the neighbours.'

'New shores,' I said enigmatically. 'New shores.'

I hurried the four children down the jetty, away from my memories of drowning. Chloe and Ruby bickered together, Tom and Seth bowled on ahead: my mixed blessings, the lot I had somehow chosen. We clambered aboard a boat that was magically waiting, shifting its bulk in the sluggish estuary water. Looking down from the deck into the shadows and impurities in the water, I seemed to see a body moving amongst thick weeds and darkness. The dead eyes stared up and I turned away, embarrassed by an inability to read myself. When I licked my lips, they were the sea and I thought how miraculous things were, how subtly veiled. I could hear the slosh of water against the side of the boat, the sucking of a restless tide. I had seen Clare's slim body alive in that marquee, drowned yet still afloat, and in her green sceptical eyes I had read that she was me and I was her, each of us bold or weak in turn, and each waiting for love's next theft: the caress of a woman, the new child to suckle, a man to excite us. *What else is there?*, she seemed to ask.

Mist – 1971

This is often how it is: you think something has ended, then find it's a new beginning. But sometimes it's neither – or both of these.

So it was for the couple – lying on the prickly grass, welcoming the lengthening shadows, wondering what they should do. Gauzy dusk had settled in the ruined abbey; and Mali, her boyfriend, and the musicians were wrapped together in an ebb and flow of light. The last few visitors were drifting away and soon the girl and the boy would go home too, back to Cardiff where they would finally need to make up their minds.

All around, the ribbed walls of the abbey stretched up, and the arched and broken windows gave out onto a darkening sky. The river was over to the left, the field with indifferent cows to the right, and ahead the funny little band played on as if their lives depended upon it. Perhaps, thought Mali, the song held the answer; perhaps the words, like an ancient rune, would be her guide. She did not expect much from Benedict.

There were five musicians in all: two women and three men, and for the past hour they had been singing and playing on wooden pipes and stringed things, conjuring a medieval atmosphere for the weekend tourists. Now and again, they paused or shuffled music around, swapping instruments and talking to one another quietly. It was in these moments that the birdsong grew clear and Mali couldn't work out if it was a robin or canary, if the thing was caged or free.

'I like the bird better than the band,' she whispered, just to speak and to make Ben look at her. Before he could turn away, she tumbled on. 'Have you noticed how that man's the joker?' She layered everything with a hint of mockery, as if, like Ben, she was above taking herself seriously. 'And that older one's in charge.' The grey haired man tapped his foot impatiently whenever the tempo went slack. Mali was not sure if it was worse being the man in the silly hat, turning from one woman to the other to make them laugh, or being the bossy one counting everyone in. Taking life seriously was doomed, and so was making a fool of yourself.

'That old man's like my dad,' she said, after a pause. 'And I bet he takes his irritation out on them.'

Her father would have been getting cross by now, tired from concentrating on something that had failed to make the grade. The old infection of hopelessness would be seeping through, as inevitably as the chill of evening. Mali shivered and put her hands under Ben's T-shirt, feeling the warmth of his body, the curling hairs of his chest. Her father had been handsome; it let you get away with things, gave you power.

'Do you know?' she said, and this time she needed Ben to pay attention, for if he drifted away it would prove something. 'My dad and you, you're alike: only children, both with a parent in the police force. Dad said that only children hate rivals. He was right.' She did not add *and you're both too handsome for your own good.* Ben narrowed his eyes as if nothing Mali said made sense, or was shrouded in a meaning that there was no point in unravelling.

'Is that so, little Goosie? And I know another thing; it's you that hates a rival.'

It was early evening and the mild weather had made it misty. Once upon a time, monks would have settled where they lay, would have rested on the stone seats of the cloister, reading before Compline. Maybe they too waited for grace – as Mali did now. Perhaps the scent of rosemary and lavender, mingled with mossy words, would have conjured places they'd rather be. Might a boy rest his finger on the page – slide his mind from the prodigal's return – and taste the roasting calf, see his mother cooking and his father milking cows? He'd look at bent heads, men mouthing delicate verses, the shrouded rivalries. Were those careful Cistercians, the young especially, as prone to wanting what had earlier been lightly cast aside?

Mali considered her childhood. Her father had been powerful and no one – least of all their mother – had thought to check him. It had made his children – Mali, Alun and Dai – wary and too quick to please. She wanted to tell Benedict so he would understand, would know why she wanted to put things right now.

'We called Dad, Spap – secretly, of course – because he'd asked us to call him Paps. A ridiculous name. Like he was Lord of the Manor. So we spelled it backwards.' She looked at Ben and he was watching, but she didn't know if he listened. 'He used to hit us hard – slaps, or, rather spaps. Once he washed our mouths out with soap because we lied – protecting each other.' She didn't say how, in its back-to-frontness, the word pushed open a gap, revealed the truth that everyone was evading.

'Poor Goosie. I would have run away,' Ben said. 'I would have run away or hit him.'

Later, Mali's father died in a car crash – her mother driving. They'd gone out of the door arguing and an hour later they were in hospital. Her mother got better; her father never regained consciousness. When Mali was seventeen, her mother moved to Brazil where she joined a cult and wrote long letters telling her daughter that guilt was negative; people must learn to let go: blood ties, ownership of property, family demands.

Mali and Ben had travelled up to the abbey in the university coach. It was an alumni trip and they had taken it at the last minute, knowing that friends had bailed out, leaving spaces. It had seemed a good idea, as if physical distance from the day-to-day might give emotional distance too, a little objectivity. As soon as they were on the coach, with all the stupid chatter and gossip – Lyn coming to sit by them, pretending nothing was going on – they realised it was a mistake. Mali felt sick even before they got to Newport and though she tried to sleep, people kept singing, as if they were on a school trip, not serious university graduates and post-graduates, taking a visit to a historical site.

At the abbey Ben told the organiser they'd make their own way back and the two set off alone, walking a path Mali remembered from childhood. It was not as long as it had once seemed, and she wondered at her earlier self, complaining about tired legs even before her family had left the paved section. Memory played tricks, she found, sweetening the past or demonising it. Trees straggled along the lane, nettles and dock grew everywhere. She and Ben tramped, hand-in-hand, following the broad sweep of the river as if it could lead to the unexpected, could even mystically advise, with its lapping and urgent swishing.

Eventually, after they'd draped themselves over a gate to stare at reeds, and at a field with a fat horse, Ben spread out his Aunt Fanny's picnic rug and tossed down his jacket. Lying on the grass they told stories of childhood: the sort of thing they might have expected to swap at the beginning, but were only just coming to, three years on. It had always been a back-to-front relationship: friends at the beginning, moving on to casual lovers, only becoming intense when her flirtation with an old boyfriend, followed by Ben's affair with Lyn, made them more possessive. It was as if they had barely known each other before. Yet she was not sure if his stories were true, nor if she believed the ones she confided to him. It was only with her brothers she could risk being honest.

Mali looked across at Ben, sprawled on the grass of the abbey. If she screwed up her eyes so that he was less sweet looking, she found him more handsome. He was too moody to deserve such regular features. The incongruity irritated, as if he was cheating on her in this too. Things should be as they seem, she naively thought; the surface of life should reflect what lies beneath. One or two university friends had warned her about Ben when they'd first split, suggesting he was predatory, but then, the instant they were a couple again, the friends denied they'd said anything. She vaguely wondered if it was she who'd invented the warnings, misery giving her insight.

The gang would be back in Cardiff by now, sitting in a pub, drinking their way into the weekend. They might be closeted in their houses, gossiping about Mali and Ben, about whether she would drown him, or he her. She had no idea what bus would get her and Ben home, or even if such an escape existed. They lay on the grass as if turned to stone. If she had not looked back that first time, but had walked away from him, they would not be here today, facing something too big for either of them. She thought of their slummy flat with Lyn living upstairs, pretending to be a friend.

The older musician glanced up and frowned, perhaps considering what to do with the interlopers. He looked down at his instrument, as if only just noticing the strange thing he held. Someone called out that the cafe was shut, someone else was walking around closing up for the night, although there was nothing much to close. The crumbled walls, doorways onto nothing, steps down to grass dead-ends had been battered by wind and rain for centuries, by vandals too. The young musician looked at his watch and turned to one of the women, frowning as she mimed having a drink. Mali wondered whether they had been secretly laughing at her and Ben lying there, behaving like silly children.

She picked up another slice of fruit cake and Ben checked her.

'It's deadly stuff, Goosie. Enough is enough. Do you want to make yourself ill?'

But I am ill, she thought. He ran his finger up and down her arm, then over her face, tracing her eyes, her nose, her broad lips.

'We haven't decided yet, Mals.'

But we have, Mali, thought. *You've made things perfectly clear.*

'Have you noticed,' said Ben, 'the military metronome? When he's not counting his band in, he's goes on tapping – hand and foot. Like he wants them to march to his tune. Left, right, left right.'

'I suppose the rest are a bit ragged, like they're floating in a world of their own.'

'Like you, Goosie. Just like you.'

He blew smoke-rings into the air and watched them drift, then dissolve. She took the cigarette from his fingers and drew in smoke until her head swam. That was when the young boy turned to the band and raised his shoulders, and the friendly woman in the black velvet hat, a hat Mali might have liked for herself, nodded back, communicating things without words. Like her parents. Like the twins, Dai and Alun. Like Benedict. The little band pulled itself out of weariness for the last number, and once more music poured into the limp afternoon.

Mali wondered if the band were as washed out and empty as she was. She had barely slept the night before and had just walked four miles. She presumed this was how grown-up life would be. Superficially doing things – talking or pretending to have a nice time – while inside you were pulled this way and that, confused and acrimonious. She was, perhaps, her father's daughter after all.

If Mali were the leader of the band, she'd probably point out the lack-lustre performance. With the young boy, in particular, she'd be sharp, for he was the one whose concentration had gone. He had glanced over when she and Ben had burst onto the scene, looking up to laugh at their shrieks. Ben had been stuffing grass down Mali's back. Not so very medieval, the boy's look had said, a breath of fresh air. So they had felt welcomed, felt it their right to tumble onto the grass with rucksack and sandwiches, spread out their old blanket in the grassy nave, roof broken to the sky. The young man – handsome, with fine cheekbones, long hair and a quizzical expression – had been looking over ever since, staring at Mali in particular, at her bare stomach and flared trousers, her legs tangled with Ben's, their sprawl of picnic stuff: cola, shop-bought sandwiches and soggy dope-cake. She half suspected he guessed what they ate.

Mali did not know why she and Ben lingered. Was it to prolong this moment? Never make a decision? A gaggle of Japanese tourists filtered down the aisles, down stone steps and out into a courtyard, as if they were lost or a hallucination. She could hear strange receding voices, comforting and alien; and the sounds were all out of tune. Mali was no musician – she'd got no further than grade one – but she thought the mistakes must come from the young, long-haired boy, not the metronome man. Perhaps her and Ben's show of youth made him want to escape back into the twentieth century, away from the austere black notes on the stave, away from the wobbly music stand. Perhaps he too was facing something ugly, a decision that meant he would lose out whichever way he chose.

The pair had managed to sit on the grass for almost an hour, holding between them their unspoken problem. All day they had been pretending they had not brought it out, that this was just an ordinary outing. All along the river walk, in the pub and then back in the tearooms, they had behaved as if the last six weeks had not happened. If anything, they had been more cheerful than usual. Someone looking at them might think they were in love, two students who had just met and were trying hard to impress. She took another bite of dope cake and thought of the baby, or seed, or whatever it was. Everything's fine, she told herself, my life's just hunky-dory.

The last of the sun's light slanted in through arches and doorways. Mali imagined monks preparing food, then reading, perhaps singing in Latin. She would not have told her friends but sunsets, books, solitary walks, the monks haunting her now – all these were her religion. But it was a religion she had no intention of revealing; mostly she acted like she enjoyed a good time. When she got back, she would make fun of the musicians and declare they were utterly forgettable. Earlier, the band had played quietly enough, but now had they snatched up strange instruments and the sounds grew louder and more discordant. The boy held a curved thing like a hockey stick and took deep breaths, puffing up his cheeks to make rasping sounds – like an animal in pain. Up until this point, the tunes had suggested medieval decorum, but this stuff was gut instinct and primeval survival. Someone else picked up a weird piece of wood and began baying, the howling song weaving dissonance into the pagan dance. This was the first time Mali had paid proper attention. Though the music wasn't tuneful, she felt in the echo around each strangled note something authentic and strained, a world less concerned with artifice or compliance. The notion comforted her – much more than the sweeter music had done.

The hairs on Ben's arms were downy and Mali fingered them, wishing that she could transport herself into a world where people knew better than to cover up their lies with sophisticated sugaring, layering more lies over the top of the old so you didn't know where you were and what to believe. She wanted her relationship to have the directness and honesty of this baying music, although she knew she was seldom honest herself. Ben said he still loved her, that he thought they should marry and that he wanted lots of children – only not the one in her belly. This child was a madness and a mistake. Surely, he'd said, even you can see that. I have a part-time job and could support it, he'd said, but I don't want to be trapped. And you shouldn't want it either, not if you've any sense, any intelligence. He had been standing in their Victorian flat with his back to the window and the light streaming through made her squint. She could not see his face properly, could not read the expression there, but she did notice that when he heard footsteps in the flat above, he paused a moment and strained to listen to whether it was one set or two.

Ben turned and circled his finger on her stomach, around and around her navel. His eyes had gone vacant from the dope, but he looked sadly at her, as if sorry that all this was happening. The circling movement made her feel vaguely nauseous.

'We could get a room,' he said. 'A treat. What about that bed and breakfast up the road?'

She imagined stepping into the claustrophobia of the thatched house: flowery curtains, an unsettling smell, the pair of them pretending to be married, a bed made up in a tiny room and the sounds of the host family filtering its way up to the chintzy bedroom.

'I have to see the doctor tomorrow. Remember? You were going to take the morning off work.'

'I have. That's why it's okay to stay; we can go see the doctor another day.' He took her silence as compliance. 'It's a shame we can't sleep here,' he whispered. 'Here in the nave.' He leaned over and licked her ear. 'We could ask them to marry us. Or do you think such sacrilege merits a bolt from heaven?'

She looked up, out of the ripped apart nave, into the open sky, at the soft purpling clouds and wondered if heaven had a bolt that could hurt her as much as Ben had. The blasting fragments of music, quixotic and Arabic, floated high out of her reach, up into the broken arches above the musicians and then out into free air. Gone.

II

Five years into her second, disastrous marriage, ten years since the day at the abbey, Mali is filling time, wandering around the shops of a small market town and buying things: a battered Wordsworth, olive oil, food from the market, a wooden sword. There is no pregnancy to complicate matters, but although she wants to leave, week after week she puts it off. She has only come away because old friends arranged the weekend trip, and until the gulf is ripped irrecoverably open, she and Des will go on pretending that life is fine – their world is hunky-dory.

Old cars chug along the narrow street, making their way to the vintage car rally in the castle car-park. Fumes from antique exhaust pipes billow up, making Mali feel sick. Her husband has already parked the Lanchester – she had first met him when he bought the car from Ben – along with the others; each one proudly displaying, then enviously looking at cars grander than their own. She has grown tired of people exclaiming about shiny bumpers, leather seats and wooden dashboards, of people gawping and pointing. She has begun to feel like an exhibit herself and, with this husband, she always has been. She knows now what she did not register when she married Benedict – that her oddity is attractive, with her wide mouth and brown eyes and asymmetrical face. But perhaps she is not attractive enough for her present husband, and probably a bit too clever. Once some men have got the measure of looks, the come-on they seem to offer, they are less eager to deal with the complications beneath.

In the car-park, she had wanted to tell a giggly woman with a low-cut top and hooped earrings, leaning into the car and exclaiming how she would love just to sit at the wheel, that her handsome, smiling husband is quite boring really, that he spends hours in the garage, and when he is not with the oily rags or attending car shows, he is visiting his secretary, pretending they talk over legal case history.

To get away from the stench of exhaust fumes, and because she is buying things she does not want, that she will no doubt leave when she eventually packs to go, Mali turns into the castle grounds. She pays an entrance fee, barely registering what the chatty woman at the counter is saying, and drifts in, preoccupied. She must look weary and fugitive, she thinks – and as old as time. Immediately she is beyond the castle walls, everything is eased and a peace descends, thickened, perhaps by the place's history. She wonders if the soft air, lulling and soporific, obeys some unintelligible rule of physics, counterbalancing the castle's slaughter with an energy altogether more healing. There are wide patches of grass, neat paths and beds of full-blown roses, as well as other plants she can not name, but which grew – possibly still grow – in her childhood home.

The rubble walls of the castle rise up, smudged sandstone, pock-marked and battered with age, the deepest gouges patched with a rough mortar. She reads that the walls have withstood burning, cannon fire and civil war, and that bodies once littered the entrance. She moves quickly away, over the newly mown lawn and stares at the crumbled turrets, the seagulls circling. Through high arched windows and blasted walls, rooms still balance, where lives played out or unravelled, just as her own is doing. Mali winds her way up steep stairs, past scarred rooms displaying information about kings and queens and facsimiles of the castle in different centuries. Like any human life, the building has known mixed fortune: wealth then poverty, importance, followed by obscurity. She climbs and climbs, first the clanging metal stair-case and then up the uneven, shadowy tower.

If she leaves Des, he has made it clear she will have no money – stupid to have married a lawyer, adept with more than one type of machinery. Halfway up, and unsure whether to keep going, she rests, getting her breath back.

She thinks about the reality of divorce and balances the bag, full of things she has bought with his money, against her shaky legs. How ludicrous to have with her the wooden sword, as if she takes the place by storm. She looks down the shadowy, precipitous stairwell and carefully turns, places her hand back on the cool rail.

There is something consoling in the effort of the climb, breath huffing out, fingers sliding over metal, over a wall scored with old and new graffiti. She is aware of differing shades of grey as the stone tower finally rises towards the unseen sky. Several times she pauses, balancing on the dipped steps, gripping tight, letting her breath steady. She should exercise more, get fit before she gets old. Wasn't that last year's resolution, or was it even the year's before? Or was last year's that she should get another job, even if Des made work so difficult? She presses her face close to the slatey wall, to the layering of murk, then sticks out her tongue and licks at the black, dark matter. It tastes of emotions kept at bay, of the tang of illogic.

Above, she sees the shifting flickers of sunlight but is dizzy from too much turning. She secures the bags against the wall and then drops onto all fours, crawls up the narrowing gyre, her hands splayed on the cold, smooth stone. When she reaches a small door, she hauls herself upright and takes a quick step out onto the walkway – a precarious shelf that winds around the tower, a place that would normally have scared her. She edges herself along a circular wall that has felt the weight of medieval bodies. The river meanders away ahead and the pretty town with its red roofs and gardens dances around the castle, then spreads back up to the distant church where a bell rings, fades and rings again. The ground is a long way down and when she steps over to the railing that stops people falling, she sees how easy it would be to topple herself over. This last year, she has been depressed. Has taken to bed and pulled the covers over her head, breathing in mustiness, a misty absence. She thinks of Benedict, although for years she has pushed him from her mind.

She imagines stepping out from the edge of the tower, the plunge into cool shafts of air. If she could fly as Icarus once did, she would soar over the houses, over the silly toy cars parked by the harbour, then escape out into the broad estuary, away to a new life.

Mali is leaning over the parapet, high over the estuary, shifting herself forward and back, rocking as she sometimes does, hunkered in her room. Down below, the tide recedes and the broad sweep of the bay has turned to mud and runnels: tussocky clumps of grass at the edges and faint tracings of shiny water glinting across a wide expanse of brown. The distant hills are a smudged grey line and Mali thinks she could live somewhere like this, a place full of stillness and perpetual motion. Small boats lie upended in mud, tilted precariously near deeper channels of water; soon the tide, flowing back in, will obscure the pattern, the route to the sea.

This is when she feels a moment's panic. Perhaps Des, somewhere down below, watches and knows what she thinks. He does not see why she should leave him; he has said his sons – though they are not hers - need security. Her thoughts are tiring and circular, just as they are at home in the immaculate house she both likes and hates. And then the strange music starts – an eerie sound that washes over and fades, just as the bells' ring did. She turns from the low turrets of weathered stone, and moves towards the cavernous doorway, and the sound comes funnelling up. This is not music, she thinks – this is the wailing inside me.

Stepping into the tower, away from bright sunlight, the darkness is startling. She is tempted to crawl down backwards and wonders what it has amounted to, the long haul up and the ignominious shuffle back. What has she learned? What will she ever learn? The discordant music comes in fanfares, the gaps in the castle wall offering strange, truncated bursts. Mali grips the cold rail, and, rather than crawling backwards, shuffles forward blindly, one foot after another. When the rail gives way to string, she sways, thinking how ironic it would be to fall now, when she has pulled back from that other edge. The steps are worn and slope in odd ways, the rail and smoothed walls polished by too many hands, too much history.

It is more precarious making her way down than it had been struggling up. Each time the circle of steps reaches an opening and a large turret room appears, she is relieved and pauses, stands in the huge space, imagining its press of lives. What does the trail of history or the imprint of one life amount to? She reads the information boards – sons killing their fathers, daughters eloping to safety – and these stories offer one sort of lie, her imagination another. The excavation of truth has never been easy, perhaps because ease is what Mali hopes for.

The castle is hosting an event – some sort of historical reconstruction – so they have set up a café under the trees edging the castle walls. When Mali gets back down, her legs are wobbly from the tremendous effort. She feels unsteady and wanders across to where people behind trestle tables serve homemade cake, biscuits, cups of tea. She will add sugar, she thinks – something restorative. The music has stopped, as if she had invented the wailing. If she leaves Des, she will hurt his sons, the youngest of whom she has bought the wooden sword for. They will miss her; she will miss them. She struggles to remember if her signature also signed away the boys. But that is too medieval. Surely Des cannot stop her visiting his sons and having them to stay? As Mali pays for a cup of tea, a voice interrupts her.

'Don't forget your purse.'

She turns and a man smiles across, his hair short and dark, greying at the temples. He is holding out her tapestry purse. For a moment, she wonders where she knows him from and if he is one of the tiresome people Des plays golf with, or invites to dinner. It even occurs to her that Des might have had her followed. Not for one moment does she make a connection with her past. Too many other things are spinning.

'Or are you leaving my band a bequest?'

And it is when the man laughs at her confusion, that she is transported – to that other day, that other decision. Here is the man who played badly with the band, the man who smiled at her and Benedict – only in those days, the man's hair was long and he was young. How had she not guessed when she first heard the baying music? And how can he not see how momentous this is? Ten disastrous years have settled like a drenching mist. And this man is the revelation of mistakes made over and over. She talks as if he must surely intuit this.

'That tune. You were playing the weird tune, like you did at Tintern, years ago.'

It is his turn to look perplexed.

'The wailing. It made me come down from the tower. I was thinking about throwing myself off.'

She does not know if this is the truth. She registers the man's startled look, the way her voice has trembled out the words. He replies as if she jokes, but fixes on her uneasily.

'We're not that bad are we?'

She glances around and sees that other musicians are taking their tea to sit on the grass, but they are different members and now they wear black, modern clothes and the one like her father is not there. She tells the man – though she barely knows him – about the disastrous day in the past. If the gush of personal history is too much, he does not show it.

'Funnily, I do remember the last time we played at Tintern – and perhaps I remember you, too.' She wonders if he is making this up. Being polite. But he is frowning, staring at her and beyond her, at something just out of sight. 'My friend left the band – moved abroad. Later he died. And I remember how everyone who came to listen seemed happy.'

She half-smiles. 'We were dealing with grim things.'

'My band, too. Peter had a ticket for Australia; a way of dealing with cancer. His wife thought it madness – she was staying. We kept on playing and playing, as if we could seal them together. Stop him going. Stop him dying.'

In the distance, a horn hoots, one of those parping things that people put on old cars. Mali frowns.

'It's the stupid vintage rally; people playing at olden times, simplifying history.' Then she sees his face. 'But I didn't mean…'

He shrugs and gestures at the jolly castle.

A child pushes past to get cake and smiles up. Mali smiles back and almost touches the soft black curls. 'A lot of my life's a blur, I'm afraid. It's strange that I remember you.'

'Look, will you stay a bit? I need to sort a few things out, but I'll be back.' He gets up and goes to rearrange chairs on the stage, edging them closer together, then moves across to talk to musicians sitting beneath the pock-marked tower. Mali wonders how she had got the little band so wrong, her own reconstruction of their history as flawed as the confident placards in the tower of the castle.

She takes her tea and rests it on a wall near the entrance and realises that she is waiting for the man to return, for him to flirt. She wants him to be her sanctuary, so that when she runs away again, she once more has somewhere to go. And it is because she understands how history repeats itself, and people seldom learn, that she leaves her tea half-drunk and slips out of the entrance, making her way back down to the estuary with its muddy swathes of ground, its rope-like patterns and blissful, ever-changing light. The early mist has cleared and the sound of curlews cuts through, a piping music: *peep, peep* they cry, *fly, fly.*

A green bus sits waiting, and without looking across to where her husband fiddles with his car, bonnet up, she steps aboard, smiles at the driver and rummages for coins. Later, the tide will ease its way back into the estuary. Later, her husband will look for her in the fancy hotel. Much later she may be with her brothers or perhaps a friend. The clothes packed in the bag at the hotel belong to her past. She can hear the faint music that has started up again and she wonders about the man, wonders if he thinks she's Cinderella.

The bus engine thrums into action and the next moment their charabanc sets off, people chatting, bags full of shopping, children looking out of the window. Mali feels something excited and fluttery inside. And then, as the vehicle struggles up the steep hill and along the busy high street, she realises that she is sitting on a local bus and that it will take an hour to get to the nearest town, and even longer to get back to Cardiff. They pass the bent church, perched upon a hill, beech trees all around, stretching back into shadow, with the church bells once more ringing. Mali looks down into her basket and registers the bizarre plunder she is taking into her new life: shiny oranges balancing on a tin of Italian olive oil, a teach-yourself piano book, the intricately carved sword, its handle knotted with red string. And she is also holding a book of poems. There is no logic to the strange collection, but perhaps the randomness is fitting, as intelligible as the rest of her life. She supposes that what she is doing is starting again – not exactly being a monk, but perhaps, becoming self-contained.

She lets her finger rest on the open page of poems and the bus bumps up and down, making its way towards sleepy villages and unknown, distant places. Mali remembers Benedict again and how, when they were staying in the bed and breakfast near the abbey, with its orchard and low ceilings, its bowls of vivid fruit, its open fire that sent them to bed smelling of wood-smoke, he surprised her by playing the owner's baby-grand. She and the host family sat in the deep chairs and listened, while Benedict played Chopin and Beethoven, feeling his way into a past that he said was only misty, crumbling away. She remembers him finally shutting the lid, and then looking across and shrugging, while they all clapped and he smiled. Later, they went up to bed, holding hands, up and up, past the tiny windows and the eroded riverbank, up until they reached the fragrant attic. This much she remembers, like a good poem or song, haunting and strangely sweet.

On The Fiddle – 1981

When you make a fire out of doors, especially on the beach, where you choose to build is key, and the twigs must be dry – old driftwood, not new. If you square your back against the oncoming wind, sheltering the flare of match, cupping the thing in your hands, you can dip down quick, offering flame to paper, hoping something will catch. Maybe the paper does burn, flares out, singed bits flaking and drifting away. And perhaps the wood begins to crack, the small twigs flickering red, the larger planks, licked by flame. You think that things have really taken off: the blaze flickers and dances while wood smoke blends with the tang of seaweed. So it is safe, perhaps, to slither meat basted in olive oil, salt and oregano, onto the warped pan. The pan that balances on a rigged-up trivet that someone else must have made. But it's in this instant that the fire turns sour – shape-shifts into a different sort of beast – all smoke and hissing, an acrid taste, and no heat at all, no hope when most it is needed. For me, love has often been like this: the best bits an *almost* and so much smoke, you can't even see what's in front of your red and stinging eyes.

I was twenty-two, and had been working on the buses for nine months when Chris made his appearance. He didn't seem surprised to find me in the canteen, as if he'd been expecting to bump into me some time or other. I was having my first break, half way through the early morning shift; it was sunny outside, but in that windowless, neon-lit room, there was only ever one season. Colin, a driver I didn't much like, was sitting next to me, muttering as he read the paper. He took up too much space, his legs sprawled, his elbows on the table and *The Mail* opened over my bit of Formica. He was liking the sex, the violence, I could tell, and he was stirring his four spoons of sugar into the strong, dark tea. The women behind the counter knew how he liked it – two teabags in one cup, sugar sloshed in. Patsy had just exclaimed, as she did every day, how Colin's teeth were growing blacker and that no woman in her right mind would put with someone who dared not smile. I was thinking that there were many things women put up with, and black teeth were the least of it.

Three new recruits were shuffling around the room, trailing behind the personnel officer; she gestured at us as if we were in the zoo. There was a tall man in his forties, hair slicked back, looking like a teddy boy; another lad with sharp eyes that took us all in – and then Chris, the youngest and best looking, whom I'd spotted and was trying hard to ignore. When the metal door had first swung open, I'd looked up from the crossword, expecting nothing – another trawl of hopefuls who'd jump ship after they'd done a week of earlies. But as soon as I saw Chris, I guessed it would be World War Three; I thought about dropping something under the table, perhaps dashing to the loo. Maddy had once hidden for a whole day in the loos – the day she'd driven the bus over Ted's new bike.

'Hiya, Sell-out,' said Chris, loudly, but not threateningly, as he threaded past our table and nodded in my direction.

'You know each other?' Colin asked, curious that I might have a life outside. He had stopped stirring, but the liquid went on centrifugally, carrying around motes of tea. 'You met before?' Colin insisted, like he was some sort of investigative journalist.

'Not really,' I said, refusing the memory. 'We came across each other on holiday.'

The training woman who had brought in the recruits to show off the food, comfy chairs and pool table, was trailing them back out again. We stared and they all stared back. Chris, tall, dressed in a suit that must have come from Oxfam, fair hair flopping across his face, gave me a salute.

95

The conductors and drivers had watched the show many times; they knew the latest bunch would either fit in or not, and that it was difficult to tell at this stage. If the three weren't trainee drivers they'd be allocated a crew and would tag along for a week or so, watching and getting the hang of conducting. Sometimes it could be fun to mentor, other times a drag. A few months before, I'd had someone fall off the back as we went around a corner. She'd broken her leg and I got the blame.

For the past nine months I'd done a pretty good job of being one of the gang. I didn't talk posh. I read the tabloids like everyone else. I kept my book tucked inside the ticket box. When I made my way to the bus and the driver offered to carry the brown box and machine for me, I let him, like most normal people. I wasn't stupid, like the Socialist Worker girl who ripped it out of men's hands, saying she was perfectly capable of carrying it herself. So the drivers preferred me to her I reckoned – protected me like I was a species of shy animal, often walking me home if it had been a late shift and was past midnight. And only one had tried to kiss me. I was too much the same age as their daughters to be chatted up. And the short hair put them off, as if I were pretending to be a boy. Perhaps they thought I was the same way inclined as Alan and Ted, whose oddity they tolerated with a weary and protective humour. So I wasn't comfortable when Chris arrived to mess things up. Perhaps he would bring what I had done in Spain flaring out into the open: using and being used by men.

If Chris hadn't spoken that day, I doubt if he would have been allocated to my bus. The debacle of the broken leg – which hadn't been completely my fault – might have meant I'd be left alone. She'd been three days in, that trainee, and a bit of a know-it-all, and I saw her topple as the bus did its slow turn, her feet stumbling forward, lemming-like, to the edge and then off. I froze, didn't even stretch out a hand, and watched her walk on air.

Despite this transgression, when Chris said how he'd like to work with me because I was young, like him, Jackie probably thought she was doing me a favour. The next day, I put her straight.

'The other one fell off; this one I'll push.' She flapped a timetable in my face as I pulled out my box from the locker and checked I had a spare roll of tickets.

'I've given you country routes to start him off, then busy town ones at the end of the week. At least he can add up; the other two need remedial maths.'

'He isn't what he seems, you know. He needs remedial social skills; he'll offend the passengers.'

'And you lot don't? You're all as weird as each other.'

She had a point: there was Jim, the muttering professor who'd had a breakdown; conductor Bob, with his tell-tale, residual make-up; and Karen, his on-off girlfriend who grew plumper and battier by the day. I worried, too, about Karen's driver, who was erratic enough to get the sack, swinging the bus around tight corners and breaking suddenly, flinging passengers from side to side or pitching them forward. He once confided how he drove thinking of Gardener's Delight and ridge cucumbers, of roses and sweet peas – the scented flowers he picked and placed in the bare canteen. Privately, I wondered if he fancied Bob and saw Karen as a rival – wanted her to fly off the back, as my trainee had.

And these were not the only weirdoes. I looked around at the conductors cashing up on wooden counters, shuffling coins into piles, and at the drivers with newspapers stuffed in their pockets, staring into the middle distance. I wondered how I put up with it – especially the racists and sexists, the left-wing activists. The socialist girl kept striking up conversation, trying to nudge me leftwards, calling me comrade and sometimes even brother. I knew she'd drop me when she realised I was a graduate, just as she was.

'But Chris is weirder than any of us – and he doesn't like me, whatever he says. He'll want to get his own back.'

'Well that's nothing to do with me. Train him well and you can get rid of him quick – send him out on his own bus.'

'Thanks a bunch.'

On the first Monday that the recruits were to start, I complained to Rose, one of the older conductors, that the new boy had the problem most males have when they've been to public school – women are sex objects, mothers or enemies.

'He'll fit in well, then,' she said. 'It's not just the public school boys who feel that way.' If I was hoping to spread rumours, I'd chosen the wrong person. Rose fished a chocolate bar out of her bag and gave it to me. 'Some sugar to make things better: we all have things to hide.' And she looked at me quizzically; as if she knew I might be running from the truth.

When Chris turned up, half an hour later, I was with my driver getting the float ready, threading tickets into the machine and checking out our shift. Chris immediately put me in my place.

'Your lucky day, Becks: two men to share. Which one of us do you want first?'

Mike, my driver, who I thought I'd trained better, chuckled and said, 'She's all yours, mate; I've had her for nine months.'

I blushed, and hated myself for looking like a silly kid. I'd worn a greyish foundation for the first few months, knowing about men's comments. But now that the drivers had left off trying to be unsettling, I'd foolishly neglected the make-up. People kept telling me I didn't look so ill these days, but any time I blushed, I felt as if I were someone else: someone who might get hurt.

I turned my back so Chris wouldn't see the red cheeks. 'You'd better listen up; you think you know things: you know nothing about me – never will.'

I trooped out to the front of the building, where the air was cooler, cursing myself for not having said something witty. The Wilbraham bus was due by in five minutes and it would stop to let one crew off and us clamber on. Usually I liked that moment, the possession of someone else's bus – the people staring, me a pirate taking over, my bright clothes making them smile, my presence a more cheering act than the one that had gone ashore.

Mike came sauntering over, whistling, and wrestled the ticket box from my hand. 'Cheer up. It might never happen.'

But I wish it would, I thought. *I'm so tired of trying to stop things from happening.* He turned and waited for Chris, then the two strode ahead. For the first time I was disempowered, made into a girl behind a wall of maleness. I could see what the socialist feminist was getting at. Mike offered Chris a cigarette and he gestured back a roll-up. Neither passed anything to me.

'I've heard there's a way to make this job cost the company, not us.' Chris was speaking softly but I could hear what he said, knew how to read his asides or muttering.

Mike appraised him coolly. 'You're a bit keen – day one and thinking of fiddling.'

'Just don't want to be out of pocket, that's all.' They grinned at each other: Mike the working class man, and Chris the privileged rich boy.

'We don't fiddle on this bus,' I announced, thinking I spoke for us both, thinking that I could keep theft and complication out of this new life.

'More's the pity,' said Mike, not looking back.

It had taken me two months to work out why the conductors clamoured for the busy town routes, encouraging me to swap shifts for the dusty country lanes. At first, I thought they were being kind, for it was pleasant – and easy – bumping through village greens and dreaming out of the windows, reading a book while no-one got on. But I wondered if even I might get bored of flat fields, a view stretching to the pale horizon, sleepy villages, quaint houses and huge farm machinery, trundling forever across level acres – that eventually I, like all the other conductors, would hand over the country routes to anyone who'd take them. Strangely, I didn't think it likely, for I enjoyed the thrumming engine inside me, the drone of nothingness that filled up my own troubled space. It was Rose who eventually put me straight, Rose who'd worked on the buses all of her life and was now near to retiring.

'You're like me, lovey,' she said one day, after her empty bus had slowed and I'd jumped through the open doors to get a lift back to the station. It was the end of a shift and I was on my way to cash up. It was common to take this sort of a ride after the work had finished, up from the busy town centre, to the bleak depot; it was a part of the camaraderie. You could get a lift anywhere, any time, even out for a walk on a Sunday. Buses you hailed, and sometimes even those you didn't, slowed to a walking pace, and then – as you once judged the thwack of the school skipping rope, timing the right moment – you jumped and were aboard: life a fairground. And just as at school, the art was to do things casually but with poise, as if there was no question of tripping or missing the platform.

Rose was tiny, with a tight perm and delicate hands. She talked at me all the while she did the stuff of managing a bus: ringing the bell, taking and giving tickets, adjusting the machine at different sections of the route, keeping her eye on passengers, on the road, or on her driver up in his cubby hole; she never looked at me directly, even as she spoke, but seemed to know things about me that I didn't know myself

'It's not worth copying what the men do; you're better off – like me – on the country routes. It's all very well doing the busy routes to fiddle, but if you lie or have secrets, it'll come out in the end.'

I braced myself against one of the rails and stared hard at people walking on the city streets, rushing this way and that, ravelling up their lives.

'I don't like secrets,' I said.

'Cheers, Dearey,' Rose said to one of her passengers. 'See you tomorrow, then. You can tell me if he proposes or not.' And she helped the woman down from the platform, as if the person were old, though the woman with the shopping was half Rose's age. 'I wouldn't have lasted forty years if I'd spent the time stealing.' She was smiling at a man who, as he clambered on, offered her a packet of chocolate biscuits and then swung his way up the steep steps to the upper deck. 'Thanks, my lovely; you'll be making me fat, you will.'

Rose fixed on me, at last, as she slid the biscuits into the cubbyhole where her empty box was stored. She spoke in her soft, London voice, scrutinising my dyed hair, woollen scarf and floral skirt over the company trousers. 'You're not like the rest, so I don't know why you're trying so hard to fit in.'

She could have been my mum. All the while she was solid as a rock, pinging the bell, seeing people off and on and smiling at regulars, like she would be there in a hundred years, while the world sloshed this way and that, duplicitous and cunning. I pretended I knew what she meant and next day started watching the others.

I don't know how I could have missed something so obvious. When you bring in the rush hour crowd – or take them home again – you can never get around the choked up bus before it's sweeping into the town centre or back up to the estate, and everyone's churning out. I had a technique that just about managed the mayhem – bending to the left, then the right, taking money from two at a time, chatting and smiling, doling out change, while the ticket machine rattled like a gun. Sometimes, though, things went wrong and I was slower because people didn't have the right coins or the damned tickets got jammed, so I'd scuttle back to the front just as they surged for the door. I held out my hand and they'd toss coins and notes – too much and too late to reel off tickets for. Perhaps I should have known what the other conductors were doing all along: that they were not trying, and I was trying too hard.

When I cashed up, I never questioned that I should declare the extra, since the company gave surpluses back, perhaps to encourage honesty. While I was placing numbers in columns, reading off the details from my ticket machine, worrying in case they deducted money (which they did, if the sums added up the wrong way) everyone else must have been stashing money in wallets, their pockets, even in their pants. I understood too, how the drivers were in on it, keeping an eye out for inspectors, not stopping if they were spotted and turning a blind eye to money spilling over the platform. Later in the day, they no doubt bargained for a cut.

Once I'd worked things out, I often thought it odd that I didn't join in, since I had no objection to stealing. Possibly, I just needed a rest, needed not to worry. University had been full of evasion and accommodation: paying people to write my essays, the odd bit of theft from the bar, sleeping with people whose wealth made life easier. I told myself I was too honest these days for the bus capers and, anyway, it was nice to fly into the flat Fen landscape, reading a book as the world spun by. Much nicer to sit peaceably on the village green as Mike told me his kids were camping in the garden that night, and Mrs Thornaway brought tea and biscuits and we waited our innocent twenty minutes before sailing, unperturbed, back to Cambridge.

My performance at work was perhaps a different form of theft, for it mattered that people liked me; appreciated the flowery dresses over the faded jeans, the red hair and uniform jacket, decorated with badges. I cheered them up they said, had a nice smile and was helpful. I could act well, and liked it that the men eyed my bust and bum, that the mums petted me and the girls were jealous. But the smile, I knew, was covering the places my mind kept travelling off to, as regular in its route as the number 184 bus. And once Chris turned up, I smiled a lot less because my mind started going in loops, what with the past and the present haunting whichever way I looked.

That first day out on the bus, Chris settled in straight away, sprawling his feet across my seats, going upstairs for a quick ciggie so he wouldn't have to listen to my training mantra, smoking with Mike when we took a break, eyeing up the women. He made lewd jokes, performing like some stupid notion of a 'working man', one who puts women down. It was no wonder I turned sour and defensive, just as I had at the end, in Spain.

Whenever I try and remember how things were, it's the film set I recall, high in the Spanish Sierra Nevada. A pretend, cowboy world perched in the clouds, left behind by American directors. I was probably travelling in the bus or camper van at that point, because a man, passing joints, told stories of how he'd worked as an extra. When I look back, it seems we were all extras and all wanting to be the star. I was eighteen and had an inter-rail ticket and a place to do History in Cambridge – although I was the wrong class to be going there: I wasn't that clever, just had a memory that my teacher said was brilliant.

When my inter-rail ticket ran out, I slept on beaches and imagined I would never go back. What I remember now is how the campfires wouldn't burn, and how the wine grew less rough the more you drank. And I remember sex accompanied by the sea's music and a tugging wind flapping away at consciousness. The details have become smudged – perhaps because I have chosen to erase things, or perhaps because these things are no longer important. I'm not sure I could even find the campsites and beaches, the tapas bars, a derelict house, that sinking house boat we once rowed out to. There were long-haired boys and hippy girls and dubious older guys – and always meat roasting, sometimes burning over the spitting fire. A world of almosts: a constant coming and going – saying goodbye and weeping and hugging, then saying hello again, with even more hugging and tears. What a splintering and re-joining – people pairing and hitching to famous places (and other countries), then returning to the camp site, searching out the familiar, erasing the difference they'd been so desperate to explore. This, at least, is the memory I allow.

Once, as we'd sat around a camp fire, cooking bits of meat or fish that were raw inside and burnt on the outside, I remember Chris and how he talked about Film Noir and the Hayes code and how smoking was used to suggest the sex that could not be shown.

'What does this mean, then?' I'd said, puffing a cloudy plume into the unbroken Spanish sky. 'What am I saying?'

'That you want to go to bed with me.' He blew me a kiss and everyone laughed.

Then I think I told him nobody wanted that – unless they were drunk and hopeless themselves. He smiled back, perhaps already knowing I was someone who would never tell the truth.

Much later I found out that Chris hadn't got the grades he needed for studying film, that he'd known this even as he told his stories. He eventually got a place at a technical college in Cambridge. Strange that we hadn't bumped into each other before he came to work on the buses. But even if we had seen one another, we would have probably brushed it off as a bad dream, a memory that needed to be escaped from. In any case, my all-female college was some way out, and I didn't spend much time with the alien upper class, nor with the town's roughnecks either. I drifted around reading and avoiding, as I had done before: avoiding essays, depressing thoughts, female students and most – but not all – Cambridge men.

By the second day of Chris's training, I was snapping at people to hurry up. He was brushing too close, watching me too much. Near the end of the shift, I even rang the bell as men and women came rushing from the train station with heavy bags, the rain spotting, the wind blowing cold through the broken bus shelter – an hour wait for their next bus. We rushed gaily past, busily on our way to nowhere, Chris lounging on the platform, flicking through my history of Spain: library copy, never returned.

'You reading this?' he asked, impressed, while the bus flew into space.

'It's for my dad,' I lied. I didn't want him thinking Spain was anything special.

'I thought you didn't have a dad.'

'I've had too many.'

Later that day, I didn't even help the woman struggling with a pram, leaving Chris to ineffectually lift her shopping, while she heaved the contraption up the step, bit by bit. It was then that I decided to leave the job, though I knew leaving was my answer to most things.

I gave it a few days, all the while thinking, if he's behaving like this now, soon he's going to let everyone know, soon he'll get revenge for those stupid things I said, the stupid things I did. I wondered if he was biding his time, punishing me by choosing the perfect moment to make everything impossible.

All that week, I was aware he was about to pounce.

Even the good bits – like when my driver avoided the folk festival, driving the back streets so we wouldn't have to pick up the hippies: even these bits no longer felt like fun. Even when we made an unscheduled stop outside Mike's house to see the new climbing frame he'd made in the front garden, letting the bus settle for a while in the suburban street, full of its staring passengers. I was trying hard to enjoy it, but it was like I'd forgotten the lines.

I began looking for other jobs, spent the afternoons mooching around the market, asking if the bookstall, record man or bagman needed help. The record man said perhaps, and would I meet him for a drink to talk it over. He grinned at me, like he knew I'd be easy. By the old churchyard there were tall trees, ancient and bent, and when the wind blew, they set up a rustling, high in the sky, like a sea of possibility, a whispering of some dawn beach. I wanted to turn myself upside down, be up with the turning leaves or find myself in a battered bus by the Spanish sea. Walking home, I reasoned that if Chris told on me, I might counter that he was a public school boy, conning them all. I don't think anyone would have believed me – his act was too good. And if they did, it was something they were used to in that city of misfits: working people stepping up a class and the rich adopting socialism like it was a new trinket.

By the middle of the second week, Chris was talking less and seemed less eager to trail me up and down the stairs. He was indifferent to how I took the money, gave out tickets or rang the bell to start and stop the bus. Sometimes, though, he bent over me to flick the machine's dial onto the next stage of the journey, just to show he was on the case. Mostly, he had stopped trying to goad me. I was probably as surly as he was jokey.

'This job's easy,' he finally said. 'Let's all go for a drink and discuss what I do tomorrow. You can watch me and I'll take the early shift; if I can mange the rush hour, I'll manage anything. Perhaps I'll be able to get out of your hair this week.'

I said no to the drink, because I didn't want Chris spilling the beans to Mike, the driver – although I was certain he would talk at some point; how could he not want to humiliate me, as I had done him? How could I stay once all the old boys knew I'd fucked someone as old as them, on demand, and had even agreed to a threesome.

'You want me out of your hair, right?' insisted Chris. 'You're not exactly being pleasant.'

'You've messed things up for me.'

'And you didn't mess me up?'

I knew what else Chris would to do the next day – he'd fiddle like the best.

Fridays were often busy and by 7.45 the bus was already filling. We were on time at the far end of the estate: people piling in – the smokers going upstairs, the teenagers up there, too, just so they could inhale the smoke. Then downstairs, the mums, the younger kids and the workers who looked too sleepy to want a fag so early.

'On your own,' I said to Chris, unslinging my machine and passing it to him. He was meant to start in the countryside, to wait until the third week for working the city, but the training was a joke. Outside it was just getting light. I'd flicked the dials to the right place and as he hoisted the machine across his shoulder, he scrutinised me.

For a moment, I thought he was going to say something nice, but he just declared, 'It's better on your own. People let you down – in bed, in life.'

I looked away, so he wouldn't see my face. Mike was staring back at us through the partition window, wondering what on earth we were doing. *Get a move on* – he mouthed. Once the traffic got bad, the minutes could slip away until you'd lost your morning break and went straight out on the road again: no coffee, no fag. I rang the bell for Chris, two bright tings to get us started. That was the only thing Chris forgot – the bell: one to stop, two to go, two if no one was getting off and the driver could weave up some precious extra seconds. So I stood near the front on the nice modern bus, electric doors swooshing open, letting in gusts of cold, but keeping us warm the rest of the time. The old buses, the ones where you stood at the back, the ones where you could fall off, were reserved for the country routes, the vehicles as geriatric as the people they picked up.

Each time the bus stopped, more people pushed their way on, bundled up in winter scarves and thick coats, coughing and sneezing. I rang the bell to start again and meanwhile Chris went pushing down the aisle past the standing passengers, collecting fares and giving himself a good amount of slack to rummage for change. By the time we got near town, he was back up the front, only half the fares collected, waiting for the jackpot. I half wished it was me flouting the rules, making life exciting, but, for some reason, I squared up to him, pointing out a woman he could give a ticket to, but he twiddled with the machine dials, saying they were stuck and then positioned himself at the bottom of the steps.

'You could have got upstairs,' I said, as the surge began, annoyed that I didn't know what to say or do, that I couldn't work out what he was thinking.

'I don't think you're the one to lecture me on honesty.' And he brushed his hand across my chest as he turned from me to the pressing crowd. 'Fares, please,' he hollered, smiling with utter assurance at the grumbling people, magnetting money from their bags, from the pockets they fished in. They too played the game, taking their time, as if they found it hard to remember where they'd put those coins they thought they had a chance of keeping, and they waited, all the while, for the doors to swish open. But Mike, up in the driver's seat in his little box, kept the doors closed, working with Chris, putting the pressure on. It was another of life's games.

Chris stood there, blocking everything, and people handed cash over, like it was an old dance they all knew the rules of, but each time, a dance they hoped might change. When a woman demanded a ticket, Chris sliced one out and I knew it would have a nought on it, but he did it so boldly, she didn't even think to look. Then the doors flew open, everyone was tumbling out and seconds later the bus clapped the doors shut and lurched off again, nosing its way across town and back out to the other estate. Mike, from his driver's cubby-hole turned and put up his thumb up, knowing he'd get a couple of pints from that morning's shift. It was then that I knew I'd probably lose my driver too and that Chris, who was such a poser, such a liar, would be more accepted than I had ever been with this motley assortment of drivers and conductors.

'Congratulations,' I said. 'Your first wages. Success.'

'The wages of sin?' he queried, flicking his arm over to consider his watch. 'I'll take it the profit's mine. You can take it off what you owe me.' He looked at me with his grey, nondescript eyes, full of irony and evasion

'I don't know what you mean,' I said.

He laughed then. I had played into his hands, done what he expected. 'Or you could pay off your debt tonight? There'd be inflation.'

'You didn't used to be such a joker.'

'It's no joke; you stole money from me in Spain.'

'To get home. I sent it back later.'

'That's what you say. Anyway, I'd left by then.'

The bus was stuck in a traffic jam; it had disgorged the workers and only a few people were left, travelling to the far side of the city, up near the hospital. They stared out of the windows, and if they listened to our hushed talk, they gave no indication that they understood a word.

'Why did you come and find me? What do you want?'

'I could have found you any time I wanted. I knew you

109

were in Cambridge. I saw you once, biking across Parker's Piece. I followed you home.'

'That's stalking.'

'I had better things to do than stalk you.'

'Getting a 2:2?' Now it was his turn to be surprised.

'Who told you that?'

'You did. I read that interview you gave after your band played at The Man in the Moon.'

For a second, I had the advantage, but then we both looked up to see the inspector, standing at the bus stop ahead, clipboard at the ready, arm thrust out. I pinged twice, no intention of stopping, ignoring the woman who'd stood and made her slow way down the aisle. As we sailed past, I feigned surprise, staring out, with my hand across my mouth and then set up an urgent pinging, tutting at my driver who I knew would stop when we were far enough away. Chris and I barely spoke for the rest of the shift. Perhaps both of us wanted to be the one in control, the one who knew all the secrets.

I let Chris work the whole morning since my mind was turning in circles. We did the estate run and I watched him flirt with the schoolgirls and charm their mums. Upstairs, I knew, he'd be more detached, squaring his shoulders, so the men would think him their equal. It made me sick – the pretence, the way he could pull things off better than me. In Spain, it had been a different story. He was better looking now, with his stubble and long hair – and nowadays, his guitar playing wasn't so out of tune. And even when it was, it just seemed contemporary. I'd slipped in to watch the gig at The Man in the Moon, but had hidden at the back – jazz punk wasn't really my sort of music.

On the green at Trumpington there was a twenty-minute turn-around. Mike was taking a nap in the cab, so I got out and went to look at the pond. Sometimes, it felt like the whole of East Anglia was slowly sinking and the sluggish water was waiting to bubble up and drown me. I often biked out into the fens on my days off and each way you looked was flatness and ditches and slow moving water. Chris came and joined me. I pointed out the little bubbles, insects just below the surface.

'I look in this pond for proper fish, but it's always empty, like it's sulking.'

'Not like the sea, then. The sea lets its emotions go; this water's boring – stagnant.'

He kept hinting at Spain, dragging us off there, as if it meant something to him, too. Chris leaned on the fence beside me.

'Like people bottle things up?' I asked, my breath held.

'Is that me or you?' he asked.

'Perhaps it's both of us.'

We could see the occasional person clambering onto the bus, finding somewhere to sit out of the cold; we'd have to make sure we got the fares before we started. One of the inspectors often got on at the next stop – rumour was, he had a woman in the village. Chris considered me.

'You didn't bottle things up in Spain – not towards the end, anyway. You told me lots – and I told you stuff, too.'

'Like you loved me.' I said this in a throwaway voice, so he wouldn't think I'd been dwelling on it.

'I thought it was mutual.'

It was too risky to keep going, although I wanted to. Soon, I would have to hurt him before he hurt me.

He was half-smiling. 'When we were in Spain, you told me you'd decided not to pack-in Cambridge, that it was a fool's game living on the beach and I should go back to study. I'd half intended staying away for ever.'

'Do you blame me for that too?'

'That was one of the better things you said. But after you stole my money, I almost didn't make it back.' He was not smiling now.

'I didn't think you'd leave the place so fast. You had a

girlfriend, remember? And, the weird thing is, I didn't even need the money. A lorry driver gave me a ride, then took me over on the ferry. All I had to do was carry some extra duty-free.'

'And that was the only service?'

'Fuck off, Chris! For Christ's sake – I was just getting home, hitching a ride.'

'Fucking off seems to be your solution to most things.'

It always went sour between us; he could never let things be. I tramped back to our bus, remembering how, in Spain, it was him that told the crowd I was sleeping with the old guy. I remembered how no one spoke to me when I turned up back at the camp to share bottles of wine and sleep rough for a night or two. It served him right that I'd finally nicked his money.

That evening I was called into the office.

'When we put trainees with a crew, we expect a good example. You don't let them take the whole shift too soon, and when they can't manage the load on the busy runs, you don't let them stand at the front, not giving out tickets.'

'Who said I did that?'

The Inspector scrutinised me. He was usually friendly; sometimes let me finish my evening 'spare' shifts in the bar of the social club. After all, he was the one who'd tried to kiss me as he'd walked me home. He was about forty, good looking enough to try stuff on, but wasn't like the other men, didn't go nasty when you said no. He looked me up and down, in my flowery skirt that wasn't proper uniform and the jacket with its clutter of badges.

'I saw you. I watch over my staff. You especially.'

'I'm glad to hear I'm watched out for. But I didn't ask for a trainee, and this one wanted to get started so he could get a bus of his own.'

'If either of you want to go on working for the company, you'd better look out. Send Chris in after you've counted up.'

I didn't say that he'd need proof; we both knew that. And I wasn't going to land Chris in it, but I knew my takings must have looked fishy. Chris had worked out how to fiddle, but his calculation about what to keep and what to hand in was all over the place; I would have managed that deception better. Later, Chris and I were going to the pub to share out our winnings. At the last minute, Mike had said to count him out; he'd take whatever we gave him, but he needed to get back to his missus. Up in the cab, he knew he was probably out of the firing line and whatever anyone planned for the future, it was best he knew nothing of it: he didn't intend to lose his job, even if we did.

The pub we'd chosen was well away from the depot. It squatted near the weir and filled with students on summer nights. It was early spring and the place was empty. As I waited for Chris to get our drinks, I fidgeted with the beer mats, turning them over and over and staring at them, like it was my life I was examining. I watched him carry over a tray, cool and assured, as if he were already a pop star.

'Here you go. For old times. A bottle of wine.' He put two glasses and then the bottle onto the pine table. 'I'm sorry I've landed you in bad stuff today. I didn't mean that to happen. But I've already decided something; I'm doing an earner again on Monday.'

'But they'll be watching, now. It's stupid.'

'That's just a frightener,' Mike said. 'They do it to trainees.' He was pouring the wine, eyeing me. 'I want to check we can trust you, that you're not a sell-out. Mike said if you told, no one would work with you.' Chris let that sink in.

'Is that a threat?' I slugged the wine back and felt the burn in my throat, in my guts. He looked around at the window, floors, the big tables and wide glass windows that gave out onto the backs and meadows.

'You know about threats, I reckon, Becks.' So he hadn't

forgotten everything, after all.

I had been sleeping with the old guy for about three months, but hadn't thought to save money; first thing I'd wanted to do was buy clothes that didn't smell rank. I also spent money on lunch out, keeping out of the way because Todd sometimes brought friends over, always suggesting a threesome. He laughed when he said this, but I knew he wasn't joking. I found myself thinking of going home to mum and her endless boyfriends. One set of misery was as good as another, I decided. I was lonely, too. People on the beach didn't have time for me, and Chris was hanging around with a Canadian. It was summer – long hot days and then evenings that brought a breeze, like a vague memory of something happier.

This particular night, I was down in my room and Todd came tramping down, put his head around the door. 'It's party-time, honey – down on the shore. Rhoda and me just had another bust-up. Why don't you come?'

Rhoda was Todd's on-off girlfriend. She often moaned – not about me having sex with Todd, which she knew about – but that he didn't spend enough. Todd and Rhoda had found me at a British Council party where I'd gone hoping to get free food, which I did – and free wine, too. I was sober enough to know that his weathered face, all chiselled lines and tan, meant he was at least forty, maybe older. He'd had to leave America fast, someone said, and Rhoda too. Someone else said he owned a boat, that he'd inherited money. This was probably why my poverty, when he picked me up, amused him. He said I could be his cleaner.

Each Wednesday I caught a bus to his village and polished things and mopped the floor. Then we drank wine. One day, when Teresa, the cook, was out, he came up as I bent over the sink and pressed himself against me.

'You're a lousy cleaner,' he whispered, kissing my ear. I

114

froze but made a quick calculation. After that, he paid me more and I cleaned twice a week. He was renting a pretty house with a swimming pool and antique furniture. There were ten rooms, Teresa the cook, and her husband who gardened. Eventually, Todd gave me a room in the basement. It had an iron-frame bed, like they have in hospitals, an old chair with a hole under the cushion, a rag rug and a set of drawers. He could have kitted it out new, but he said he liked the feel of coming down and slumming it. Sometimes I stayed in his bed upstairs, and if it hadn't been for Rhoda, you could have said that me and Todd were a couple. But I'm not sure I liked him and wasn't sure he much liked me.

All the way to the artist's house, Todd complained that he'd bought Rhoda expensive jewellery and she'd immediately sold it. As he drove, he pulled a wad of notes from his pocket and threw them, one-by-one, out of the window. I thought about re-tracing the route and picking all that money up: it could be my fare home. After he parked, we walked down the track, his arm draped around my shoulders, fingering my breast. I hoped he wouldn't suggest sex in the bushes, as he'd done before. I knew he was getting bored. There were things I wouldn't let him do, things I couldn't imagine people wanting to do; he'd said he might need my room back.

Once we arrived and he'd chatted to people he knew, he got busy flattering the artist, telling her he'd buy her paintings, that he had a girlfriend who liked expensive things. She was laughing back at him, flicking her dark hair from her bare shoulders, so I knew she'd end up in his bed that night, with or without me. There were people in every room, squashing into the kitchen and through the lounge and even out of the front door. There was music playing inside and, out on the patio, a guitarist was strumming: it was a song I vaguely recognised.

Todd was used to getting what he wanted. One of the beach crowd said that he'd had a boy beaten up; that girls, once they stopped living at the house, disappeared. I wasn't sure about this, but when he got mad, we all knew to keep out of the way. And the day before, he'd locked me in my room until his friend came down so both of them could slum it for the afternoon. The artist's house felt safe; it didn't have locks on the doors and was balanced on the edge of the dunes and was more of a beach hut than a regular house; there were huge mirrors in each room, nice fabric spilling from the ceiling, good food spread out in the kitchen. Everything about the house was homely and made me feel sad. Todd had said the artist was Portuguese and renting so she could daub the colours of the Spanish sea, catch the water's shifting emotion; she'd made a career at being an outsider, living in one country after another, painting the colour of different moral codes.

Chris had propped his guitar up by a chair and the Canadian girl, as usual, was talking at him. I registered that he must have left the beach crew way behind, just as I had.

'I've got a flat these days,' he announced when he saw me. 'Down in the old town. I'm Linda's administrator.' He slipped his arm around the girl, and I knew that wasn't all he was. They were both drunk.

'Lucky you. I don't have a flat – I'm just plain flat. Emptied out, in fact.'

He went to give me a hug and I pulled away, not much liking the feel of any man's hands.

Later, as I became drunk, I noticed that Chris and his girl were arguing. I swayed over after she'd flounced off. He told me she'd gone to stay at a friend's, that he was to see the flat was okay and wasn't to let no-hoper friends stay over. He pulled a face.

'I think she means you. Fucking slave driver. She gets her money's worth. I cook as well as clean. And I do the

116

translation work.'

He was better at languages than most of us, had become almost fluent.

'Well, if you love her,' I said philosophically, staring out at the band of white waves breaking again and again on the shore. I remember thinking that those waves would be breaking as I went through my life's mistakes, and even when I was dead, the cold white waves would crash against the shore.

It was then that he said, 'Actually, it's you I love.'

We were both so drunk we could hardly stand and when we kissed, our bodies banged against one another clumsily. We wandered away from the party and when he pressed me up against a stunted tree in the darkness and fumbled at me, all I can remember is the hardness of the tree and the smell of eucalyptus. Light flowed from the house, like water pouring, and inside Todd was probably wanting sex too, while Chris was taking it, just like those men of my mother's. Everybody wanting something. Everybody sad.

Later, we went back to Chris's flat and made tea and toast, and opened another bottle of wine. We leaned against each other, squatting on the balcony, waiting for the day to come. He told me stuff, not so unlike my own stories, and we clinked glasses, congratulating ourselves on survival. I told him – and this was the truth – that I'd liked him from the beginning; he said that he respected my toughness, that I made him laugh and that he couldn't fathom me. A lizard was pressed tight behind a mirror, propped against Chris's wall and I watched it as we made love again; this time our bodies soft and friendly, and life was okay.

Sometimes I let those moments come back, like cool shards through a blur of drink and time.

It was at the end of the night, after I'd said how I thought Todd might be dangerous and that I was thinking of going home, that Chris turned to me, as if something had just occurred to him. It was a small flat with three rooms: the bedroom, a living room with a pull-out settee, and a kitchen. I guessed we were in the living room so the girlfriend wouldn't know I'd been there.

'Is that the only reason you're here – because you're avoiding him and have no other man to use?'

'Perhaps you deserve to be used – spreading all those rumours about me.'

I half meant it as a joke, half as my revenge, that he had let me go off and sell myself to Todd when we could have sorted out something better. He flopped onto his back, with a loud sigh that was almost a groan. We lay in the stuffy, silent night, with Spain all around and the sea pounding away beyond the harbour walls.

His voice came out cold and vindictive. 'What I said earlier – I didn't mean it, you know. I just wanted to screw you. You'd be the last person I could love.'

'Well screw you,' I said, and turned my back. And it felt like we were siblings and that we might forever be squabbling.

Later, when he went to sleep, I stole his money and tiptoed out of the room. I wanted to start over, be someone else, whose mistakes were different and perhaps not so sordid. But as I stood outside, with the smell of fish coming from the boats unloading and people talking to one another in loud voices and me only able to understand a few of the words, I wished I could be back inside, that I had not shut the door so firmly.

I remember how, before I left, I had watched Chris sleeping and wondered about boarding school. It didn't surprise me what the older boys did to him, especially when there weren't any girls. There'd been a younger boy called Rob whom he'd protected, whose mother had committed suicide. He'd told me, too, about one of his father's exes – Mali. She sent him letters that grew longer and longer and he could never think what to write back. Before I left the flat, Chris still sleeping, I thought of writing a farewell note, but I was drunk. The scribbled words came out like a threat – because I didn't want anything coming back to haunt me, rearing up in my new and shinier life. At least I was good at moving on: my mother had shown me how.

Chris and I had been sitting in the pub a long time, not saying much, just drinking the wine, occasionally staring out of the windows. And then he came back at it again. He pushed his long hair behind his ears and looked, for a moment, like that lonely boy in Spain.

'You think I'm making threats, Becks? I wouldn't dream of threatening you. You're too much like me – a misfit. You'd turn and bite the hand that feeds you.'

'I'm like you?' I could feel the wine and expectation taking hold. No one had ever told me they loved me, but him. A woman opened the door out onto the balcony and I could hear the ducks quacking, making their usual commotion. Someone must be feeding them pub food again, slinging bits of chicken and crispy fried duck to those cannibals that paddled the pond.

'I'm not threatening you, but you must have worked out you're going to lose your driver, that he'll want to work with me.' Chris was staring hard, like he was thinking one thing but was saying something else. 'Mike reckons you're some kind of weird goody-goody – too honest by half. I haven't disabused him, though I could. He says I should warn you off informing.' He smiled at me then, half tenderly. 'I said you wouldn't dream of it.'

Chris wasn't saying the things meanly; his smile was like we were in it together, sidekicks in a film, mates who could beat each other up or be a team, and it was all pretty much the same thing. He lit up a cigarette, handed it to me and blew out smoke like it carried his message.

'I remember Spain all the time,' he said. 'Nothing else

119

has ever matched that time, everything happened there to change me.'

'But nothing did happen,' I insisted.' 'Nothing proper happened, and nothing's happened since.' But I said this softly, as if I only half believed it.

'Perhaps we're not so similar,' he said, lighting up his own cigarette. I was about to say something, to risk the thing I'd been wanting to say all week, and the thing I thought he wanted to say too.

It was then that the girl came in, the one I'd seen dancing at his gig. She was prettier than me, with tousled hair and eyes that peeked out from a long fringe. He stood and collected up his shoulder bag.

'I'll see you tomorrow, Sunshine. Don't forget what I said.'

That was the problem. I hadn't forgotten anything he'd said, as hard as I'd tried. So I knew there was only one thing left – my tried and tested route. I'd be packing up and inventing a fresh self in a different city. I'd ride a new place until it tossed me off, like those cowboys I imagined riding the Sierra Nevada. I'd go to London, perhaps, where the river kept surprising, with its corkscrew bends, giving you chances to see things differently, to surprise even yourself.

There was a job I'd applied for in a lesbian collective, making a film about runaway children; there was a squat floor to sleep on, and a chance to research stuff, to travel some more. There'd be an opportunity, too, to forget the thing I'd almost risked, for it could have led to a re-run of Spain: us tripping each other up, pretending we were things we weren't, and scared of who we actually were. As he walked out of the door with the girl he'd probably marry, he turned and blew a kiss, ironic and wry, then we both smiled and he was gone.

Perhaps Chris knew I wouldn't turn up for work next day, otherwise why would he have left that letter on the floor, the one all crumpled, not addressed to me but with his father's name on – Des Williams – and an address in South Wales? Maybe he was wiser than me and knew I had plenty more spitefulness to use up; he would just wait for me to turn up like his bad penny. Or perhaps that's all romantic nonsense. But I kept the envelope anyway, with a few other bits and pieces, in the terracotta pot I'd lugged back from Spain – an appropriate place to be burying my friend Chris.

It was years later when I thought about contacting him again and pulled the scrap out, still telling myself he meant nothing. The paper had turned soft and yellow and the address had faded away, was no more than a dream. My young son, Kit, was balanced on my hip and I stared at the crumpled envelope, bleached by the sun, as if this was something Chris had planned all along. That same day, I tried chasing his ghost across the Internet, to Singapore and back again, typing a name that was so common, it turned out there were thousands. I was thirty and had just split up with the man I'd lived with for two years. He was Spanish and had taught me the language, but not how to be kind. On the counter lay red roses he'd sent, thorny, with no scent and a cheque towards bringing up our son.

Sometimes I glimpse Chris's shadow, or someone like him, flitting through Paris or Madrid and he turns and laughs at my games, his ghost telling me that all love is corrosive, that we have been kind to one another, keeping so far apart. *There is a lot of mileage in almosts*, he says.

I am remembering him today. Here, as I finger the white sand, stare at the foreign waves breaking by the shore. It is morning and I have been playing with Kit, me on a lonely holiday, consoled by the child and by the notebook that rests on a red towel. I have jotted down a list of good bars and cafes, the Spanish food that people may not yet know, also snatches of history and a few brief drawings of things I must remember. Tonight, as the child sleeps, I will finish the article and tomorrow it will be sent to London.

I research for a film company and write bits for a travel magazine; when I have something in the *Daily Mail*, I smile as I think of the bus drivers reading me. I whisper to my son, as we make a castle, patting down the damp sand, saying that life is a problem, really, with its echoes and overlappings – but all you can do is keep riding. These days, I do not risk falling; bones break easily with age.

'I've done with cheating myself, Kit,' I tell him. 'Now I have you.'

He laughs back, his brown eyes soft, his teeth sharp, his tawny skin browner and stronger than mine. I doubt if he agrees, but he likes banging away at the red bucket and pointing to the secretive sea, hushing away, down by the tatty fishing boats. Someone has made a smoking fire and a family is cooking meat, opening a bottle of wine. I can smell oregano, seaweed and spices. Over by the harbour, the car park boasts a funfair, and a merry-go-round filled with young children and a few courting teenagers, sets off once again. The tinny music filters through the air and Kit turns, quick to watch the dancing movement, the boys and girls astride like cowboys, and one girl sitting side-saddle, like she's a lonely princess. I lie back down on the beach, and listen: Kit's laughter, a barrel organ, the sea rushing towards me, the sky tilting down and everything just for once, adding up nicely.

Premature – 2001

This was the part Maggie remembered as she stood, fingering the glass and gazing into the garden. In the dream she had been giving birth, but with none of the usual paraphernalia – was both mid-wife and mother, swapping between roles with a giddying ease. The child full-grown, with tight curly hair and dark eyes, laughed and then demanded a camera. *Or better still*, said the baby that was no baby, *pass me a joint*. Maggie's arms encircled the fragile thing that smelled of milk and cigarettes, and when she pressed the child tight, it disappeared, slipping away into darkness.

The window had steamed-up, and Maggie rubbed, as if to scour the troubling dream. Her own ghostly reflection was visible and beyond that the frost, pasted thick over lawn and bushes. In the sky floated a ghostly moon. Yes, she thought, that is how life arrives and that is how it goes. And she considered – as she hadn't done for ages – her mother, who had hated pain, yet had nevertheless given birth, not once, but three times: *Premature, you were*, her mother used to say, *I hoped you'd be streets ahead, but somehow you've spent your life trying to catch up.*

Later, Maggie stared into the garden again as she stood at the kitchen counter. She had made sandwiches –cutting off the crusts – and was grabbing at the things she needed for work: hand-cream, a box of rubber gloves, files. She jammed a map into the top of her basket and squashed down the apple and bar of chocolate. The darkness had thinned, and in the midst of overgrown bushes and a still whiteness, she spotted Sophie, her niece, wearing a flimsy nightdress and Maggie's old coat. Was this what all teenagers did? Or just Sophie, thrown out of school again?

The ghostly figure, gathering up the fragile light, was pulling at stems and flowers, then cutting off branches, one by one. The girl carried a bundle of seed heads, leaves and dried blooms: grey eucalyptus, hydrangea, cornus, honesty; her hands looked frozen and the scanty dress clung to her. There she was, a rare plant in the garden – a garden that had always seemed to Maggie, who had grown up with a field beyond, like a back yard. Each year, the place offered its modest seasonal show: bulbs, then apple blossom, shrubs, clematis, roses, tenacious honeysuckle: sometimes even visitors – once a hedgehog, then in the shed, a homeless woman living. In the unkempt, nettled corners, Maggie could feel a spinster's presence, digging and planting her world, not yet knowing the house was to be sold, and then split into shabby flats.

Sophie looked up and gave a cheery wave, holding up the bunch. She trudged back towards the kitchen door, and in the gloom and half-light her presence was luminous. She yanked at the handle and spilled into the room, bringing with her the cold, cupping within her body the dankness of soil and brackish air, the earth that held them all. She shook off the Wellingtons, sprawling them away in different directions, then slung down the secateurs.

'You said you liked flowers, aunt Maggs. I've bought you some.' She thrust the uneven lengths at Maggie.

'Don't you mean brought, Soph?'

'Bought – out of my sleep time. I wanted to get up and give you a send-off, a thank you.'

'Well, thank *you*. But I like it when you stay – even when it's... unexpected.'

Maggie put the flowers on the table and bent to kiss the girl's untamable, woolly hair. It surprised her that this child, her own relation, was so physically definite. The rest of the family seemed washed out. Her own hair, when she didn't dye it, had a dusty colouring, her skin was delicate and her build had stayed boyish, as if, even in her thirties, she was making up her mind which gender to be.

'If I'd been on time, Sophie, I'd have missed your unexpected present.'

'Being late has compensations – I tell my teachers this.'

'Don't tell them what you told me last night. It's the sort of thing I once did – and it brought only grief.'

'But I can live without weed now – or men. When I go back, it'll be flowers and cups of tea; signing on at a college.'

Sophie was shoving stems into a green jug and water puddled over the surfaces. She was beautiful with her tawny skin and brown eyes, looks that ravelled up her mother's Welshness and father's Ethiopian poise.

Later, as Maggie left, she called out: 'Clear up the mess and make it up with your mum.'

But the girl was already watching a film and probably didn't hear. Maggie thought of good and bad mothers, and how her own mother had fashioned a first-aid kit: pill boxes filled with sweets, asthma spray, syringes, plasters and real thermometer, all packed in a shabby, leather holdall. Maggie and her sister – Sophie's mother – had taken it turns to be doctor or patient, poking at each other's bodies in ways their mother wouldn't have approved of. Maggie sometimes felt, as she carried the delivery box to the car, that being a midwife was as provisional and odd as those childhood games. Soon, her dead mother would rise from the graveyard, make cakes, call them in for tea. Today would be Instant Whip or jelly mixed with Carnation milk and her mother would stir this up with improbable stories: happiness, the children a success, her own knots eased away.

Scraping at ice on the windscreen, box at her feet, Maggie wondered why her mother had pretended that the man she had married (not Maggie's real father, but the only father she'd ever known) hadn't had affairs and didn't hit her. Even indoors, her mother wore dark glasses to cover the swollen eyes: the puffiness caused by tears, rather than blows – Stan judiciously placed those elsewhere. With the curtains drawn, Maggie, her mother, her sister and brother watched endless telly: cop shows, black and white films, doctors with white coats flapping or kissing nurses in corridor.

That would be a nice job, Maggie's mother would muse. *You could be nurses – get a doctor.* Later, when Maggie didn't do well at school, her mother bought a movie camera in a car boot sale. *You could work on the TV,* she said. *There's nice older men on TV.*

Maggie found observing life through a lens steadying, and the fragments formed a significance her own life seemed to lack. She never aimed the camera directly at her father – he might have lashed out – but she filmed her siblings; dawn sunlight in a wood; her first boyfriend undressing; bonfire night and the fence catching fire; a neighbour chopping down his shed after the premature baby died. When Maggie found a job in a film company lugging equipment, she pretended she didn't mind the men's bawdy comments. And because she was sleeping with one of the camera crew – it was he who had got her the job – she stayed; even when nothing wonderful happened, even when she was tired, overworked or bored. When her college friends married, bought houses and had children, she stopped travelling, stopped pretending she hadn't noticed the man's other affairs.

By this time her mother had been dead a year, her father had disappeared to live in the Far East, her sister – surprising them all – had become a doctor, and her brother had escaped to Brighton. Becoming a midwife had seemed, at first, like a good idea, even if the fast-track training was hard and the real thing harder. The uniform was unflattering and one shift was never like another.

Everything merged into a surreal dream: urgent requests to send this patient home or stay with that one; demands for epidurals that she was worried were too late; drugs that never seemed to help; needing to anticipate Caesareans, breach births; tears; cards saying how wonderful she'd been. And none of the busy doctors wanted to marry, or even sleep with her. She craved what she had just thrown away – being the other side of the camera – observing, not performing.

She would have left but she got a job in the community, and work suddenly eased. Now there was less rigidity, a better uniform, no fussy Sisters tutting as she caught the baby's head speeding out, having forgotten, again, the sterile gloves. Driving through the winding valleys, where sun softened the hilltops, she took a grim interest in towns where life was complicated and poor: generations of families born to mine coal, now with no jobs; men and women watching TV when she arrived, not even turning it down when she talked about a birth-plan. Some houses were messy, others ferociously tidy. Unlike the hospital (where staff thought her inadequate) here, she was accepted. Women – and men, too – trusted her coolness. She moved around the tiny terraced houses, or the modern homes, examining the furniture, the cupboards full of tins, the bedrooms and cheap cupboards spilling toys and clothes. She liked these people. Liked the way they kept the drama for themselves, played out their vivid lives, but didn't expect her, except for the moment of birth, to join in.

This particular day, after Maggie had left Sophie, an accident on the M4 made her late for clinic. At the surgery, a queue had already formed. A Bangladeshi man stopped her as she rushed in to ask if she could see his wife first – she was having contractions, he said. Then Maggie was late visiting a client up near Cwmbran. The car had overheated and she'd needed to pull in to a lay-by and let it cool. Each of her clients, that day, wanted more of her than she had to spare. The first woman she visited was a doctor, who at forty had become a mother. The woman cried and said she'd made a big mistake – she couldn't cope with this thing two weeks old. At the next house on the outskirts of Newport – large with an electric gate – a woman cautiously opened the door in her dressing gown. She had a black eye. Had banged it on a cupboard, she said.

In Cwmbran, in a tiny house that looked out over fenced farmland, Maggie made a cup of tea for Lisa – nine months pregnant. Lisa looked no more than sixteen or seventeen. Sophie's age.

'Sugar?'

'On the shelf.' Maggie pulled out cheap looking white cups, while Lisa rested her swollen legs. When Maggie took the cups back into the room, the girl smiled up nervously.

'I'll be okay, won't I?' She was pretty, despite her size. Last time Maggie had been there, Lisa had listed hazy medical problems, but maybe it had only been because she was lonely. The girl complained of rashes, palpitations, indigestion, and nightmares. Or perhaps these things were real.

'You'll be fine. Ring the hospital, or get your husband to ring if… if you're worried, if the contractions start.'

'I never thought we'd have one so soon.' The girl stared down at her swollen stomach, spreading itself across the armchair. 'And Mam had only cream paint left, and now that's what the baby's room is. A nothing colour.' She paused, as if she had offered too much. When Maggie did not reply, she muttered something, half question, half statement. Was it, 'Like my life?' or perhaps, 'Like your life'?

'Things will feel colourful when the baby comes.' Maggie was taking the girl's blood pressure, drifting into her own thoughts and wondering if she'd have time for a shower before she went out.

'It's not due yet, is it?' Maggie could taste the girl's fear. She was staring in a way that was almost rude, perhaps because she had noticed the midwife's eyes: one hazel, one green. Even Maggie's features could not make up their mind. Maggie disengaged from the hot clutching hand and glanced at her watch. 'Well, is it due?' the girl asked, petulantly and began to cry. Maggie patted the plump hand, with its rings shifted to the little finger.

In the kitchen, where the tissues were kept, Maggie stared out over the muddy back garden that would not be planted until spring and might never be planted. The girl would like it if she stayed, if Maggie sat on the settee, folding Lisa into her arms. Or perhaps it was Maggie who wanted this. Lisa had a pleasantly clean smell, like talcum powder or lavender. And then Maggie's mobile went.

'Aunt Maggie? I'm hungry. Do you have any food? Or weed would do.'

Standing in Lisa's white kitchen, with its microwave, fancy kettle and wooden units, she assumed that the girl was listening through the walls.

'No, sorry. I'm just finishing off here, but we could hold that meeting when I get back.' She hissed, 'Pizza in the freezer,' and clicked the phone off. Scooping up the value pack of tissues, she hoped that Sophie didn't rummage in the cleaning cupboard and find the Tupperware box labelled *Weed. Killer*.

In the other room, Lisa had a hand on her distended belly, massaging the lumps that rippled their way across the flesh. Her eyes were red. Maggie passed her the box, then sat on the edge of the chair.

'So will this be my life? This baby?' It was as if the thought had only just occurred to her. Maggie looked around at the bare room.

'It will fill up your life.' She thought of her own existence – sometimes miraculous, other times stillborn.

129

'You'll love being a mum. I expect you'll want lots more.'

The girl smiled back wanly.

'I get up at nights. Look out into the fields. I think of the darkness… and other things. Is this the sort of world to bring a child into? I don't know if life's a curse or if I'm one of the lucky ones.'

Maggie sat back down and held the girl's hand. She was not so naive, after all, this child.

That evening, Maggie had been invited out by people she barely knew. He was something to do with the university, his wife, Lyn, an architect. The two women had met at a community centre where both had taken, then promptly dropped, a black and white photography class. The week after they had left Lyn invited Maggie for tea, insisting that Maggie's camera tips, not the useless teacher's, were what she needed. The house was Victorian, three storied and elegant.

'It's too big for us – we rattle around,' Lyn said. 'I bought the house as a project – when we thought we'd have children. I suppose now it's become the child.' She gestured at the impressive fireplaces, chandeliers, doors that swept back to reveal a dining area and conservatory beyond. As they stood in the huge living room, the collie sniffing Maggie's legs, Lyn sat down at the baby grand; she played a single note. 'I thought I'd learn some day.'

Lyn's husband was on the tiled path when Maggie arrived, perhaps looking for her. He held out a hand.

You must be Maggie. I'm Benedict – Ben.' He flipped off his glasses, as if they prevented him from seeing. 'It's nice to meet you at last.' He squeezed her hand and scrutinised her, no doubt sizing up just how dumb she was; Lyn had warned that he could be critical. Ben gave a curt, but not unfriendly smile, dropping her hand. Other people threaded their way up the path, pushing through the straggle of bushes, past the bare lilac and dripping magnolia. When they reached them, Ben stooped to kiss the woman – heavily pregnant, petite, with blond hair piled up – then shook the man's hand. The three visitors stood there, looking at one another, waiting for introductions, but Ben flicked his eyes to the sky. 'I'm stargazing,' he announced, as if this was explanation enough. 'Learning to navigate my boat the ancient way.' He squinted into the darkness and popped his glasses back on. 'Look! There's Betelgeuse.' He gestured at a faint redness above, a dot in a blurred constellation. 'And Sirius, the Dog Star. There are myths about stars' beginnings, you know. Ironic, since some of them are extinguished by the time we receive their light.' He moved closer to Maggie, pointing into the distance, flying her into space, to the triangle of three bright dots. 'Betelgeuse, Sirius and Procyon. All in different constellations, but you wouldn't know it without a telescope. They look like they belong together.'

Maggie could feel the warmth of his body until he backed away and abruptly introduced her to the couple: Kerry and Dai. They murmured hellos and smiled, but only saw bits of each other in the darkened, intimate world. Maggie could hear Benedict's breath, could sense he was staring, but all he said was, 'So you're a midwife?' As if it were the oddest choice. And then, 'You should chat to Kerry, here. You've lots in common.' His voice was ironic and musical.

Inside, Kerry took off her coat with heavy concentrated movements and smiled at Maggie. Maggie gave a half-smile back, following the men into a lounge full of people, hoping that she'd be able to smoke. Trays of drinks were set out. On small tables, nuts and olives lay heaped in pretty bowls. There were about twelve people in the room, some by the fire, some standing around the settee near the bay window. When Kerry followed Maggie in, she was given a seat. The pregnant woman looked across hopefully, but Maggie had joined the knot by the fire, talking about a film they'd seen the night before. Some liked Greenaway, some didn't. The hostess, Lyn, flicked her eyes over to the other group and back again.

'Greenaway gives such a strange sense of space, don't you think?'

'That's because he uses a wide-angle lens.'

'Maggie was in the film business,' Lyn added, neatly offering her friend, like a dip or bowl of pistachios. She slid away and, as the talk went on, Maggie watched her introduce Kerry to people, spinning conversational flax. As people asked Maggie things, she felt the familiar swelling inside, problematic and pleasurable. She hesitated.

'Actually, I was in routine documentary most of the time. No glamour.' It was unusual to be so honest. A woman – French, with dark coiled hair and immaculate make-up – considered for a moment as she flicked ash into the ashtray. She looked across at a smaller group where people talked in loud voices.

'Creative work's routine, but hard, too; some people with academic jobs don't appreciate that.' She nodded over to the other group. 'What they don't know is, if you're any good, you give glimpses of something bigger, of strange connections.'

'Or disconnections? My film would explore fracture, but I'm never sure what sort.'

'Do us! Document our lives.' It was Lyn, arm linked to the man she had brought over. 'Rob, meet Maggie. I've sat you next to each other; the rest of us are just boring couples.'

At the table they argued about Iraq, student loans, the new Welsh Assembly, fast food and wearing the hijab. While they spooned strange tasting soup with mint and coriander or forked at tender lamb made with pickled lemons and spinach, people caught at words, twisting and turning them inside out. At first Maggie enjoyed the drama, was relieved how easily conversation flowed. No intellectualism – just opinions, heaped in a colourful pile. Rob, next to her, did not so much ignore her, as communicate, tactfully, that he assumed neither had any interest in Lyn's match-making (someone had mentioned that Rob and his wife had just separated). A man with a goatee beard, who earlier had said little, was becoming cross. Twice, he had come back to a subject they had all let go.

'You can't have a student sitting in your tutorial not making proper contact, covered in the hijab from head to toe.'

'But Russ, people communicate with speech, with words.' It was Nadja, sighing this out, as if she, the liberal Muslim, was bored having the same conversation over and over. Lyn's husband, half addressing Maggie, was musing, as he broke up bits of pitta bread.

'The notion of God is a nothing, isn't it? Yet it's spawned substance. That's a true virgin birth – substance out of nothingness, belief born out of ignorance.'

He smiled across, as if Maggie appreciated the joke. The others ignored him, more interested in the simmering argument and the fragments of conversation they'd started up earlier, the half consumed delicacy of talk they still wanted to finish.

Russell broke back in. 'I want to see my students' faces – to communicate properly, for God's sake.' The man scored his serviette with a knife, piling up the fragments.

'You don't like it, because you can't ogle them.' It was his wife, Claudette, the French woman. Earlier, Maggie had thought her imperious; now she wondered if she was just unhappy.

'But it oppresses woman.'

'Well, you'd know about that, wouldn't you?' The words were barely audible, the woman taking a swig of her wine. She turned to offer a fixed smile to the person next to her and brightly asked, 'Have you seen that painter in Cardiff like Paula Rego; do you know the one I mean?'

The man she spoke to looked uncomfortable. Claudette's husband leaned forward and Maggie watched him put the elbow of his cream suit in a patch of spinach. Other people seemed to know what would happen next: this being a re-run of a film they had watched again and again. They were all eating or talking in an exaggerated way, as if to draw fire.

'Oppressed? Daubing paint on canvas all day? I'd put my hand up for that sort of oppression.'

Kerry was ripping strips off of the blue napkin, as if she were trapped with birds of prey: fragments of torn or scrunched up paper now littered the tablecloth. Lyn poured drink into several glasses, whispered to her husband and then handed a postcard of an exhibition to Claudette.

'Wonderful,' Lyn asserted. 'Dramatic.' Benedict looked across at Maggie and said how sailing at night was like launching into other countries, washing up on alien shores. Maggie smiled back, wondering why his conversation always seemed to have bits missing.

'I filmed in Pakistan; at first I wore the hijab, but later I cut my hair, wore a cap and baggy trousers. Became a man. Being a man is easier.' But Maggie wasn't sure she believed this and didn't know why she'd even said it.

'Really?' asked Rob. 'I'd love you to tell me how to make it easy.'

Lyn brought out the pudding – an Arabic recipe, she said, given to Benedict by an Iranian PhD student. Empty red and white wine bottles cluttered the table, the voices getting louder with each bottle opened. Dai, the pregnant woman's husband, smiled out and rubbed his wife's hand.

'Baking bread and having children is what men should do.'

Benedict, topping up the wine looked over at him and pulled a face.

'If you weren't so drunk you'd appreciate that I'm your

role model. I made the pudding, cleaned, even chopped the wood. New man. I'm thinking of having a baby next.'

Lyn lifted her glass to toast him. 'Well, not with me, honey.'

Then everyone was talking at once; the easy affiliations of female versus male loosened. Maggie felt stupid, as if she was in a different orbit to the others, along with the silent, pregnant woman. She noticed how Kerry had barely registered her husband's words, but was daydreaming, stepping out into the lightness of herself, as if nothing else mattered. The girl stared into the dark garden where lights lit up the fountain, the arbour and garden house.

'I don't know if I want a boy or girl,' she said to no one in particular, 'but I suppose I ought to decide soon.'

Earlier, she had leant across to Maggie, about to speak, but had dipped back, like a deer retreating to the flecked shade of trees.

The apricot pudding was spiced and foreign. No one spoke as they scraped at china bowls and took more when it was offered. Someone mentioned Instant Whip.

'Awful! But didn't you love it when you were a child – wasn't it bliss?"

'My cleaner makes it for me. Our secret snack.' It was Rob, smiling ruefully at Maggie. She wished he had talked more; he seemed sensitive, she thought, or perhaps just evasive. Interesting. She could tell that, like the others, he wanted wealth and sophistication (he was an accountant, he'd said) but needed it salted by the plebeian. Just like her. Why was no one happy with what they had? She was suddenly bored by them. Bored by herself.

No one had spoken to the pregnant woman. Maggie, who had been at work all day and now felt off duty, had not asked when the baby was due nor what it might be called. Why should she take a professional interest? As if she intuited this, Kerry scraped back her chair and quietly left the room. Then Maggie felt her mobile vibrate. A text.

Wot u doin?

She tapped back to Sophie, *Drunk, dancin on table —*

The reply was immediate.

Wots nu? — Cn I smoke ur weed

No

Y not?

'I think I'd better go. I'm needed at home — my niece, the one I told you about.'

Benedict looked up.

'I'll see you out.' He was pouring black coffee into cups and fiddling with the strings of peppermint teabags. That was what the Cwmbran girl had smelt of — some sort of mint or lemon balm, not lavender. Maggie waved the host back to his job.

'It's fine. My coat's just outside, I'll see myself out.'

She noticed that the cheap bottle of wine she'd brought had not been put on the table with the others. She squeezed through the heavy door, acknowledging the goodbyes. They would talk about her when she was gone. Benedict followed into the hallway.

'Call me.' He slipped her his card, slid a hand around and touched her bottom as he kissed her goodbye. Then, as a voice shouted his name from the other room, he was gone.

She wasn't sure if it had happened, but she held the printed card, felt the soft place his hand had rested. She picked up her umbrella. The Victorian tiled floor was intricately patterned, each piece fitted together in a neat and ordered way. Life had once seemed like that — or at least, its surface must have. Now it was more like her own tiled floors: a jigsaw of cracks, with pieces missing that could trip you up. Affairs. Loneliness. No sense of where you belonged or what you should do. She moved past the end of the curving staircase, with its hardwood newel post, its dramatic span of polished banister and heard a grunt, animal-like. An escaping shock of noise, half whimper, half exhalation. Then a sharp cry of pain.

Maggie climbed the stairs and threaded her way down a dark corridor. She kept the map of these Victorian houses internalised, the permutations on a single theme, the layouts she paced and explored up the valley and in the city. Behind a stained glass door that flooded light was the bathroom. The door was locked. She tapped gently.

'Kerry. It's me, Maggie.' And then she added, 'The midwife.' And she felt she *was* a midwife, not someone just acting the part.

The bolt slid back and the girl – for she could not be more than twenty five – stood there in her soft green dress, bent like an old woman, confused, with pleading eyes. Maggie saw her as she had avoided doing all evening, and understood something. We communicate in complex ways, shroud ourselves even when our bodies are naked. Give ourselves away when we are covered head to foot. That was why the man had touched her, had known she was a possibility; she sent out that message.

Kerry looked helpless, as if she needed someone to sort out the mess, the dreadful inappropriateness of what was happening. Maggie guessed she would not panic – unlike that girl in the valleys. The dress was wet at its hem. On the floor of the large bathroom, with its claw feet bath, wicker chair and piles of fluffy towels, there was a pool of water.

'Second child?'

'Uhuh.'

'Contractions?'

In answer, the woman doubled up, gripping herself, and moaning. Her face was sweaty, but her arm was cold.

'Can we get you to a bed?'

She groaned again, crumpling to the floor, holding her stomach and rocking to and fro.

Maggie grabbed some of the towels, rolled the girl on to them, padded one for her head, murmuring to her all the while that she was doing fine, telling her how to breathe.

'We need to get your pants off.'

'Why?' Kerry stared up hopelessly: it couldn't be the baby; she was not letting it be the baby. Maggie checked the dilation, then called on her mobile for the ambulance, asked for paramedics.

'You'll be okay,' she said to Kerry, then went to the door and shouted for help. A huge moon was shining through the dark bathroom windows, and the girl fixed on it as she breathed and rode the pain. After a while, she latched back on to Maggie's eyes, watching them as the pain came faster and stronger, trying to read if something was going a little wrong or badly wrong. Her blonde hair was wet and her make-up smudged.

'It's not due for another week,' she managed in a breath's gasp, as if she could send this child back, make it wait its proper turn. 'I feel sick.'

Maggie grabbed a china bowl decorated with delicate roses and the girl heaved into it, the orange juice and mint soup swilling around the patterned sides.

'Are you alright up there?' It was Rob's voice, echoing from below.

'I need a hand,' Maggie called back, turning her head, but keeping her hand on the perineum. First Rob, then Benedict and then his wife, Lyn, and someone else crowded in at the doorway. Maggie pushed up the woman's knees under the long skirt as Kerry's husband struggled his way into the bathroom. He bent down to his wife, then stood again and turned to the people collecting on the stairs.

'For Christ sake *do* something. *Get* someone.'

A woman stared back at him blankly. He bent again to grab at his wife's hand, to feel her forehead. She shook him aside, focusing instead on Maggie.

'Call an ambulance, for Christ's sake,' he entreated.

'I have.' The man looked at Maggie, as if he didn't recognise her, hadn't been sitting opposite her all evening.

'The ambulance is on its way. Give me some space. Get me a clean towel, a plastic bowl and clean out the sick bowl; I'll need it again.'

'She's a midwife,' someone said uselessly, as if she'd been making it up earlier. Lyn took over the other tasks: washed out the bowl, directed someone to a bedroom to get pillows, while someone else pulled old towels from a cupboard in the corner; the room was so big, with its fireplace and cupboards, it had probably once been a bedroom. Several of the guests were backing away, saying they'd go, get taxis home; that they were in the way.

'You're doing fine, Kerry. I can see the head. Can you push, now?'

The girl writhed and moaned, 'I can't. I can't. It hurts.' She was making strange noises – short exclamations and groans, wheezed out as she breathed, then longer shriller ones as the contractions took her and intensified.

'Is she going to be alright?' Maggie flicked her eyes up to Kerry's husband.

'Fine; she's doing fine.' But the pushing was having little effect.

'Can you just turn on your side, Kerry, if I help you?' Maggie gently rolled the woman to her left and moved her knees towards the shadowed world under the bath. It was not ideal, but on her side there was less resistance for the baby's downward thrust.

Kerry turned, making a low, long moan, like a cow, mournful and alone. And then she pushed and the head was there, ripping its way out.

'Pant now, Kerry. Pant.' And as the girl panted and Maggie felt the head and saw the new child being born, there was a hiss or gasp from someone behind. The husband could see nothing because he was crouched down, holding his wife's hand while she dug her nails in, gripping like she would never let him go.

'Is it alright?' he asked. 'Are they alright?'

The baby, perhaps in shock at the light, the noise, the moon sailing above, let out a whimper, with his head stuck out and his legs and body firmly inside the woman. Even as Maggie carefully held the head, wishing the people would have some decency and go away, she thought to herself how strange it was for this baby to speak.

'He's fine. Kerry, keep panting.' She felt the throat for the cord and gently freed it, slipping the jellied rope over the baby's head. 'Push, gently now. Push again.'

The girl pushed, Maggie pulled downwards and then up and the bloodied baby slipped out into the ready towel. Maggie wiped the child's nose and mouth, then placed it, with the trailing umbilical cord, into its mother's arms.

The baby gazed up, with intelligent, cloudy eyes, examining Maggie's flushed face. It looked, to her, as if he knew that this would be one of the last babies Maggie would deliver, that soon she might make documentaries about birth – in the Valleys, then later abroad. As if he knew, with his crumpled, penetrating stare, that whether you're premature, or late, life is what you make it. And Maggie read all this, as if the baby had given her second-sight, and the communication was mixed with wine, thoughts of Sophie, a boat sailing under stars and the yellow moon, laughing through the window.

'A boy,' she said, knowing she would be the only one to register. The father was still moaning, as if he could not stop, as if this huge thing had unhinged him. He was muttering, incanting – *Oh my God, Oh my God.* Those crushing in at the door, watching the baby suck, started to talk.

'How wonderful!'

'Look at him; it's a baby!'

'Kerry, you were marvellous.' Lyn was crying, leaning against her husband, someone else was kissing people out on the landing, hugging them each in turn.

The baby, woad-like with its blue membrane and

draped in the strings of blood and tissue dragged from the womb, puckered its face and cried at the welcoming committee, at the moon, at the strange heat and cold, the hunger of existence. They think it's all over, Maggie thought to herself. They've forgotten the afterbirth; they always do.

Someone else's documentary would probably have swung the camera to the crowd, lingered on the long fingered baby, whose ears stuck out a bit too much and then softened the focus. They might have shown the abandoned dinner table, the crumpled napkins, a cookery book, its cover splashed with oil, upturned in the kitchen. It would be sentimental – complete and satisfying.

'What a night,' someone was murmuring.

'Thank God you were here,' the husband said. And it *was* a bit like a film, ending with the glorious yet nebulous moment of birth, ending with the champagne corks popping.

'I need the ambulance, the equipment.' And for the first time, Maggie was worried, though no one was listening.

She waved at the green plastic bowl and someone handed it to her (it should have been ready; she was making mistakes). She pulled gently on the cord, waited for the smudging of blood, then pulled again. As the trickle increased, she positioned the bowl to catch the blood, the clots and liver-like substance that oozed and pulsed from the womb.

'Unbutton your shirt more; get the baby comfortable, let him suck again.' (She should have opened the buttons earlier, been more prepared. Next time she delivered at a party, she'd remember). She was checking the membranes of blood, peering at the stuff that smelt like metal and raw meat.

Downstairs there was a hammering at the door, while the blood rushed out and the baby sucked. Someone was already dashing down, letting them in, then running up the stairs, telling the story, as if it was the first time this mystery had ever happened. Maggie could hear, and blocked out Rob's voice, giving snatches of the garbled story. Then the ambulance man was there.

'Stroke of luck you being here, love.' He was bending down, inspecting her job. 'Everything okay?'

Maggie shook her head.

'The bleeding's too brisk.'

'We'll take her in for a check up.' The crew were setting up a drip, injecting Kerry in the leg. Maggie felt relieved she was no longer centre-stage; that she could at last go home.

'Take me?' The woman looked up, her face washed pale, her eyes dreamy as she watched the thing that nuzzled and gnawed at her breasts.

'Get you checked up in the hospital, love.'

'Will you come?' Kerry stared into Maggie eyes, as if she were her mother, as if they were bonded.

'Of course.'

They carried her in the stretcher out into the dark night, wind rustling the branches of the trees, shaking rain down onto the rough blanket and the baby wrapped in clean towels.

'They just brought one in as we left – delivered in the ambulance, shouting and screaming, that one – from Cwmbran, she was.'

The ambulance man was cheerful as he helped Maggie and Kerry's husband up the steps and inside, as if this part of his job was the gift, making up for arbitrary death. If any ghosts trailed him, he didn't seem to notice them – at least, not right now. Maggie knew it would be late by the time she left the hospital; by the time they'd found a bed for Kerry. She would probably be so late, she'd see the darkness thin, would glimpse the uncertain dawn and the frost as it rimed the lake and painted her precious, ragged garden. She thought of her niece, planted in her life – perhaps the only child she'd bear.

Maggie's own film, she decided, would show the amazed face of the mother when she had given birth, the look of wariness she shot at her older husband, who showed some fussiness she sensed and mistrusted, but which would not surface to trouble her until years later. Maggie's documentary would reveal the hot afterbirth, tell about haemorrhaging, the loss of lives across the centuries, the design fault built into women's bodies. Then it would pan away to the indifferent moon, the trees waving their branches in the cold night. Hinting at the complication and work that lay beneath life's surface. But even this film would not be the truth, just a version, conjured from that night or that day's apprehension of things. She would need to keep looking, making the film over and over again, searching for what she had missed, the clots and blocks that stopped her understanding who she was and what life was really about.

Umbilical – 2004

Here we both are, as if we are one. Wherever you go, I go, and although this is not of my choosing, nor of yours, either – regrets, planted deep, set up the strangest reverberation.

In the small front room, you pick up objects and wipe with an absent gesture, all the while wondering how long to give the new job. Looking back, there have been other failures, but, mostly you've done well: a scholarship to boarding school, becoming a doctor, marrying, giving birth to two beautiful children. You dust the art, literature and medical books, the lamps and stereo, but barely register this. It is natural to be busy: to walk through a room and collect up papers, carry things from one place to another, to type with a phone tucked under your chin. Natural to make endless lists, plan each meal even as you browse the medical catalogues. And natural too, to remain a little absent, to hide – from yourself and from others.

You seldom ponder on me, yet do not avoid the subject either, for you are not self-pitying, nor the slightest bit self-indulgent. But I sometimes wonder if all this deliberate work, this obsessive furrowing is connected to the loss? I know that when people slow, they remember: the dark hinges open, and memory, that strange dream, comes unfurling back.

The house in Swansea is Victorian. Your mother, who thought all possessions unnecessary – a hippy before the term was even invented – would probably have called the place cluttered. There are splash-of-colour dishes from Spain, the delicate Japanese raku bowl – a birthday present from Shimi, your ex-husband – and the chiming clock your brother says his grandmother meant him to have, not you.

You dust the sibling rivalry from the mahogany case and decide, once again, that, when you next visit Brighton, Max can have the cursed thing. But it is not your fault he takes life so seriously, nor that he's nearly an alcoholic; he should give up being a teacher. In the mirror you see your frowning features, and it's your brother's crossness that leaps out. You could have been twins. The rest of the family consider it an irony that eldest child is sick and the middle a healer, but you know better, you who are ill yourself.

Pleasant surroundings do help. Beauty, you have always thought, can dilute the toxic. There are paintings propped near the door and you shift them aside, mopping at the hidden dirt. One day, you think, one day, the dust will eventually clear. Whenever Jim, the most recent lover, stays, he arrives heaving a great canvas through the door, chipping paintwork and struggling with the scope of his latest vision – he doesn't go in for glimpses. At first, such gifts were flattering, but there are only so many walls in a small terraced house. And still the paintings come, as if he thinks this house is his workshop, or perhaps a place to hide the collateral. He has hinted that he'll maybe take them back once he leaves Izzy, and that he'll need most for the London exhibition. So you began to see all his artifice: the paintings that are gifts and yet not gifts, the flowers, apologies and regrets – a strange story you've been sucked into, a narrative full of lacunae and self-deception.

Straightening, you assess the colourful daubing, head on one side, your hair looped and elegantly clipped. The messy canvases remind you of Chagall – deep blue backgrounds that might be the sea or sky and attenuated women floating towards the viewer. Even with your reservations about Jim, you have come to like these gaudy things. The paint is perhaps too thinly layered and does not suggest the complexity Jim thinks it does, but you have secreted a few in the attic, knowing that when he retrieves the others, these may be overlooked. The more you live with the deep blues and reds, the more urgently you need this brew.

Later, good friends are due for dinner. They are a part of the old life in Cardiff and – understandably – seldom visit. They will find the new house transformed; Swansea is cheaper than Cyncoed and the surplus cash has added a conservatory, an extra bathroom and bedroom in the attic. You will tell your friends (will there be an edge of triumph?) that the new job, which still feels – though is probably seen by them – as failure or capitulation, has, in fact, become a pleasure. You are not sure what you will say about the paintings – or if you will mention Jim. You know that they will see through the bravado for, even before you took this job, they were telling you it was foolish. Why, they exclaimed, would anyone leave Cardiff? And why move to Swansea? Everyone makes mistakes. For, of course, they knew why you had left. It wasn't just the exhaustion, or the ex coming back to work at Heath hospital; it wasn't the rows with a daughter who missed lessons and smoked dope. It was something else.

As a blood donor doctor the stress is negligible and the mistakes of less consequence. Today, drifting into the session, shopping bag over one arm, green coat flapping open, it was as if you'd chanced upon the echoing church hall transformed into a temporary hospital, as if the white coat you put on, the stethoscope you slipped over the top, were not even real. You dumped your bags in the kitchen, where Jenny brewed tea and laid out rows of pale green china. The girls, with their scant training and nurses' uniforms, were like extras. They had learned – for the purposes of their daily performance – how to extract a pint of blood, stop a faint, deftly administer a plaster. But in

146

reality, they knew more about make-up and fashion than anatomy or the transfusion service. You always notice their make-up, the thinly pencilled eyebrows, dark liner and thick foundation. You have started being a bit more careful about your own appearance.

Today, the donor session was busy. Rows of people sat waiting to have thumbs pricked and their blood tested. Several people went up to the administration desk and complained, saying they'd leave unless they were done quickly. Others, who'd been accepted and were waiting in the second queue – just in front of the beds – also grumbled. The girls were slower than usual, dawdling out to fetch the next patient, leaving beds empty for minutes at a time. Something was in the air – but there was no full moon and no one was getting married. Half way through – you had a sixth sense about the inevitability of something – Jade, one of your nurses, gave a strangled cry and turned to the man she was meant to be minding. By the time you rushed over, Jade had the tube out and the plaster on, but her hands were shaking, and you could see how much she'd taken. A dreamer, she is, especially when in love, and different to the other girls.

'It's nothing to worry about,' you promptly said to the man. 'You're just looking a little pale.' And you got his feet up, the pillows from under his head. He had no idea that Jade had taken a pint and a half, but he obliged us, for the colour drained from his handsome face. 'Just lie there; stay where you are so we can keep an eye on you – in case you faint.' You admitted nothing. But felt his pulse, took his blood pressure and, all the while, Jade flustered and you cut her off each time she spoke.

'Keep focussed, Jade.' You nodded at the blood that had pumped into the squashy sack. At other beds the plastic bags, tucked out of sight, were filling, the blood oozing out a deep, dark red. A gauge registered how much had flowed in, and after a pint, each patient would need to be tapped off. Most of the girls are experienced, practiced at managing the calming talk, watching the gauge, keeping things moving, and drifting in and out of their own thoughts.

When one of the girls came to collect the man's sachet of blood (Shelly was good at weaving up and down, eyes sharp, prompt at swinging away the full sacks and latching up the new), she could see by your face that this was a reject. She whipped off the container, carrying the bulging bag half concealed by her apron. 'We'll just let you rest here a while,' you said to the man, patting his hand and noticing how his dark curls were damp against his dark skin. And all the staff could see he might faint – a rugby type, and they often do. You smiled, as if all this was natural, and then he relaxed and you went to your desk to scribble some notes, keeping an eye on him, making sure he got no worse.

Patrolling up and down was Jenny, the team leader, ready to pounce, the person really in charge, despite your status as doctor: it was always a dance between you, compliment and complaint, the shifting hierarchy of rivalry. Everything slowed as Jenny came over and the girls watched to see what would happen – for they liked a drama and someone in the wrong, especially if it was Jade.

But today, you and Jenny were a team, and nothing terrible happened and the perigee of crisis passed. Time sailed on, despite things later turning bad-tempered and scrappy: two faints (the rugby man one of them) and a spilt hot tea and a woman's arm bleeding and bleeding, needing plaster after plaster. And it was so stuffy in the badly lit room, with its low ceiling that by the end everyone was yawning and wanting to be home. By four o'clock the girls were folding the chairs and clattering the tables aside and you finally took Jade over to a corner. Earlier, you had watched Jenny tell her off and you felt sorry for the girl, sniffing into her hankie, trying not to catch anyone's eye. In your hand was a last cup of tea and the girls were chattering about boyfriends, about what to wear out, about wanting babies. Jade, who had red eyes, kept saying sorry, sorry about the mistake, yet you didn't even mention the oversight. These things happen. You reflected on your own mistakes. How that young girl had been new to your practice, how it was probably too late to get the thyroid tested and stop the inevitable. Her parents had just died, she told you; her husband had left. She'd been anorexic in her youth, was exhausted. You counselled her, gave her the anti-depressants she asked for, made a note to arrange an urgent blood test: what more could you have done?

It was as you reflected on this that Jade – toeing the ground, preoccupied with the parquet floor – blurted out the other thing. Three months gone and she'd only done the test that morning. Her boyfriend, when she'd told him – and perhaps this was why she'd not done the test sooner – told her it was over.

'I feel sick all the time. I can't concentrate,' Jade said, and you felt sick too, remembering how it was. 'And I can't bear the blood.' Jade looked up, tears glistening. Her beautiful clear skin was downy and pale, her eyes palest blue. Youthful and pretty and about the same age as your daughter. You told her to go home and rest, told her to contact HR and not to come in for a while. You touched her shoulder – she was soft and warm – and asked if she'd spoken to her family. There were NHS or private places, you said quietly, that could sort out an abortion, if that was what she wanted. Behind, the beds were noisily dismantled, but you sensed people listening as the chairs were stacked with a hard clattering. You were preparing to drive a mile up the road to the good supermarket and needed to get to dry cleaner before the shop shut. Jade might have said something earlier, you thought. But there is never a good time to reveal things or a good time to make mistakes.

Your Cardiff friends say you're a good doctor. That you were a good GP. Your friends say you worry too much. Carry around ghosts. So you are thinking now, as you tidy the room, how you might have done more for Jade, that you could still get her number, could phone and be motherly. You pause, holding the duster aside, as if my whispering is audible, after all. Pick up the wooden bowl, black, etched with green and stare at it blankly, not fully appreciating its beauty. Something is at the back of your mind, something to do with your daughter. Propped behind the bowl is a shadow puppet and beside that sits a brash pottery dish, like a sunflower, with yellow petals and lumpy fruit, made when your child was little. Sophie crafted it that last summer she and Menelek were thrust into the hospital play-scheme.

Here is your orbit, revealed in an array of objects, partly sentimental (a marker to people and events) but also a deliberate artifice, placed so everything looks its best. Your mother would be wrong to call it clutter. I call it art. Do you know that I covet the bowl of ornate eggs, bought one by one – your strange, greedy indulgence. The black marble egg from New York (first anniversary trip with Shimi); the green one from Spain (an escape after you divorced) and from France comes the ornate papier-mâché, bought by Jim. You choose a white egg to hold, caressing in your palm the coldness. What might life have been if I had not remained a secret?

When Wayne and the others arrive, they will like the new house, the confection of colours, the Turkish rugs, old wooden trunk, the well-chosen objects. But Wayne, who is an architect, will understand that outward appearances are constructs, like photos or memories. They hide as much as they reveal. To your friends, you are kind, shrewd Lizzie who dutifully attends to people, objects, books, the open fire, the armchairs. And all of your old friends, who really

150

do like one another, will nevertheless circle politely, as if the time for confessional friendships has gone. Are you glad that you have learned to manage surfaces, that life is less uncertain, or do you, like so many others, yearn for what is lost? What your friends probably don't know, whatever they gossip about in your absence, is that your thoughts, wherever else they go, are eventually brought to heel by the tug of an umbilical cord, ferocious and insistent.

You are dusting a sort of doll, peg and cloth, made in Egypt or perhaps Africa – rough unhemmed material attached to a stick. The doll is part of a set: one woman carries fire-wood, the other holds a baby; two children, draped in the same rough material are propped alongside the matriarchy. It has always been a sort of superstition that the group should stay together. In the absence of men – the stick males gone to war perhaps or merely feckless, and lounging in the sun – this little group clings. Even when your daughter, Sophie, danced the dolls up the stairs, or out into the garden, you'd insist (too sharply, perhaps) that the group belonged on the mantelpiece. Dust has settled in the cracks and folds of clothes and the blue dress is grey (though you still visualise it as sky blue) while the pink wrap of the scarf has faded to brown. Their fifteen year existence is a marvel – these thrown-together gewgaws for the tourist market. What would the person who made them think, to know that despite Elizabeth's enviable wealth, her Aga, caravan in France and pretty house, she has enthroned these flimsy bits of rag for all to see? And it's because of them, with a jolt, you remember me.

The smell of beef bourguignon, your standby since the seventies, threads through the solid and newly decorated house. The phone rings. Someone asking about the convoluted route, perhaps.

'Mum, it's Sophie.' Contained in the voice of your daughter a black hole of misery, a hole you don't want to acknowledge.

'Hiya, love. Has your phone been out of battery? I've been trying... lots.'

This is a lie. You've tried twice, but otherwise have been swept up with the job and the new man. Whenever you did thought of your daughter, it didn't seem an appropriate time to call. Mostly, it was too early in the morning: she worked the festivals, seemed to be away most of the year. You wonder if your voice carries unspoken messages as eloquently as your daughter's.

'Oh Mum!' The groan, the helplessness, the need for rescue, a constant in the child's life.

'What is it darling? Where are you?'

Just as you say something reassuring to Sophie, the phone goes dead. When this has happened before, you have been left lying awake and worrying, hearing the rattle of the upstairs window, the wind howling in the chimney. You often get up, pace the house, while your self is horribly sliced in two, one part straining for the phone's ring as you imagine the field, road-side or bed-sit that your daughter lies crumpled in. The other part blocking these imaginings, insisting there is no point in worrying – even as you do.

For some reason, all the time you try to reconnect, you are remembering your visit to Ethiopia where you took Sophie as a baby and Menelek to see their grandmother. The old woman looked down at Sophie's pale brown skin and shook her head, saying softly that girls brought only trouble. At the time, you were cross and noticed how the girls and the women were the ones who took the trouble: cooking, cleaning, waiting on the men, on you too, as a guest. Shimi's cousins and sisters, draped in beautiful fabrics, scarves tied around their hair, chopped wood, and cooked stews of spiced meat and giggled behind your back. As a guest, you weren't allowed to help and so had nothing useful to do, but irritatingly, you were not allowed to huddle with the men, smoking and talking politics.

Nineteen years ago you thought the country an exotic and tender place, an adventure, though Shimi said the women considered you odd – mannish in your dark trousers and loose shirts, your skin pasty white. Thought you didn't fit in and were a strange sort of wife. You did not translate for yourself, the deeper implications of this foreign visit, the bargain where women are cherished yet take second place. You did not feel you needed to; Shimi might be Ethiopian and you might be Western, but you were both educated, equals and doctors. You returned to Cardiff with silk shawls, spices, embroidered bathrobes made of soft cotton, and two spoiled children. Shimi – though you did not know it – returned with something more complex. He grew impatient: with the children, with your liberality and wooliness, that he said was, nevertheless, controlling. He said the marriage had been a mistake.

You are just picking up the phone again when it rings at you, insistent and querulous.

'Mum; it's Sophie. Why did you cut me off?' Before you can reply: 'He's left me.'

Her white, rough boyfriend, smiling and restless, who liked Sophie's Dreads, her brown skin. Who was shocked to find her mother white and disapproving – a doctor. You cannot say to your daughter: *this boy was bound to leave you. He's not educated, not even tame. How could you expect your toughness, tears and mockery, to not, at last bore him, though your difference might keep him interested a while?* You know, by now, what you might or might not, hazard with Sophie.

'Where are you? Are you coming home?' You can do the counselling thing with your patients – like a mother or a kind aunt. With your daughter you always sound like some sort of administrator, planning the next AGM.

*

153

You have been driving an hour when you register that you're on full beam – have been for some time – blinding others, as you were blinded by Sophie.

I'm in the tent on a beach. Everyone's doing drugs. I'm pregnant.

Staring into the darkness, you drive on auto-pilot, noting the other cars, as if they are a pasted scene against which the drama of life unfolds. Red lights and white lights run together, a fairground of movement. There are sudden pits of darkness, cars emerging or cutting across, lorries sometimes holding their ground or monsters that bear down, then overtake. Your head aches. At least you thought to grab the migraine tablets. You fix on the motorway signs, rehearsing the route the computer outlined. It is an impossible distance – a distance you would have thought twice about driving in daylight. Swansea to Plymouth. Why didn't you phone Shimi? Is it because he would have taken over, blamed you, suggested you'd let the children go off the rails? No university degrees – a shame to the family.

You still have a hundred and fifty miles to drive; over two hours for Sophie to sit alone in a tent. She had asked if the cramps that hadn't let her sleep for days were a sign she might miscarry and you told her, no, cramp is common in the early stages. *Get a hot water bottle; take paracetmol.* And then once she'd put the phone down, you'd worried that she might take an overdose. You have put the medical case in the back. It makes you feel in control, but you are not sure that there is anything in it to help. It is the motherly stuff Sophie needs; warmth stripped of judgment. If she smells censure, she'll be gone again, slipping away to be a pregnant stray, producing an unwanted baby in some barn or squat.

Half an hour later, when you pull off of the motorway for a break, rigid from straining into the darkness and gripping the wheel, it's not just migraine tablets you take. In the services, you make for the toilets and listening to the roar of the hand dryer, the cajoling of a parent who splashes water and soap over the hands of a tired child, you swallow the amphetamines. Not since you were a student, and then a new practitioner, have you resorted to the 'tricks of the trade'. In the late seventies, when you trained at Addenbrookes, the students who didn't take the pills used beer or wine to keep going. You often wondered about the sort of injections or stitches they managed when the call came bleeping through, after they'd been in the pub since six.

You could have swallowed the tablets in the car, but perhaps thought a camera might record your plunder from the box in the back. So, sitting on the loo seat, with the stench of unclean toilets and menstrual blood, you rummage in your leather handbag for the tablets you have put there. You swallow and hope they'll work quickly. The motorway services – a surreal space-ship that people have docked in, is too brightly lit, full of people who squint at signs and at money, who are unable to make eye contact, to walk straight and only just manage to buy coffee, chocolate or burgers. As if everyone is on drugs. You drift into the shop and stand while people push past. It is late; for a minute, you do not know why you are there, and then you buy chocolate and coffee, realising, as you pay with cash, that you have no credit card and the tank is nearly empty. The rest of the way, you keep the speedometer on fifty: conserving what you have.

When you reach the bay near Plymouth, the tide is a long way out, but the smell of seaweed on the damp salt air, the gusts of wind and energy, make you a child again, awed and exhilarated. Even as you uneasily scan the horizon with its smudge of sea, and then the dunes and the boarded walkways for a glimpse of your daughter, you feel a bubbling impulse to drop your handbag and run, full tilt, to the sea. To stand and scoop handfuls of grainy sand, let them sieve through your fingers or be blown free by the wind. You think how, in the scrape and grind of the everyday you have forgotten about the elements, forgotten about life's pleasures. And then you see her. Like a peasant woman carrying water, or wood, or carrying a child perhaps, the girl comes trudging from the distant dunes, the crescent moon slung low in the sky behind her. She is a tiny figure, head down, like someone beaten.

When you reach Sophie, you grab your child and it is a disappointment that the moment feels so normal, so lacking in the significance that two hundred miles should have given it. It is only Soph, after all, her hair matted and smelling of smoke, her body sweaty and thickly covered; it is just the familiar curve and heat of Soph. It is when, with your arms wrapped around the child, explaining that you cannot go home yet, that there is no petrol, but that you can stay at Aunty June's B&B, for you have phoned her and a key has been left out (hung in the peg bag), it is when you have said all this and are tightening your arms around the shivering child, who is stiff against you, embarrassed, no doubt, by your awkward murmurings of comfort, that you see, in the distance, another figure trudging out of the darkness.

It does not look like the murderer your imagination had earlier conjured, who might have slaughtered mother and daughter on the isolated beach to create the next day's headlines. This figure is tall, with lumps and packages on its back – probably a tent of some sort – and plods forward in a dogged and hopeless way. Sophie follows your gaze.

'He's sorry now, that he left me alone. He went and got wrecked because he was frightened. But we're going through this together. It's you he's afraid of.'

And the blasts of sea wind, that are colder second by second, buffet and you both wait, like moored boats, for this swarthy boy to wash up against you. Your lips are dry and cracked, your cheeks raw from cold and the place where your cardigan is unbuttoned allows the cold to slice through.

Next morning, Aunt June has finished cooking the official breakfasts by the time her visitation wakes; the real guests – the paying ones – a family from the North, eye the rucksacks and tent in the porch and you let them pass without the usual pleasantries. Let them think what they want about the tears, about being woken in the night. Aunt June has never been one to care about propriety. She serves toast, honey from the bees, and makes strong coffee. The lemon cardigan she wears, is tightly buttoned over baggy dungarees. She is short and stocky and the grey hair, which she has cut herself, has a fringe that winds off upwards, then loops down to cover one of her eyes. She puts her hand into the dungaree pouch and pulls out a fifty-pound note.

'For the petrol. Pay me when you can.' She blows upward and the hair of her fringe rises and reveals a hidden green eye.

'Why haven't you come to see me?' she demands. 'You spent every summer here when you were a child. And you used to bring little Soph and Menelek, too. The place needs youth.'

How can you say to her that you need your sentences connected these days; that coherence and control have grown to be important? You promise to visit properly soon and set off, waving goodbye, declaring that Sophie will be sure to buy a better tent next time, that she won't let it collapse in the middle of the night, nor need rescuing. Soph and Dan smell, despite the shower they have taken. The day is cold, but you wind the windows down, drinking cans of red bull that you bought earlier from the dreary village shop. The journey home, despite your tiredness, seems more straightforward than the one going out.

Hours later, when you finally park outside the Victorian terrace and haul the dirty bags into the hallway, it feels as if, in your absence, the precious house has reconfigured.

Places, however much they bear an imprint, have the ability to reshape with the tide of each day's events. Sophie seems to intuit this and inspects each of the rooms suspiciously, then reoccupies the room she was allocated after the move. The space has been made tidy for the guests who never visited, who were hastily put off with a story so strange, even Aunt June might not have believed it.

When you go up to the bedroom to ask what Sophie and her boyfriend would like to eat, to ask whether or not they are still vegetarian, you see that they have strewn the room with sand, tent, clothes and cigarette butts, somehow making it into the beach they have just vacated. You shut the door sharply, leaving the chaos. Downstairs, you check on the computer that cover for work has been sorted and you think about Jade, the pregnant blood donor nurse, sent like a premonition. If you were not so tired, you would scoop her up as well.

Reflecting on the drive, you are in awe of your own virtuosic dash, of how you drove hundreds of miles and did not crash. The lies to your aunt – the story of a migraine, a broken tent – sort of hung together, though Aunt June would not have cared if you had said that aliens had landed, or if you had told of the pregnancy. At breakfast, the boyfriend, Dan, had flustered and filled in too much detail, less good than the women at deceiving. You noticed, with satisfaction, how he was marginalised as the female complicity wove its narrative.

Now, you chop salad and toss in olives and feta cheese, rehearsing how you will one day tell the incidents of this event as a funny story, how you will describe Sophie and Dan dozing in the back, emitting an animal scent of sweat and sex and something else – dank and tramp-like that forced you to open windows and gulp air, then shut them when Sophie complained it made her stomach hurt. You will not, you think, ever tell your friends the real reason for the midnight adventure, but will invent a plausible version, will pass this on to Sophie – to Dan, too. Meanwhile, you make the necessary phone call about an abortion, ringing your colleague in the Marie Stopes clinic, then check prices on the web for a place that will get things done even quicker.

The scent of last night's stew fills the house again, as if the world is ordered, purposeful and calm. You have already had the contraceptive talk with Soph in the car while Dan snored, and you think that this emotional jolt might make her re-think her life, perhaps consider the need for more education. You eventually grow tired of waiting for them both to come down and take your own plate of food back to bed, hoping you will sleep off this new nightmare.

By the next day, mess has spread into the living room and kitchen. Sophie appears and makes tea as you haul sleeping bags from the drum of the washing machine.

'What's that note to me on the table, Mum? What do you mean, you've arranged everything?'

Sophie is wearing Dan's pyjamas and a brown zipped up cardigan. Her thick stripy socks have more holes than wool. You watch your daughter scattering sugar as she carries the full spoon from one side of the kitchen to the other. There is a puddle of water in the tray where the electric kettle sits and milk trickles from inside of the fridge onto the floor.

'I thought you needed to recover yesterday, so I just went ahead and made the calls – then I had a headache and had to sleep it off.'

You are not sure what Sophie is angry about – that the choice of clinic had been made by you (it is you, after all, who will pay) or that she feels everything has been done in too hurried and clandestine a way? It is just like her to suddenly embrace this sort of thing, assert it for all to know, as if abortion is a badge of honour.

'What calls have you made, Mum? I'm perfectly able to deal with nurses and midwives and hospitals myself.'

You are staring into the garden, holding the damp sleeping bags, noticing that the pale yellow roses have pulled free of their support and need pinning back to the wall. Without meaning to, you sound impatient, as if your daughter gets more stupid by the day.

'You wouldn't see a midwife – not for an abortion.'

Sophie blows across the rim of the full, hot cup and then stops to look across.

'Who says I'm having an abortion? I love Dan.'

And she carefully puts the cup down, smoothing her flat stomach in a way that you find ridiculous.

'But that's why I came to get you! And you said in the car, it was the wrong time, an awful thing. You'd be trapped.'

And as you stare at this strange and perverse child, so separate, you realise you've got it all wrong – again. You are about to say you wouldn't have bothered to risk all their lives on that treacherous journey, that if all Sophie wants is a child, then she is stupid and can look after herself, that children are stupid, that they stop your life from being calm and happy and perfect. But instead you start to cry.

'It's alright, Mum! I'm fine. We'll manage somehow. Dan's got a new job starting. It's in Glastonbury, digging ditches; he's got a place to live. I was scared I was going to miscarry – and bleed and die, like they do in films. It was great what you did.'

But you can't stop crying; like some valve has opened and you are crying about me, not just about your daughter. You feel hot tears on your cheeks, the end of your nose, your chin, and running down your neck. Your nose is so blocked, you have to sit at the kitchen table and fumble for tissues. Sophie pushes the harlequin box across. She stands over you and smoothes your hair, pats the neat bun. Even in the midst of your grief, the gesture irritates, especially when Sophie takes a slurp of the tea and something hot drips onto your new dress, which will now need to be dry-cleaned.

'I've hatched, Mum. I left the nest a long time ago. You don't have to worry any more.'

And Sophie puts her cup down, leans over and squeezes your shoulders hard. For a second, you feel looked after, as if you are the child. You know there is no point saying, but I do worry, and always will. Because, in less than a year, Sophie will understand.

'I can see a grey hair,' Soph says, giving a preliminary tug at your scalp. 'Shall I pull it out?' And she rips it up from the roots, blowing it from her fingers as you yelp. 'I don't need what you need, Mum. I don't need a perfect world – a happy one will do.'

And at that moment, Dan drifts in, looking sheepish.

'Made that tea for me yet, Curly?'

It was the day you found out your husband was leaving, leaving you and the children and moving to London – with a girl he'd met in Brixton. You had been waiting to tell him when he arrived back from his conference, that you were pregnant again. It had not been planned and was not exactly convenient. Sophie was three, Menelek nearly five. But you thought it might unite you, although the other babies had probably done the opposite. Like a coward, he had phoned, rather than come home.

It's no good. You know that as well as me. It's better if I stay up in London. You can't have two careers in one family.

He had said something like that, although the order and emphasis may well have been different. You have a story you offer out, which will do as well as any other: he was finding reasons to justify the affairs, his need for distraction. You delight in telling people how he did not stay with that girl, nor the one after. When he wanted something, Shimi was determined, intransigent; it had always been a quality you'd rather admired.

For days you took time off from work, walked the streets, were monosyllabic with the children. You asked yourself whether he was right about you failing to support him. You felt horribly sick and could hardly get up, were so tired you needed to rest every afternoon, while the children grizzled and poked you as you lay on the sofa. One afternoon, Sophie pinched you awake and you slapped her, shook her by the arm; after that, you spoke to the counsellor at work.

The day you drove to the abortion clinic in Bristol, you were early. A security person guarded the door so you walked up Park Street, looking in windows at the Christmas decorations. Although you wore fur boots and leather gloves, it was bitterly cold. You went inside the shops to keep warm, and in one that was closing down, bought the crumpled stick dolls that stand on the mantelpiece. For years after the operation, you had vivid dreams about me, the child you never bore. I was always a boy, although in some I had dark brown skin, in others I was more like Sophie. You still think, when you can bring yourself to face the subject, that you made the right decision.

We go on making up versions of our lives, managing surfaces, as Sophie is doing now. She is probably wondering why she has upset you, and perhaps, this time, you should tell her the truth. There is a time for bringing things into the open. Your daughter's skin is tawny and perfect, like a creamy coloured shell. You are on a ledge, looking at your life, observing your daughter's choices. You feel yourself float out, against a backdrop of sea, or maybe sky. You open your mouth, and, as she looks at you, the carapace of silence splits apart.

Fires – 2005

The first time Chrissie set fire to the flat, Tom thought it was an accident. Perhaps she had been smoking in bed. Maybe the ashtray, with its half-extinguished stub had burrowed into the duvet, down into the tangled sheets where only an hour earlier they'd been making love – trying to create a baby. He had left, rushing off to work so he would not be late, but first he had turned to kiss Chrissie's hot forehead. She was propped against the pillows, his dark angel, scowling at revision notes.

I'm off to the underworld, then, he said, lightly, but she did not glance up nor smile, was descending into her own dark labyrinth. Hours later he arrived back from teaching and found papers, charred and floating in the sink, the white sheet slung back and the mattress boasting its black scar, singed and smudged at the edges.

The second time Chrissie set fire to the place, Tom knew it was deliberate – as deliberate and cold as when she had once slapped him. It was strange how he could still feel the imprint of hand against cheek, could almost see the red mark, blotchy under his stubble. He had been telling her that it was all right if she never saw her mad parents again.

I looked out for my mum, Chrissie – for my sisters, too; I'll care for you. She had glanced up from the doodles skidding across her A level notes and had scrambled up to face him, peering into his eyes, as if she was having difficulty recognising who he was. *Honest, Chrissie, it's okay. Who cares if you fail exams, that you're dyslexic, that your father said such stupid things*. Even as he had used the word, father, given their age difference, he knew it to be misjudged. But, for a moment, her face had softened and he remembered thinking, I'm not sure I want to play that game, to be Daddy. He thought she might caress, as she often did, crooning *come to bed, make love, make babies*. But she had glared and then slapped him, hard.

That was over two years ago, but he can still feel the reverberation. Its shadow is there like something gauzy, a spider's web that clings to the teacups and walks in the park, the writhing limbs in bed. The slap happened a few months after they had first got together and, because he didn't know what else to do with it – everything was so new and precious – he packaged the incident away, stored it in a file marked 'the unexplained'. There are other files in his head with that title. Mostly, he likes to forget them: his father's alcoholism; the stillbirth of his only child; his ex-wife's letters when he left her – her scrawl of insults keyed across his car. He has carefully placed Chrissie's useless violence (and her tearful explanation that it was the stress of doing A levels) in a flat brown envelope that he has sealed up and locked away.

After all, Chrissie had been tender and quiet for days after she had lashed out, often meeting him from the bus when he got back from work or holding his hand as they walked, silent, to the studio flat. She was a strange sort of housewife, baking unpromising meals, often forgetting to shop and leaving her make-up, tampax – even her bra and pants – sprawled across the kitchen surface in a way that would have shocked Tom's real wife. Although, probably nothing would shock Tom's wife anymore, now he has run off with a girl twenty years younger, who used to go (intermittently) to one of the schools he taught in.

It had not surprised Tom's male friends: the girl was stunning; his wife was depressive. And, he told himself, it wasn't just because Chrissie was young, with olive skin and Eastern features that he loved her; it was because, at last, he was properly needed. She had once confided her father's dreadful accusations, spat in the arguments he had with her mother, constantly ricocheted around in her head:

How fucking stupid do you think I am? Do I look like a fucking chink? She hasn't even got my colour eyes. Do you think I'm going to spend my life keeping a whore and a bastard child? Get out on the street and earn your keep. Stop giving away your cunt for free. While Chrissie said these things, she looked as startled to feel them issue from her mouth as Tom was to hear them.

When Tom and Chrissies' lives had first collided, she had been barely able to meet his gaze. She sat apart from the other pupils and paid great attention to everything he said, but dropped her eyes whenever he, or any of the boys, looked across. Tom had liked to think that it was *his* music lessons, *his* teaching that had given confidence. He could not remember now, if she made the first move, or he did, but after meeting in a café to discuss what second instrument she should take, there had followed a second and third and fourth assignation. Finally, they met secretly in a country pub. On the way home, he turned down a muddy lane and stopped the car under an oak tree. For an hour, as the wind scattered leaves and acorns on the car's roof and bonnet, they kissed and held hands; he'd never realised how erotic such things could be, how the tang of lust grew saltier with self-denial.

Because neither had anywhere safe to go, their rendezvous were initially coy: throwing bread at ducks in unfamiliar parks; drinking coffee in the upstairs rooms of cafés – always watchful of the stairs; driving out to isolated beaches. But on the beaches, you take too many clothes off, so, one day, on the way home he swerved into a motel. After that, there were plenty more hotels, nights spent sucking on each other until dawn, then that deep and guiltless sleep that made him late for work.

Tom and his wife were already sleeping in separate rooms. He told her that he stayed with the friends he played music with, and since he always made sure he ostentatiously carried instruments, she didn't seem to care *what* his explanation for absence was. Andrew, an older friend – a father figure, almost – who taught in a primary school, made him take care. The girl was in the sixth form; Tom would lose his peripatetic work if it got out.

So Chrissie and Tom kept things secret for a while, trying not to let their fingers touch as he moved around the viola players, listening for good and bad notes and also for that hidden thing that turned notes into music. It was hard to do his job, hard to listen when other noises kept clashing through his concentration: her wispy breathing, her soft perfume, her way of watching ironically as he hummed out a note to someone when they strayed out of tune. He could hear her when she was most silent and he had always liked things that way. He had come to mistrust words as if they missed the point or made things leaden. He preferred intuition and the allusive – life as an unfinished score.

Closing his eyes, Tom rests on the hard seat in the corner of the room, trying to filter Mozart's oboe concerto into his mind. He wants the cadenza towards the end of the movement to flood into him, to clarify and heal things with its intensity and complication. He picks away at the flaking paint on the narrow bench, not registering what colour it is or whether, outside, evening has arrived. The musical notes he is chasing repeat themselves, circle, then fall away, clustering in the dusty corners of the room. If he were to spend long enough locked up inside himself, he thinks that he too might go mad – or perhaps something else could happen. Perhaps solitude would change his compositions. He writes music for a drama company; people compliment him, but he senses that there is something lacking, some want of energy or intricacy.

Tom leans against the wall and pries apart the sequential moments of his and Chrissie's relationship, forcing himself to go from beginning to end. He is trying to work out how it can have gone so badly wrong and why he had not seen this coming. He supposes the dissonance, the negative things in her, must have always been there, pushed down deep, hidden in crevices. He finds himself placing the love-making, confidences, the day-to-day banter, under a microscope, straining to see the canker sealed within. His mind, unused to such reflection, is making things blotchy and in the wrong order; like a symphony begun at the end and scraped back to the beginning's flourish. He peers into the jumble of life and sees the flurry of shape, colour and movement that has been his existence, but finds it difficult to identify anything whole or definite. He fixes instead on the girl, as if this will provide the answer, but realises he doesn't know much about her either, what she really feels or thinks. He has never asked, has failed to properly listen.

He can visualise Chrissie, though: tall, thin (almost anorexically thin), with almond eyes peeping from her long fringe. He remembers their picnics on the Gower, humming her tunes while she crunched on ham and sand sandwiches, sprawling against him, fingering a seashell and telling him that she supposed she loved him. He remembers thinking how other men must have considered him lucky. He is not bad looking – fair, with a warm, ironic smile, quite young looking, really – but those boys and men on the beach must have noticed how beautiful she was, how striking. He hoped they didn't think he was her father.

There is the smell of soup – Tom supposes it's his lunch, some tinned concoction that will make him ill. But he's not sure he can feel any worse. His head is already throbbing and his eyes are having problems focussing. He would like to wave the lunch away when it is brought, as if to prove something – innocence or moral rectitude – but he is fainting with hunger. Normally, when he gets like this, he has to stuff himself with chocolate to stop falling over or veering into people, stop himself from talking nonsense.

He didn't sleep much last night and neither has he eaten breakfast.

He remembers, with a clarity that is startling, the second time Chrissie set fire to the flat. He loops up the uncompromising trail of thought, as if he is fishing and drawing ever nearer something large and ferocious. It was a bright spring day and he had arrived home early to hear Chrissie clanging in the kitchen, radio on. There was a strange smell and he wondered if she was making soup, brewing something foreign and spiced. The Welsh school he was due to teach in had had a burst pipe, so he'd been sent away as soon as he arrived. He'd joked to the piano teacher that these were the sort of surprises he liked best and he could go home now and practise for the concert he was playing in that night. He'd got cakes on the way back – French, with custard, the ones Chrissie liked best. When he slipped in like a thief, wanting to surprise, it was she who surprised him. Closing the front door quietly, he'd held his breath, tasting something acrid, something he did not want to swallow.

Chrissie was on her knees in front of the greasy oven. She was striking matches, trying to catch alight a bundle of stuff that was pushed inside. Her hair was flicked behind her ears and he noticed how one ear was oddly shaped – was surprised that he'd never noticed the defect before. A pile of dead matches littered the vinyl floor, some having made little dark burn marks. On the windowsill, the new DAB played Radio 1. He knew at once Chrissie was not cooking, but he thought, at first, she was having a stupid sort of clear out, making a bonfire of old files; she'd threatened she was never going back to university and wouldn't bother to try and re-sit her exams. He knew, of course, that they'd been through all this self-doubt at A level and that he would help her re-write the music history essay, just as he'd done the one for A-level Geography.

Tom wanted to reassure, gently chide Chrissie about the

fire, say how foolish it was, that she might kill herself and all the people in the flats below and above. But, as he stood by the kitchen door, holding his breath, incredulous that she could be so naïve – he watched her take out a photo from the heap and roll it up to use as a spill. It was then that he registered, and life began to unravel, the seconds slowing as his hold on the world grew less secure. The spill was one of his own photos and the oven packed with his books – even with his scores. On the floor beside Chrissie was the music for that night's concert.

What the fuck are you doing? He shouted, although he usually prided himself on not losing his temper. *That's my stuff in there; that's my stuff you're burning.*

She jumped, as if he'd shot her, and it was then, once she'd been found out, that she changed – or that is what he tells himself now. He should never have come home at the wrong time. He should not have forced open that Pandora's box of troubled self. He can see her still, a film reel he would rather not watch. Her mouth is open, like the Munch painting they visited in Oslo, and she is screaming words at him he could not have imagined her uttering. He remembers going towards her and how, as he struggled to take the matches from her, she bent and bit his finger. He yelped like a child and let go. She came at him as he stared at his hand and before he knew it she was scratching him on the face and neck. Even as he jerked his hands up to protect himself, he was wondering what he looked like, covered in scratches, yet his face holding the vestiges of pleasure he'd carried in from work.

You're following me. Why are you spying on me, following me like some paedophile?

That's what she said. But then she crumpled as if she was a puppet and he had cut the strings. She folded and pressed herself against the kitchen units, hair tangled, breath and words gasping out, face contorted by fear or anger; he couldn't tell which. She was shaking, as he must have been, and he heard her say something about him trapping her, turning her into his child.

What's wrong? he managed, before she flew at him again, hitting his arms and neck with first her fists and then her open hands.

Bastard. Can't you see? You want to keep me so fucking stupid, keep me at home, write my essays for me, so I never have to think.

He held her away from him, too startled to think of speaking, or defending himself. His mind was racing: had someone else hurt her? Had her parents contacted her and threatened her? She had told Tom that they hadn't wanted her to study, that her father hated the thought of boyfriends, that he once said he'd kill anyone who touched her.

It's too much, Chrissie wailed, *all too much.*

She was scratching at her own face and when Tom moved to stop her, she yanked his arms away and sank to the ground. She made a movement to scrabble at the charred debris in the oven, as if it would provide some clue for Tom, for herself.

You'll burn yourself, he said gently, slipping down beside her and feeling, as he did, the expensive cake, in its card wrapper squashing under his knee. She was breathing heavily, as if she could not get air inside and she crawled away, panting out her fractured words.

Driving me mad, she said. *Can't you hear? Don't you ever listen…*

She was pulling everything back out of the oven, scattering the books and charred paper across the kitchen floor. Then she stopped. Heaved a great sigh. Stared at the bits on the floor and the mess in the oven

I'm sorry, she said, looking at her blackened hands. *It's not your fault.*

He was glad it was not his fault. They sat on the floor, breathing heavily, and with each breath charred bits danced around up and around, choreographed by sighs. She put out her hand to catch the black motes drifting and falling, shaking her head from side to side as she spoke.

I can't be a child forever.

And he was scared the words might crescendo into further rage or despair. But her tone stayed flat and monotonous.

I hate music and books. I hate sex. And I hate you, too.

As he sits on the bench, shivering and remembering, he decides to stop the tape in his head right there. *It's not your fault*, she had said. He can't quite bring himself to think about what happened after, not yet anyway. Perhaps he might let himself remember the immediate aftermath, but not the things that have brought him here today.

He had suggested to Chrissie, after that second fire, that it was time they separated. He would help her find a place of her own, help her get a job. He had felt guilty, as if he had toppled her into a place of dark chords and high-pitched lament. He shouldn't have taken a child and forced her into the grown-up world. What he did not let himself explore – although it played around the edges of his reasoning – was that she *was* grown-up. At her age – twenty – he had been married and coping with the death of a child. And he would not let himself, for now, examine just how much he had conspired to keep Chrissie infantile, how much she had manipulated him into playing that role. That was the past. *The past is past*, his mother had always said, *thinking on it is a waste. Snatch the good things while you can.* When Jack, his own child, had died, his mother said how something like this had happened to her. *You were a twin,* she said – *Your brother died in the womb, but early on. I didn't want to tell you, to upset you.*

A day after the second fire, Chrissie crept in beside him. He was sleeping on the sofa. *Babe*, she said, crooning at him, *I've got to tell you.* She smoothed his face and took his hands from under the covers to hold them. *Tomkins, I'm*

171

pregnant. She had placed his hand on her pathetically thin stomach, as she must have seen people do in films, and expected him to intuit, or perhaps even feel the kick of a seed that lay deep inside. *I've been stupid and crazy; I'm sorry. Things will be different now.* She pushed her dark hair out of her eyes and stared down, bashful and shamefaced. Then she looked up slowly and held his gaze.

How beautiful she was, how he desired her. Looking back, he realised he'd been naïve. He didn't ask to see a test, believed her when she said she'd been to the doctor's. In his mind, he conflated what his ex-wife felt when their child died – the terrible emotions that drenched her – with what women feel more generally at being pregnant. It was all to do with hormones and animal instinct. If Chrissie was pregnant, then the outbursts made a sort of mad sense. Because his first child had died, it was imperative to nurture this second carrier of seed, as if pregnancy were a blessing against life's vagaries.

This was how it went on: all the next week they were wary and ridiculously polite to one another. He moved back into the bedroom, cooked all the meals, did the washing and kept asking Chrissie how she was. She eventually seemed to soften and become grateful, apologetic even. She would not say anything that made reference to that other Chrissie, the mad one. It was as if certain events had never happened. The books were back on his shelves, the photos pressed flat under the big atlas. On the Monday morning, less than a week after she'd announced her pregnancy, he had been showering while she cleaned her teeth, spitting paste into the Victorian bowl, holding her drape of hair out the way. He noticed how creamy her shoulders were, how her long back sloped, making you want to trace your fingers down and down. He rubbed his hair dry, thinking that he would have to rush so he was not caught in morning traffic, but he would have liked to stay so they could make love. She turned to him and smiled shyly, like she had so often in the beginning.

I'll have to start buying some proper clothes now I'm four months gone. Do you want to meet me after work? We could go shopping. I'd like to look at prams and cots.

For a moment, he was going to make a joke about time flying when you were having fun, but then he stopped, let the towel rest on his shoulders.

What?

And we'll have to move, now. Get more space.

But how can you be four months? You're only four weeks late for your period. What does the doctor say?

Even as he spoke, he felt the ghosts swooping: the incongruities he had never examined; the strange mood swings; the clinginess, yet ferocious independence. She stopped smiling and glared, bending towards him. What was she trying to read? How far a lie could go? She grasped the edge of the sink and he hoped she would cry, for then it would be all right; he would know what to do. From the flat next door came music, snatches of classical lightness, foolishly consoling as it floated into their imperfect world.

Chrissie pulled herself upright. *I knew it. I knew you'd do this.* She took a step backwards, as if all she had seen – his scepticism, the muddled thoughts inside his head – was contemptible and, even worse, predictable. She flicked her hair over her shoulder. And it was a stagey gesture, as if the whole scene had been planned.

But what have I done?

He appealed, knowing neither he nor she could answer this. She pushed past and flounced from the room, and the strap of her nightdress slipped from her arm, exposing the curve of golden breast. As he pulled his work clothes on, he could hear from the bedroom the clicking open of a suitcase, shoes emptied from the basket under the bed, tumbling down to thud, thud on the floor. If she was packing, he should tell her to stop, but he did not want to look in the dark hole she had opened up.

He went, instead, and sat at the kitchen table, smoking one of her cigarettes, puffing ineptly, pulling lose threads of tobacco from between his lips. This was a crazy nightmare world, emptying its spectres into every pore of their home, polluting the good things he had strained to build. He kept going over the dates and timings, kept thinking back to what Chrissie had just said, as if ordering the calendar of their life might swing all the madness back behind the door it had sprung out of. Was she pregnant? Was this new confusion part of her strange instability, or worse, was she deluded about everything and everyone? Had he misheard? But if he had, wouldn't some simple response from her have cleared up the confusion?

He turned her hairbrush – left on the table by the bread – around and around, as if in winding the tangled mass of hairs clotted in its teeth, he might deliver himself from hell. What should he do? Call a doctor? But they'd just moved to this area and the doctor scarcely knew them. Or should he try and make contact with the elusive family, the family he'd never met? Chrissie had been staying with an aunt when she'd been at his school, but he knew the woman had gone back to Scotland – Chrissie always said she didn't know where in Scotland and hardly cared. She'd once told Tom that her parents lived in Liverpool, but he could hardly drive through the city shouting out Chrissie's name, offering back the damaged goods. And anyway, he didn't want to return her. He wanted a fairy-tale life with her at the centre.

He had poured himself a second brandy and wondered if the best thing might be to drive Chrissie somewhere safe, like a refuge, but then it struck him how ludicrous this was, and that it was probably him who needed the refuge. He took another gulp and felt stronger. When he glanced at his watch, he saw he'd be late for work, yet it was impossible to do anything but stay. When he went to hammer on the

174

bedroom door, he could hear Chrissie crying. She told him to go away, that the door was locked. He thought about going for help, but if he left her alone – even just outside long enough to phone Andrew on the mobile – she might set fire to things again or, worse, smash up her instruments, and his too.

This didn't feel like one of Chrissie's usual scenes: about university, her lousy parents or the failures at cooking. Those usually ended with them kissing, talking, drinking themselves senseless. He could hear her making a phone call, whispering to someone things about him, then he caught the word, *taxi*. She sneezed three times and he found himself muttering 'bless you' at the white painted door, with its scratch marks and layers of old paint, the layers of lives lived there before. When she finally creaked open the bedroom door, she frowned at the drink in his hand.

It's no good for you, she said, *having brandy for breakfast*.

When he peered into the room, he saw she had packed several suitcases and bags – far more than she had come with.

It's alright, she said, following his eyes, *I'm only borrowing your bags; I'll give them back*.

It's not that, he said, *I don't care about the bags*, although he wondered how many of his own things she'd pushed inside. There was his father's pocket watch in the bedside table; she'd liked to play with it, rest it on her chest and listen to its measured ticking. *I don't care about stuff. I'm worried about you. I don't know what's happening between us*.

He sounded like a scene from one of the soap operas she liked to watch. She pushed past and would not look him in the eye; her face was pale and strained and she conducted herself as if she were afraid, as if he had been the one shouting or saying terrible things.

She opened the flat door and dragged the heavy cases down the wide staircase, not letting him help. He followed her out to the street where she left the tartan bags by the kerb, then followed her back in again, noticing how the light in the hallway was golden, with flecks of sunlight dancing. Chrissie had looked quickly up and down the road before she'd dumped the bags, and Tom found himself pleading as they trudged up the stairs: *it's all my fault, we could meet after work, anything you want.*

Upstairs, the next-door flat was still playing music. It was Vivaldi's Four Seasons and the snatches from Winter kept glitching and jumping. Tom stood there, desolate, yet nevertheless inserting the missing parts.

Chrissie appeared hauling more bags. When she attempted to heave the large check holdall over her shoulder, it slipped down, and as he caught hold of it, he pinched her arm. She winced, as if bruises sprang from his every touch, as if he were capable of giving more. Old Mrs Probert came out on to the landing opposite, shopping bag over one arm, looked across and muttered; she'd told him that living with Chrissie amounted to child abuse. He'd replied that Chrissie was in her twenties, and she'd scoffed back – *I don't think so*. From then on, the old hag made a point of talking to Chrissie and never him.

I'll walk down with you, Mrs P, Chrissie called out, as if she were scared of Tom following.

The two set off together, dragging the heavy bags and bumping them down the steps. When Chrissie eventually trudged back up again, she was puffing and holding her stomach protectively. She looked him up and down sadly.

You didn't even see me down. I told Mrs P what you're like.

But I tried... he started.

You go off to your concerts and expect me to tag along or just be here when you come back. Do you know what it's like, alone for days and for nights? I hear the neighbours whispering. They press against the walls and say their disgusting things about you and me, whispering all the time. All those voices. And when you come home, you pretend everything's normal.

These were the clearest things she had said in months, but none of it then made any sense. She was standing on the doorstep, her red bag slung over her shoulder and a small holdall gripped tight. She had her hair pulled back into a scrunchy band, like she used to in school, and the hair came straggling out. She'd been speaking to him quietly, tersely, and now Mr Probert was opposite, putting out his milk bottles with deliberate care, straining for their words.

At last Chrissie said, *I don't hate you. I just don't want you controlling our child, like you've always controlled me.* And she raised her voice when she said this, so Mr Probert could hear.

I don't want to control you. I don't want to control anyone, least of all a child. But – and here he could not stop himself – *there isn't one, is there?*

She looked at him as if she hated him and he half expected her to slap him again. She pulled herself up straight, very dignified and flounced away, her heels clicking regally down the stairs. Mr Probert, still stooping, bottle in hand, stared across.

And you can fuck off, Tom said, not realising how these words would later fit in with Chrissie's version of how things had been. When he went through to their tiny living room, so he could glimpse her outside, he saw a car waiting. It didn't look like a taxi. A man got out and gave Chrissie an awkward hug, then bundled her inside. From this high up, he looked middle aged. Tom banged on the window and shouted, knowing she was unlikely to hear or see. A young boy, on his way up the path with a bag of compost or coal, looked up at the pots of red flowers and the man mouthing his madness.

The policeman is polite when he brings food in on a tray, says that the solicitor has been delayed again, but should get here soon.

177

'England are 110 for 1,' he announces, as if this is meant to cheer Tom.

'Glad to hear that someone's winning against the odds,' replies Tom, but the irony is lost on the burly man.

'Maybe. Sometimes it looks one way, though, then turns out the opposite.'

The soup is less sickly than he imagined. He scrapes the bowl and then eats the ham sandwich, although he is vegetarian. He had hoped that food would make his thoughts settle, but the stimulus just speeds everything up. All the things he doesn't want to remember, those things that happened during the month *after* Chrissie left, come flashing back as he sits on his bench, staring at the plate on the tray.

For three weeks, as he taught in one school or another, the police arrived on his doorstep, delivering warnings or taking him in for questioning. First she said he had beaten her and there were apparently bruises on her arms and face. She told them his violence had made her lose the baby – that she'd been one month pregnant. Next, she claimed he had followed her, had tried to break into her new flat. And it was true that he had found out where she was living, and had gone to tell her to stop what she was up to, even though it was against bail conditions. But he had not thrown the brick through her window, nor slashed her bike tyres. It had not helped that his ex-wife had confirmed he could be moody, was even prone to violence. She was either making this up, or must have been remembering how, when the baby died, he had smashed up their shed, obliterating it, until the things he'd made there were turned into senseless kindling.

Actually, if Tom is honest, for the first time in his life, he thinks that violence might be a solution. Last night he dreamt that he dashed Chrissie's exotic head against a wall, wrapping his hands in the rope of hair. He had wrenched her body, puppet-like, this way and that and then she had

178

dissolved. As she had disappeared, he had felt a great peace, as if the nightmare had loosened. He has been put in a cell four times now and each time, when the police come to get him, he has wanted to run away, to creep into a hole, to own up to things, just so this endless cell will go away. He has not slept properly in weeks. The policemen are not as rough as he imagined they might have been. They behave apologetically as they lead him to the car, then take him to the local station; they talk as if they too think Chrissie is mad. Do they believe him innocent, he wonders, or is it that they favour men's testimony over women's?

Whenever they trudge up the steps of the Victorian police station, people stare and he feels like a criminal. He is ushered into the building and down corridors, past young policemen behind the counter, who itemise lost property or car theft and turn from one noisy neighbour to another; exasperated, the policemen write up random versions of life's muddled story. They, just like Tom, are trying to focus on what has and has not happened, finding it harder and harder to know where truth lies and who is the hero of each fairy-tale and who the villain.

Each time Tom has been arrested, he is marched past the front desk, with its regimented banality, and into a dreary back room where, he supposes, more serious crimes are scrutinised. Later, he is put into a cell. He believes it is the same one each time, but the graffiti is sometimes different, so he isn't sure if the place is routinely scrubbed, or if all cells give out the same intrinsic feel of hopelessness and claustrophobia.

Today, Chrissie has said he raped her before she ran away. She had been too scared to come forward any earlier, but wanted the police to know Tom was targeting girls in school, grooming them for sex. What Tom wants to work out, as he sits on the bench and waits for a lawyer, waits for the police to make contact with Chrissie's parents, is whether he should have seen his downfall coming. Was the

179

fatal flaw in him or her, or in them both? And do all personal dramas play out with such stupid inevitability?

Because there is nothing better to do, he starts, with careful and methodical patience, to unpack his past, pulling out the pile of stacked and sealed envelopes and placing them, one by one on the cold bench beside him. His head aches from flu and he constantly needs to blow his nose on the scrap of tissue in his jacket pocket. He shuffles up on the uncomfortable seat that is also a bed and pulls his jacket around his shoulders. Perhaps it's not so bad being in a cell. At least he does not have to face anyone.

It is getting late – a pleasant evening in August – and the shadows in the room have softened: the place looks almost homely. Tom sneezes and feels his head swim. He asks himself why he has tried to keep his life contained, why he became a teacher and never travelled, why he turned down the chance to go to London and play in a quartet, and why he endlessly looks after people. For the first time, he also asks why the beautiful Chrissie chose someone as ordinary as him. It is hard to concentrate on this self-examination because of flu-like things happening in his body: his thoughts are fragmenting and spiralling; his head throbs and there is a pain behind one eye; a hissing noise builds – the kettle inside his head, edging to boiling point.

When he looks up, to see if the sound is coming from outside, he notices, with a jolt of pleasure, that he is no longer alone. His family has arrived: his parents, his aunt with her violas, his brother and sisters. The dead, who have had a long journey, thank him and stand, patiently waiting. Who has opened that wooden door, made up of strange instruments, and let such a procession in? Chrissie, he supposes, and it must have been her who made the sandwiches, who laid out the tray of drinks that have appeared on a table. How kind. He smiles across and she gives him a sad look, as if she knows already what he will think of her in the future, once he gets to understanding just what else she has done, what she still has up her sleeve. The room is crowded, as if time has slid from its constraining envelope. Will the lawyer be able to squash in, he wonders, as the room burns brighter? And he thinks how, when the woman arrives, he will need matches to keep the room so bright. His father turns to gaze at him, a wry expression on his face, and helps himself to a large drink. *To forget*, he mouths and winks – or perhaps he is blinking in the too harsh light. In a dreamy state, Tom rises, holding the wall because he is dizzy, but Chrissie doesn't notice. He hears his father's voice. *Tom's a good musician*, and here it sinks to a whisper, *but his music's shit; it needs more edge*. Tom, floating behind, knows this to be the truth. Life is odd, he thinks, to contain such irreconcilable aspects.

Chrissie touches Tom's father on the shoulder, asking if they might dance. *Dance on*, his father exclaims and before Tom can speak, the two shuffle away. How wonderful, thinks Tom, Why was I worried? Of course, cod liver oil is the answer – or is it vitamin C? He notices Chrissie smiling at his ex-wife and thinks he may introduce himself. Maybe they will help him to understand things in a different way. For a start, why he chose them – and why they picked him. Over in a darkened corner, Gnarls Barkley plays softly and out of tune. *It's Mozart*, thinks Tom, *I need blank sheet music*. And in his head, the symphony swells: notes unravelling and twirling, as if they might soon escape. The tangents and asides, he intuits, need to be swept up with a hairbrush, and the notes belong to an older score, that well may be Bach. He remembers, suddenly, the wood of his first violin, the feel of the strings and the delicate bow, how the Jewish teacher made him listen, really listen. She would beat time, concentrating on something just beyond, not the music that escaped him, but that which was nascent. And now that teacher must be dead. He sits back down with a bump and

181

shouts, half a cry of pain, half jubilation. *Listen*, she had said, yet he had chosen not to hear. Everything is melting, fading back into the grubby walls. But he knows that the dead never melt; they stay, layering themselves inside you, for good and for bad – their last ditch attempt at immortality. And when he feels his forehead, he realises there is no need for matches, for he burns already.

It is then, from somewhere quite distant, a place that is outside yet within him – he hears a fresh sound. Syncopated and sketchy, it's a ditty that limps along: hop, brush, skip, it goes: hop, skip, fizz. Is it the tapping of bow on wood? Someone sweeping outside, perhaps. It must be Chrissie – lonely and sad, come back to say sorry. Though she has taken him somewhere dark, this is an odd sort of death. For how tired she must be, trudging back and forth to the underworld, and whether she is down there in madness or up here with men, it's all the same. They keep looking – and all she can do is burn.

Rage – 2007

On a Sunday, an early call from Ruth's son was a bad omen.

The phone had rung as she'd been on her way out with the middle one, taking him to a studio so he could make a music demo. Her weekends were full of such distractions: delivering teenage boys here and there, DIY, walks in the park, occasional trips to the farmers' market. Like so many of their friends, she and her husband kept life spinning, holding at bay the complex or unpleasant things that hummed away in the background. Ruth had been standing at the front door, holding a street map, getting light on the small print and tracing the convoluted route. She had never driven to these outskirts before, and the map showed street after straight street, and then lines that indicated streams and marshland, the landscape before anyone thought of building. It won't be pleasant, Ruth thought.

When her sixteen year old, Richie, heard who was on the phone, he carefully propped his guitar against the wall and gestured to the kitchen; there'd be time for breakfast, after all. An unspoken understanding existed in the family – Ruth's eldest reserved the telephone for crises; the rest of the time he was text man, abbreviated or evasive. In the hallway, with its oak side-table and vase of white lilies, Ruth stared blankly into the mirror, listening to her son's terse voice, listening to the way he suggested that something about the latest disaster was her fault. True, she had not checked the Pulse of Misery – her husband's phrase, not hers - for over a week, but she'd assumed at twenty four and just married, that he was at last grown-up, might even be happy.

Ruth rubbed at a mark on the mirror's antique surface, trying to work out what James was attempting to communicate. His first words had been expletives –

something about the electricity man not having arrived and how he'd been late for work: the Civil Service were tolerant he said, but not that bloody tolerant. He would have been reprimanded and any reproach would have burned; he liked to be flawless, although, in others, he soon found fault. She could see now where the conversation was heading. When he arrived home he would have taken things out on Amy.

'Anyway, it's no thanks to Amy we get by. I earn: she spends.'

Amy had been a teacher in Cardiff, but hadn't yet found a job in London; she wanted to get the flat decorated, get their lives sorted – Amy's word, not James's. Sometimes Ruth thought she should warn Amy that James was not someone you could ever hope to 'sort'.

The mirror had a scrolled gold edge and Ruth could see, reflected in the worn glass, copper leaves from the maple outside, almost the same colour as the rim. It was strange how difficult it was to know what bits of life were real, what the simulacrum. The reflection in the glass felt more significant than the tree she strode past each day and barely glanced at. Here, framed and glowing, the performance offered back some truth, to which she ought to pay attention. What had she done to her eldest to make him what he was? What was he doing now to pay her back? Richie, dark hair pushed behind his ears, passed with a piece of toast and jam in his hand. She gestured that it was dripping, to go back in to the kitchen, but he only shrugged.

Once, after one of his meltdowns, James had told Ruth that arguments were necessary. Like forest fires, they cleared old wood, made space for the new. Did she know, he had asked, that since fires were now controlled, the American redwoods were dying, choked by the canopy beneath? She might have said, I often feel choked too, but she didn't much go in for metaphor or melodrama. Instead, she told him this wasn't the States and he shouldn't scare her.

'I'm not going to overdose again; I was a kid before.'

Maybe not – she had thought; *maybe you think you're fine now. But for us, it's like a war – always waiting for the next ambush.* Images of James's childhood had flickered across her mind: surreal photos on continuous loop: tantrums, self-harm, razors, smashed windows, hospital dashes, stitches and bruises, drugs and alcohol. It was as if his every action was a challenge to her own philosophy: hadn't she always made an effort to be nice, to stop the ugly stuff taking hold? When she'd suggested goodness as a solution, James had laughed.

'Only you could be that nice, mother. Too bloody nice.' He had looked at her, brown eyes crinkling into a smile and had shaken his head, then offered her a gin and tonic.

What Ruth had never admitted was that she knew exactly how James felt; she may have hidden it, but her own rage simmered. She'd become skilled at flicking things inside out, channelling anger into work or lavish meals – sometimes into half-hearted gardening. This worked – mostly. But when James, as a baby, had hit her full in the face as she sang, when he'd smeared poo over the bed, as her mother once had, or when the shower tray listed and the ceiling collapsed under her naked body – all of these things, so sudden and appalling flipped her back: *Bastard, bloody world, fucking, fucking life.* Sometimes she cried or broke china; once she had smashed down a pile of plates after the old dog – before it was put down – bit her. Now, standing in the hallway, watching a wren making its busy way up and down her glowing tree, she caught the smell of chicken cooking, drifting in from the kitchen. The copper pan with its carcass, onions and herbs rested on the stove, liquid barely shifting. And although it seemed as if nothing happened, the flavour intensified, while on the surface, a grey scum rose – her own condensed anger.

Listening to James, whose voice had dropped to a whisper, Ruth knew how he must have wanted to hurt Amy, because Amy wouldn't have understood. The girl had no sense at all; she made ridiculous comments about politics or world debt and thought James should make money in the city, not use his degree working for the government. In public, Ruth pretended she liked Amy, but only because it helped sweeten their lives. In private, when she imagined her son slapping the empty-headed girl, it gave her a feeling of satisfaction. The problem was, if he had hurt Amy in some way, now, out of guilt, he might want to hurt himself. She could feel despair stinging down the wires. Ruth concentrated on the reds and oranges in the mirror, burning with beautiful intensity. She wanted to wrench open a small space beyond the glass and crawl in there, dragging James with her, curling up in that safe and comforting glow.

'Shall I ring you back, love – save your credit?' She tried not to let her voice communicate anything: no weariness, judgement or fear. If she was honest, she wanted time to get a cigarette, though these days she seldom smoked. She'd have liked to stand outside, autumn leaves falling, while she sucked on nicotine and stared into emptiness. James must have sensed her drifting.

'Don't let me stop you. No doubt you're in the middle of ferrying Richie or Brat Child somewhere.

'His name's Michael, and when you were that young, you had lifts, too. But I'm going nowhere; it's okay, I'm right here.' And as she said it, the thought depressed her.

Outside, Ruth could hear a machine rattling. The next-door neighbour had an obsession with equipment: gadgets to steam and scour and cut or spray. But nothing was ever completed. Piles of trimmings and bottles of industrial cleaner lined his path, a half made bird table lay at an angle on the lawn. Last week, when she'd peered into the back garden, a tower of oil drums had appeared: a bizarre art installation, perhaps, or supplies for war. Whenever Ruth spoke to the neighbour, he was mostly cheery – in fact kept her talking long after she wanted to get away. But other times, his curtains remained closed and if you bumped into him, he could be evasive or rude. Exactly like her mother had been before the illness got so bad Ruth had been shunted on to poor Aunt Megan.

Ruth didn't believe her son had his grandmother's illness. His problem was anger, not sadness, but his moods (which James called a natural response to life's idiocy) made her worry. He was telling her something now about an incident on the way home from work and she was barely listening but making agreeing noises so he'd know she was paying attention. The real story – not surface events, but the important, hidden things – would only come later and she wondered if he would notice if she placed the phone down, then rushed to the study to get a cigarette. She was not a pushover, but other people's clamourings could be overwhelming. Fixing on the table's scratch marks, as if the wood's obstinacy and endurance, despite its wear and tear, was in some way reassuring, Ruth took deep breaths, just as the teacher in the yoga class had shown her.

It was Ruth's aunt Megan who had given them the gate-legged table. Yet as soon as Ruth inherited it, three legs became wobbly, cup rings appeared although she had told the boys it was an heirloom, and the cat savaged the only sound leg. Aunt Megan would have put a brave face on this, might even have allowed for life's decay.

'It's not your fault,' she would have said – and yet it would have been. And then Auntie would have sighed, that dreadful, accusatory sigh. 'What doesn't kill us makes us stronger.' Mistaking such platitudes for optimism, Ruth's husband – initially – had named Megan, Ma Pollyanna. Stick her on the sinking Titanic, he'd once said, and she'd tell you how beautiful icebergs were. But later Geoff realised what Ruth had known all along. A stillbirth, a crazy sister, bringing up her niece and tending to a sick father meant that by her forties, Megan had given up on surprises ever turning out well.

From the phone came a cacophony of strangeness: voices, a shout as if someone had been struck, echoes, a tannoy, clunking and clicking, a baby crying.

'Me and Amy. It's over. Just don't say anything.'

'It's fine, whatever you choose to do.' It wasn't exactly fine, of course. There'd be complications, not least the £5,000 they'd just lent Amy. 'We all make mistakes. Anyone can choose the wrong person.'

She was saying this as her husband appeared, hauling the greyhound on a lead. He had been reading the paper in the study and must have heard Ruth, but he feigned surprise when he saw her standing there, chewing at a finger. She moved the finger to her lips and frowned into the mirror, noticing how, when she stopped, the lines stayed – *beginning to look my age*, she warned, *Megan died a year older than me*. The curly hair, dyed and scraped back into a pony-tail and the cardigan bought in Top Shop or River Island looked stupidly girlish. She wondered if it was time, now she was forty-six, to let the grey grow out. Paradoxically, she still looked younger than Geoff, despite him being four years younger. These days, he'd become more aware of appearance, of health issues, too: he was always slipping out in running clothes or taking the dog for long walks. Both he and the dog needed to shed pounds – but neither seemed to.

Geoff was being deliberately obtuse. He bent over, putting the dog's plaid coat across its back, so Ruth had to mouth James's name, gesturing and pulling the sort of face that even Geoff couldn't ignore. He sighed, dropped the lead, muttered *fuck*, and looked pointedly at his watch.

Soon, she could smell coffee and understood how he would bring her a cappuccino and cigarette, just as she would have done for him. The dog was wandering around, sniffing at wellingtons, trailing its lead. If Geoff had answered in the first place, it would have been better; in his youth he'd been a surfer – was more practised with tidal waves.

James had gone off on a tangent, talking about work, how he was researching child poverty and the effects of broken homes and then he jumped – reached the bit he must have been holding back on. This was what he often did: started off one way, achieved a U-turn and then the listener arrived in an unexpected, and not altogether welcome, place.

'Amy said I had a fucking temper, said I pushed her into corners. Made her evil: made her want to hurt me.'

Richie appeared at the top of the stairs and pointed to his watch. Ruth held up the fingers of one hand – in ten minutes, she signed. The younger child turned, impassive, and soon she heard methodical scales trudging up and down the keyboard. James had not stopped his flow of talk. 'I feel like jumping off a bridge, Mum.' She held the edge of the wobbly table: there were lots in London to choose from. Trains ran every hour; she could get to him by midday. He had always been the baby: born when his father was a student, when she, herself, was barely a grown up.

'Mum, I'm on my way to Paddington, coming home – for good. Amy's been flirting – with my boss this time.'

After Geoff left, dragging the dog behind him, Ruth asked James why he'd hadn't spoken to his father.

'Your dad needs to know stuff, too. I thought that it might be better: man-to-man.'

'He'd take Amy's side; he's always fancied her. And he moans and tells me stuff I don't want to hear.'

189

'You mean he tells you off?'

'Not exactly. He's just another problem. Where's he gone?'

'To the common. The usual.'

'Perhaps you should go with him.'

'I'm glad to be rid of the dog shifts. I used to do the lot, remember?' She had finished the coffee and was brushing cigarette ash from the table, feeling uneasy that she'd smoked inside. She could hear something odd in James's voice – probably guilt about the dog. 'I'm not blaming you. I know you'd have the animal if you could.' He was silent. 'So are you sure about Amy flirting? How bad was the row this time?' He sighed, and she worried that he'd eventually lashed out. Even if James had done awful things, she thought she might forgive him.

'People row. You make it sound like we do nothing else.'

'No. But you argue a lot: like it's a habit. Your father and I haven't rowed in years.' In the mirror, she saw herself utter the glib falsity.

'Perhaps you should – to clear the air. We're not all bloody saints.'

Later, when she was driving Richie and his friend to the studio, she went wrong three times. She had shown her son how to read the map and how he should tell her to turn by a row of shops, then a church, then bear right at a fork in the road. But although he held the folded sheets, turning them this way and that, scrutinising street names and calling them out to his friend in the back when he could strain a joke out of their Welshness, he only told her where they should have turned after they'd sailed right past.

'You've missed it again, Mum. It was back by there. Didn't you see?'

'But I'm driving, Richie. Looking at the road. You're meant to tell me in advance. Anticipate.'

'I did. I pointed.'

'But you didn't say anything. How do I know things if you don't speak?'

'Body language. That's what I learned in Psychology. We interpret things, just through body language and stuff.'

'Well I must be blind, then. Because I didn't see a thing – just rows of great big houses, set back in gardens and no house numbers or road signs or anything. We could be circling in this affluence for the rest of the day.'

'I'm happy to circle in affluence.'

This bit of the route was vaguely familiar. Ruth felt she'd been there before and then she'd been equally lost. And that time, too, she'd been carrying something half-formed in her mind, sentences not quite shaped, intuitions that stayed sketchy. Or perhaps that time had been a dream, a premonition of what was to be. There were guitars, drums and a keyboard piled high on the back seat with Ali squashed between them. Whenever she caught his eye, he looked down, as if he were embarrassed about something.

'How's your mum, Ali? How's the new dog?'

Ali's mother had been widowed two years ago. She had got an animal, she said, so she could accost people and talk. Now that her husband had died, she had drifted away from the Asian community she'd married into. A lost soul, Ruth thought. Ali mumbled and looked confused, as if he were aware of something vaguely distasteful in his mother's new interest.

When they were finally heading in the right direction, out towards the city's edges, Richie turned to his mother. He had crumpled the map down onto his lap.

'So what's up with bro this time?'

He was close to James, even though his brother left home when he was ten.

'He had a bad day. There was a horrible thing on Friday going home. The tube was packed and it stopped. The lights went out, people screamed. Someone sitting beside him, praying in Arabic, grabbed his hand; someone else fainted. They were stuck there nearly an hour without much air. He told me he wasn't afraid at the time, not until he reached home and found Amy unpacking bags of shopping from a designer shop, draping sparkly lights all over the bedroom and living room. He said he felt outraged, her acting like it was always Christmas. Spending money like she lived in a palace.'

'Is that all?'

'Which way do I turn now? Is it straight over at the mini roundabout?'

Ruth did not tell Richie the rest, although on a different day she might have. She was still figuring things out, reaching for something her son had been about to communicate and then had not. He had started telling her that he wanted to see someone about his temper, but that he didn't want to end up blaming her; he said that she expected too much – from everyone. He found this suffocating – always had. As Ruth drove, making random decisions about left or right, she was thinking, not just about James, but about herself and Geoff.

That week, they'd been putting shelves and pictures up in eleven-year-old Michael's room – their youngest, the one who had been a surprise (or mistake, according to Geoff). She'd been protesting about the fuss Geoff made about chores – always grumbling and letting days drift by in a haze of indecision. The back gate was rotten, no-one did the gardening, the wood-pile needed covering; it was her who planned every holiday.

'What could be better,' she'd asked – knowing it sounded sanctimonious, 'than making an effort, making things nice?'

'Making things nice for yourself?' he'd hazarded. And for a moment he was the student she'd fallen for: flippant and sybaritic.

'Always a glass half empty,' she'd rounded before she could stop herself, though his words had not implied this. 'Making me feel life's full of dregs, like nothing's worth anything.'

'You said it,' he'd replied.

Ruth had lowered herself onto the edge of the creaky bed and Geoff shook his head, telling her she didn't appreciate irony, and that's what he couldn't bear: she willfully misread things, went into a panic at the tiniest dissent, verbal or otherwise.

'You sound like I'm a weird sort of neurotic, a bully,' she'd replied.

An answer had been on the tip of his tongue – she could see that. He'd put down the hammer and turned from the picture they'd been trying to hang – an oil painting: black with blood-red dots. She remembered how she'd held her breath, trying not to look at Geoff, while he tried not to look at her. Outside, a sanding machine or saw had started up. Geoff sighed, as if he were sorry, then asked whether they shouldn't both have a gin and tonic, a glass half full to drown their sorrows. Perhaps she should have asked then what was wrong: with him, with her and with a marriage that went in stupid circles.

When Ruth and the boys arrived at the rehearsal studio, it turned out to be in someone's tiny house – Ruth had guessed that the boy they had talked of would not own a real studio. The area was poor, a straggle of streets full of boxy houses, the only difference being the amount of disrepair each house had fallen into. Garden fences keeled over at an angle and there were gaps large enough for dogs or children to escape through. Green and black wheelie bins rested where the bin men must have strewn them: on paths, against walls, with a battered one, dead in the road. Satellite dishes littered the brickwork. Ruth carefully drove around the green bin and parked up by a house with two broken-down cars. Ruth was not sure if this was the front or back of the terrace. As she'd arrived in the estate, she'd noticed each house had wooden additions, a front porch and a back outhouse – both looking much the same. The wood had faded and warped in the sun and the planks gave the impression of being provisional, like tacked on decoration. These houses made her uncomfortable. It was too much like the seedy area she'd grown up in, living with her mother. They got out and stared around.

'That's 48.' Ali had taken the lead; something of his mother's confidence layered inside him. She wondered what of her grew in her own children: James with his temper, Richie placatory, Michael who was shy and communicated via painting.

Ruth helped to haul the heavy instruments from the car so the three of them could tramp up the street to an entrance shadowed by trees: tall firs, spindly sycamores, a huge ash. A parked van blocked the high gate and, when they got there, all three had to squeeze down its side, lugging the equipment. They pushed through the chipped plank gate that caught on the ground and juddered as they heaved against it.

Inside, a mulch of leaves lay on the ridges of mud and gravel, left by builders. Like strange tightrope walkers, all three balanced and swayed across the difficult terrain. Then they stopped, uncertain, standing in the small garden of the end terrace, with its dark canopy of trees.

'Are you sure this is the right place, Ali? It's the corner house. It looks like it belongs to the other street.'

There was no obvious front door. Something that looked like a kitchen entrance was ahead and to their right was what might have been a floor length, sliding window. Threading through the air was a pungent smell, like compost or sewage. A bramble had caught on Ruth's soft woollen dress, but she could not remove it because she was carrying the keyboard in both arms. It was not fair that

Geoff had left her to be the taxi. He got out of doing stuff for the boys by being impatient, then they asked her instead. You need to learn to say no, he often told her. Stop clinging; let them be independent and use real taxis – or other parents. Richie was attempting to balance the bass guitar while he fumbled with one hand for his mobile.

'I'll give Jake a bell.'

But before he could get the guitar to the floor and find his phone, the world flung out its flipside. From inside the house came an eruption of noise: shouting and swearing, bodies crashing against walls, doors slamming, hollerings, strange thuds and someone's stifled groans. Then dead silence, a moment's pause when whoever was there took a breath; the next minute something smashed against a wall and that set off the shouting, the swearing, the wailing. A symphony of crashing filled the still morning. A deep voice, almost a tenor, kept up a litany of curses, then a boy's higher voice shrieking back, telling the person to fuck off, telling him he was a cunt, a fucking cunt.

They stood in the garden, a frozen tableau, the gentle breeze flicking over the three of them. Somewhere upstairs in the battered house, doors still slammed and the place vibrated so richly, it seemed it might collapse, cascading into piles of bricks and hopeless circling dust.

'Go fuck yourself,' shouted one voice and then they heard things thudding, as if bigger objects were being thrown. Something shattered with a clanging, mechanical sound.

'I'll phone,' said Richie. And he was already talking in a whisper, hastily moving back towards the entrance. He looked around for somewhere to prop his case, but didn't seem to trust the damp, slimy bark of the trees, the mud slipping beneath his feet. Ali was moving backwards too, his face concentrated and fixed on Ruth, as if her ineptitude had somehow caused the wrongness they now found themselves in. She wanted to say, *Why didn't you find a*

195

proper studio? Why didn't your selfish mother give you the lift, like she said she would?

But she found herself whispering just as Richie had, 'Mind where you walk, Ali.' And he flashed her a contemptuous glance as his feet squelched backwards through the mud, the brown softness sucking around his trainers. If he kept on sinking, she thought, he would reach life's molten core.

Inside, a phone was ringing, and it took Ruth a few minutes to realise that it must be Richie calling and that no one answered. Two different voices, one low, the other higher, both in chorus, chimed – *go get the fucking phone*. Ruth turned awkwardly, hoping she was not visible from inside and then a girl appeared at the broken gate. The young thing scrutinised the group, as if they were burglars and up to no good. She was fat, but not unattractive, wearing a skimpy top that showed her pale middle. Her short skirt exposed tanned, bare legs and Ruth wondered how someone so fair could have become that warm or brown in this cold autumn wind. Big hoop earrings jangled whenever she moved her head or when she coolly assessed the young lads: Ali with his straight, neat hair, Richie with his tanned skin and father's aquiline nose. The girl smiled, as if the boys pleased her, even if they were sixteen-year-old thieves. It was then that Ruth noticed a pale child, wearing vest, nappy and slippers, hiding just behind the girl's legs, a girl too young, surely, to be its mother.

'You want Jake?' the girl asked. 'You looking for Jake? You better go round the front. Creeping up on folks, you find out things you didn't ought to.'

She grinned and moved back from the gate so the boys were able to pass, but they had to press up close as they pushed their way back down the side of the van. Ruth wanted to follow but was stuck on the blackberry bush and whenever she moved, the bramble ripped threads from her dress. It was new. Pure wool. Elegant. Not from a cheap shop, but from somewhere in Bath. And she was carrying the wretched keyboard with both hands. She watched her son and his friend disappear and felt momentarily abandoned; the familiar sensation: childhood turned inside out.

'Hold still. I'll get it free.' The girl slipped into the garden and delicately picked her way across the mud. When she had lifted the bramble from the soft wool, she looked Ruth in the eyes. 'There you are. You're okay now. They ought to be fucking murdered for letting this lot grow up. It's a bloody wilderness in here. And you so nice and smart.'

'Thanks. Thanks very much.'

But the girl had turned and immediately gone. Gone to see what her child was up to or gone to watch the handsome thieves.

When Jake finally opened the door, he smiled out a welcome, as if it must have been some other demented person swearing. Ruth knew the boy lived alone with the father – that his mother, the drinker, had gone off with another man. She didn't blame the woman; why should anyone stay if a marriage didn't work? The boy's hair drooped over his sickly face and his front tooth looked discoloured. She should take him home, feed him up, scrub him into health. There was no real hall and after they'd taken their muddy shoes off in the little wooden porch, they were immediately in a living room – of sorts. When Ruth put the equipment down, it felt as if her arms still carried the load; she shook them around loosely to get some feeling back. Recording equipment filled every bit of space apart from a corner with a television and a chair pulled up close, but piled high with washing.

'Tea?' asked the boy, but she knew she wasn't meant to accept.

'Thank you,' she said, 'But I'm just the taxi – and the

cash machine. I suppose I need to ask how much it will be?'

'Eighty. But th… th…that includes t…two.' He paused. 'Two days' recording and discs.' He smiled shyly, perhaps anticipating the unbidden clashing sounds that hurtled around, that he would spend a lifetime fighting.

'Eighty?' She was echoing back the words.

'It's cheap, Mum. He's the best.'

She had not told Geoff she was paying for this recording, this latest whim, because she had assumed it might be ten or twenty pounds. Things always cost more than she anticipated.

Distracting her and looping through her mind was the stench of the garden, the garbled swearwords she'd heard, messed in with the image of a tube-train stilled by darkness. And stirred into this apocalypse was the reek of damp clothes and earthy skunk, James saying he'd wanted to kill Amy, James saying he had something else he needed to tell his mother.

'That was the best I c-c…' The boy looked at her with a helpless look. 'That was the best I…'

Richie interrupted him. 'It's cool, Mum. Ali's mum will pay. She says she owes you.'

'She does?' From the open door into the kitchen came the smell of unemptied bins.

'Oh my God! I left the keys in the car.' Ruth flew back into the porch, stopped to shove feet into shoes, then rushed up the steep path and out into a narrow walkway where kids played on scooters. She dodged past a child with a pram and then darted into the road without looking. She ran down the middle and turned into the messy street off to her left. When she skittered into the alley where the car was parked, the plump girl was already standing there, hand shading her eyes so she could better look inside the Mondeo, with its camera and mobile on the front seat. Close to the girl's midriff, the keys dangled from the lock.

Ruth could not speak, she was so out of breath, but the girl spoke for her.

'You shouldn't be so careless. I had a nice camera like that – but it got stolen,' and she nodded at one of the houses – maybe her own, or the thief's. 'Digital's better than the old sort – mistakes don't matter.' She gave a bitter sort of laugh and looked down at the child clinging to her leg. Ruth didn't know what to say. She seemed to have lost the ability to read people.

'Thanks. I'm a bit stupid.'

'You don't look stupid.' The girl picked up her child, turned and swayed off down the street. She made a funny little gesture that might have meant anything. The child kicked its plump, white legs, bending back and forwards, urging her on, excited by his own and by life's energy.

Ruth stood there while the girl drifted down to a young man who was washing a taxi. He whistled a tune, sloshing buckets of soapy water over a glistening bonnet. At one end of the street kids shouted and endlessly circled on their bikes. In a back garden, a man threw handfuls of leaves on a bonfire and smoke whirled into the bright autumn air. The world had filled itself up: people tumbling out to occupy their lives after a week of October rain. Behind Ruth, in a small garden, a giant horse-chestnut stretched up and overhead, its yellowing leaves, with their crisp orange edges burning into her.

That night Ruth lit the first fire of the season, something to make James glad. She had now heard the story from Amy, too, and knew the truth was parcelled up in everything the couple thought and didn't think about each other. On the phone, Amy had told Ruth that James was impossible and that was why she had hit him with the kettle. Ruth talked about it to Geoff, both of them whispering and standing in the kitchen, staring at Michael's latest paintings – dark blues and purplish reds splodged on an angry black canvas.

Geoff said he thought Amy's flirting was a plea for help; she perhaps felt cornered. He sounded like the social worker he was.

'But I wouldn't ever hit you with a kettle! And why flirt? Why not just go?' Ruth genuinely wanted to know. She had once come close herself to leaving.

'Things get complicated,' he murmured, and bent forward to kiss her on the cheek, smoothing his hand across Michael's knotted painting.

On the stove, the soup just needed dumplings and herbs. Although she had lit a fire, even from out here, she knew it was smoking, that the wood was damp. Upstairs, James unpacked, while Richie had phoned to say the recording session had gone well, that Ali's mum had paid and would later give them a lift home. Ruth handed Geoff the chilli and apron; they had tossed a coin to see who would cook the fishcakes and who would fetch Michael from school camp.

'So I'll get Micky and explain – make sure he doesn't wind James up, pull those quizzical expressions.' Ruth picked up the scarf – she'd got this in Bath, too, pretending it had cost half the price. 'You don't mind finishing dinner?' She didn't wait for a reply – but turned out the contents of her bag, looking for car keys. 'Try not to over-cook the rice; it can go on steaming while you fry the fishcakes.' She rummaged amongst make-up, lists and her nurse's ID card.

'I've cooked fishcakes before, you know – and your keys are jangling in your pocket.'

Ruth left Geoff mixing oil and vinegar, plucking random herbs from the window ledge; he combined flavours in ways that gave pleasant, or sometimes unexpected, shocks. Earlier, chopping onions and spinach, Ruth had kept up a loud conversation so she wasn't forced to hear James on the phone, saying ridiculous things to Amy, begging her to come and stay. Of course, James hadn't bothered to ask Ruth if this would be okay. She had strained for random words so she could work out just how doomed things were. She heard muted conciliation and dampened accusation, the accommodations of a marriage. Strange how you can spend a lifetime unsatisfied, yet never acknowledge it. Perhaps that was why her mother had chosen madness.

The street was tree-lined, with a large house full of students and a hostel for the homeless. She and Geoff sometimes complained about loud music, the swearing and shouting, the undercurrent of violence, but really, she liked the street's unpredictability. Driving the car down the street, she turned left onto the main road, then immediately remembered her purse, still on the kitchen table. They'd need wine or brandy to get through an evening with James touchy and Amy on her way. Because Ruth could not be bothered to turn and drive back up the cul-de-sac, she parked under a row of beech trees that lined the busy road. Leaves lay piled and sodden in the gutter, others had blown up, like a tight collar against garden walls. In more salubrious streets, people complained about the slippery mess; some suggested that the city's trees should be felled. She wandered back up the steep street, enjoying the trees, the smell of a bonfire in someone's garden, the Stones music, full volume, coming from the hostel. She slipped down her own side entrance, knowing that in the depths of the kitchen, Geoff would never hear a knocking at the front. The mushy leaves softened her footfall in the afternoon chill and from next door the hum of machinery in the neighbour's shed gave out its steady background vibration. The laurel kept her in shadow as she made her way into the overgrown garden and towards the kitchen where the green purse, key inside, lay fat upon the table.

Ruth did not know what made her pause, what made her stand in the dank corner near the water butt, where the compost bin needed emptying as a mulch for the roses. But she stopped, as if this moment had been scripted. She heard his voice – Geoff's – on the mobile, standing by the log pile, where once she had glimpsed a fox. Her husband had a finger in his ear, perhaps to drown out the noise from next-door's shed and he was talking urgently, his back bent, as if he protected the words he offered out.

'She just wants it safe and unchanging. James's always going to be up and down. He hit his head on the wall when he was a baby, but he likes that sort of madness. He's bored by the nice girls.' There was a slight pause, then a laugh. 'Yes, like me.'

Ruth felt the loose, cool words entering her. She hoped – though knew it unlikely – that he was talking to his brash sister, the one who lived in the States and whom she didn't like. Then she heard a low chuckle and instantly knew this was no sister: never that laugh for a sibling. Something nasty brushed the back of her neck, twigs from the maple perhaps, or a spider. She was terrified of spiders – spiders and darkness.

Ruth heard Geoff whisper and she strained to hear what was said in that tone of intimacy that she was shut out from. And in that moment, she realised how odd she'd become herself, how clipped and dry, like the leaves above her head. A woman who, like her aunt, kept up a silly brightness at home and at work, too. She felt stickiness seeping from her collar downwards, as if someone had set light to her neck. The temperature was dropping, and although she had gone out without a jacket, she was no longer cold.

Geoff cleared his throat, glancing sideways at the lights from the kitchen, spilling out over the lawn in a jolly sort of way. With one hand he held a phone and with the other he twirled around the back door key and its leather fob. 'Of course I love you... yes, her too, but differently. Maybe tomorrow. It's difficult with James home. He knows something – asked me outright today.' Geoff stopped and paid attention to what the other person was saying. 'The usual place? Sure.' He absently looked across to the next-door garden where the man was shut up in his loneliness, the light from the shed sending out an insipid glow. 'If Ali's recording with Richie again and not at home, yep, I could come round yours.'

The beech at the end of the garden caught the late afternoon light. Ruth noticed this as she strode forward. She also noticed the orange heads of honesty, the asters with their last show and, when she got closer, she would notice how Geoff needed to shave because his stubble was going grey and made him look old. There was a pile of tools propped by the lean-to, which should have been put in the garage and would rot in the rain and dampness of winter. As Ruth passed, she grabbed at a spade, resting next to the sharp rake and pitchfork. She wanted to smash his head. That he should be having an affair with the mother of her son's best friend was shaming and ridiculous. The whole world would be laughing at the boring, blind wife, the wife who was nice and dried up. He was turning now, surprised by the scuffling from the gap in the hedge, staring as if she were a Halloween apparition.

Ruth felt her mouth open, like a cave full of darkness and then her bile came streaming out: 'You stupid, fucking bastard. You fucking bastard.' Her husband's face was changing oddly, his mouth going slack, as if he was a TV actor doing a bad job of suggesting shock; his jaw had dropped, his mouth was open and he looked at her, foolish and pathetic. An old man, she thought – looks like he's finished already. She was vaguely aware that the woman on the other end of the line would be hearing all this, that she might be afraid and it gave Ruth a dulled sense of satisfaction, the idea that when she had finished here, she might drive around to Gwen's house. Geoff was muttering something and staring at the spade that Ruth had raised up high. It was heavier than she remembered, and she was not sure she would be able to smash the sense into him; she wasn't even sure what she was doing. He was preparing to fend her off, backing away and raising up his own hands, anticipating which way the weapon might swing and where it might fall.

For a moment, the two were caught in this dance and she knew that if neighbour looked out of his shed, he would be surprised to glimpse them swaying so oddly. Ruth took a step forward and brought the spade crashing down, but her swing lacked conviction and the metal bit was falling awkwardly and much lower than she had at first intended. The flat part of the spade crashed across Geoff's back and shoulder, and the thud of hardness on his leather jacket reverberated through her arm, jarring her. He gave a muffled grunt and toppled sideways, then tripped and fell. That she hadn't killed him was chance or possibly a decision made from one second to the next. Later, when Ruth thought about it – and the detail was always sketchy – she could never make up her mind how close she had come to killing her husband, either by accident or design.

As she stood in the garden, looking at Geoff sprawled on the ground, Ruth knew that if she hit him again she could do real damage. But after that initial rush of rage, she had begun to feel indifferent, as if she were now someone else and had already been set free from the effort of that other life. Out of the corner of her eye, she could see James scrabbling at the back door, trying to get out and intervene. His face was framed by the window and she wanted to laugh at the way he was shocked by her rage, as if it had never occurred to him that she might have inside her a disease like his own.

Ruth threw the spade at the idiot ground and it bounced up, making Geoff flinch. He got up on all fours and scrambled away on hands and knees, his new trousers covered in mud.

'I hate you,' she said, in a more level voice, but he must have known this. He looked sad and crumpled, as if he too hated everything, himself included. She whispered the words she had been holding inside all afternoon, racing around and around, like they had a message she needed to know. 'You're a fucking cunt,' she hissed. 'And I'm leaving you.' But she did not know if she wanted this – or just needed to say it.

Later, Ruth sat on the park bench, watching the red sun sink into a flaming sky. The beech trees that framed the park cast their shadows in straight lines across the clipped grass. She pulled up the collar of the old black jacket that she always left in the car, and stared out at the place, so strange and new, as if a visitor who had chanced upon the green square of park with its late afternoon ball games and children innocently running. Nobody quite believed how mild the day had been and now that the week's rain had ceased, people were out, draining the day's dregs, as if this were a gift before winter finally swallowed them. Soon, like all the other people, she would have to get up and leave, perhaps to find a hotel. She imagined the flat she might one day live in, where she'd feed a cat and make dinners for one.

In the last rays of the sun it was warm, but in the shade, cold. She thought how all things were equivocal; there was a soup half made and a child called Michael, whom no-one may have thought to collect from his trip, who was probably also sitting on a bench as miserable and abandoned as she was. Here she sat, someone who seldom lost her temper and had come close to murder. There her oldest son was, enraged and passionate and probably more in control of life than she had ever been; she could see that now. These were new things to think about in the second part of her life, the bit that had started after the razing of those first four decades. In her new life, Ruth hoped she would be less controlling, and wilder, too – perhaps more honest.

For a start, if she were being truthful, she had just walked out and had not been abandoned by anyone. And misery was too slight a word for everything she felt. Wobbliness was closer, the strangeness you get after illness, when you're emptied out and the only thing left is fragility, a dizzy echoing head and a tight constricted chest. Ruth did not like to think that this newness balanced within her had come about through violence. But she thought it a possibility, even as she felt its dislocation. She brushed at the chipped paint on the bench and little flakes shot up.

In the distance, figures were marching down a long path and Ruth squinted across, hopefully. But it was not Geoff or James, nor Richie or Michael, not them at all; these other people wore fancy dress, were wielding plastic pitch forks and had flapping cloaks and dark witches' hats; they were probably off to a Halloween party. Nearby, a man was biking across the grass, backwards and forwards down the football pitch, as if he were involved in a protracted circus act, amazing only to himself. He passed by, but did not unsettle a Pakistani family, all pinks and orange, a livid brew of colour. They collected up rugs and also an improvised picnic, Ruth had watched being cooked on a barbecue. Even as the group gathered up children, pushchairs and cricket bats, one child broke loose, a sister's scarf held aloft, streaming orange like a banner. It was good sometimes to be part of something large, a life that spilled out in extraordinary ways, that couldn't be tamed or made nice. Ruth looked across at the family, as if the sight were spring water.

She'd been thinking about her mother and how there are many types of madness – a thousand ways to run away. Hunched over, bent in on her thoughts, she was unsure what she should do next. A couple who lived in the next street jogged past with their young, adopted daughter, all of them laughing. Ruth wondered how anyone laugh, but she knew too, that happiness is a short season and that, since you can never net it, all you can do is let it blow through. Minutes later, Jim, the next-door-neighbour drifted past, and she was glad he did not notice her, or if he did, pretended that he had not. Bent over, he urgently sent a text, surprising some other life beyond the dimly lit shed and solitary meals that Ruth had conjured for him. His scent lingered long after he passed, a spicy perfume, suggesting something sophisticated and subtle.

Sitting on the cold wood, she thought of the music studio and the pale boy with his quizzical face. It came to her that he had not stuttered once in all the swearing and shouting, as if in rage he had discovered some lost and fluent part of himself. On the bench beside her, the phone vibrated and after a few seconds started to ring. She was startled, as if it did not belong to her, and carefully, shading her eyes from the sun, she picked it up, angling it into the raw evening light to illuminate the number. If it had been a day full of fires, it was still too early to see what was left, too soon, perhaps to answer a call from home. Behind her, by the curls of leaves near the muddy stream, she saw something move, and then, slipping by so fast that it barely seemed to exist, was a flash of light, blue and iridescent – a kingfisher. She looked more closely, but it had gone, leaving only the muddy bank, an icy steam and a nebulous pile of Autumn leaves smouldering in the dim light.

Waiting Rooms – 2008

In the chilly waiting room Rob slung his holdall onto a metal seat and sighed: no trains were running between Havant and Fareham. He glanced at the girl already sitting there, her breath huffing out as wispy strands of smoke. A thick woolly hat was pulled down over ears and her gloved hands rested on the newspaper she had been reading. Beside her, a pushchair was pressed into the corner and every now and again, the child within made a satisfied sucking noise. Next to the pushchair, judiciously out of reach, was a wicker basket. Inside, the black cat prowled, hissing and throwing itself against the caged door: occasionally, a black paw came reaching out. The girl shushed the cat in an absentminded manner, as if she'd forgotten it was not a baby. Or perhaps she knew that words, rational or otherwise, are often useless. There are certain animals, and people, too, who will never submit to captivity.

She had looked across as Rob marched in. The look had seemed to communicate: *we could have done without this, you and I.* And he imagined how, should they talk, behind her sentences would be requests: *might you hold the baby? Can I persuade you to carry the cat's cage?* Rob knew how chance conversations could be fatal, yet occasionally are salvation. Today he was tired – exhausted, in fact – and since appearances are deceptive, and since it wasn't easy to judge what he'd be letting himself in for, he merely smiled, then settled into a far corner and took out his book.

He tried to read but the tinny, whirring heater, in an intermittent, yet regular way, kept shutting off with a series of loud clicks. The machine seemed to be expiring, but the girl was obviously practised at making things go; she bundled up the newspaper and paced across before the box had ceased its rattling.

'Never say die,' she said. 'It's like me and my boyfriend: always hot and cold.'

A handwritten sign, sellotaped to the wall, stated: *To Re-start Waiting Room heater, rail travellers should please press red button.* The fourth time the machine shut down, without words, they established it was now his turn: she had been rocking the pushchair, determinedly keeping the child asleep. She smiled up, half laughing at their predicament; her eyes, he noticed, were large and brown and she was hippyish: hair tousled under the hat, battered rucksack, tattoo on one ankle, a tin of roll-ups on the seat beside her.

Earlier, Rob had tried to phone, but, as usual, his aunt had forgotten to turn on her mobile. In Brighton, where they were due to meet, she would have to wait, just as he now impatiently waited. Despite the irritation, he was conscious that things could be worse; he, at least, was not dead – was likely, at some point, to reach his destination. The waiting room, painted dreary cream, had shadowy areas where, at bench height, someone had touched up over old graffiti. He could just make out: *Dave is queer*, then under it, *Queens rool.*

As they waited for the train, other passengers intermittently entered. Some stared around glumly and went out again, onto the platform where wind swirled a newspaper up and down and where people huddled, shoulders tensed against the cold. Rob was halfway through his own journey and had been changing from one train to another when the Tannoy had announced a slight delay. It was only when he'd asked for an update over at the ticket office, an office that was up the steps and over a high bridge, netted to stop people jumping, that he was given the print-out: *death*: it said, *person hit by Southampton to London express.* He wondered at the words' matter-of-factness, as if this were a seasonal hazard, something caused by January frost cracking into disaffected lives.

Later, when the line had been cleared and his train raced smoothly on, the sea glimpsing in and out of sight, he morbidly searched. Had the person died by this smart terrace? Perhaps by that dismal shrubbery? Or maybe at the crossing with its ringing bells, which the train so effortlessly flew through? He wondered if it had been quick and whether or not it had been suicide. Recently, maiming had become a fashion: young people taking their lives by hanging from banisters or trees, or shooting up, overdosing on whatever was available. There were not many drownings, he'd noticed, perhaps because the sea, even for the depressed, was so cold. Not for the first time, when his thoughts veered here, he was led to his mother. The point was, if she hadn't drowned by accident, then why had she not thought of him, of how he'd be left alone, boarding in that terrible school.

In Brighton there was no sign of Mimi. She was not at the station and not at the hotel either, though it was now gone five and colder by the minute. For a disquieting moment, he imagined it might have been Mimi under that train. But he'd never even seen her cry and she was, in any case, travelling via London, from her hometown of Norwich. He wondered, next, if he'd got the wrong week. At work, he'd forgotten crucial meetings, had turned up for work on a Sunday, had even filed emails in the fridge. People made jokes about his vagueness, about how he ought to work in a university, but Rob knew these weren't jokes; they were warnings. He half suspected his colleagues might have muddled the dates in his diary, sending him to Brighton so they could laugh behind his back.

Yet, if that were so, why was he being given a key? The Spanish receptionist smiled, gesturing for him to sign to register. When Rob produced an expensive fountain pen, the man smiled again, turning the book around to admire the rich black scrawl.

'Bene,' he said. 'So much waiting for spring.'

The place was more ramshackle than Rob had expected – a small guesthouse in a forgotten side street, the turbulent sea at the end of the road. It reminded him of holidays with his mother. That had been when his father let such things happen – just after the divorce and before her drinking got really bad. Perhaps Rob and his mother had stayed in Brighton; it was entirely possible. The way the wind tugged at his scarf felt familiar, and the sea-weedy smell, narrow streets, the tang of fish and chips.

Behind him, the main door crashed open but he did not turn around, merely handed over his credit card. He expected to feel Mimi's hand, to smell her citrus perfume, but he heard a man's voice.

Did you see how that seagull took me out?

We should have gone abroad, a woman replied, her voice was low and plaintive. There was a thud as bags and cases were dumped down and Rob felt a sigh of coldness and disappointment. A small boy peered up at him.

I feel sick

For goodness sake – we're out of the car now. The father's voice wasn't kind.

Rob remembered his mother, how she invented lives for the people they met, how she made everything transient and impulsive; how her treats were barely treats at all, and how sometimes, she slept all day. Being in a place like this wouldn't have mattered, not even when everything else was falling apart. He had sometimes wondered what his mother made of her taciturn child, quietly watching, determinedly cheerful – always trying to do the right thing.

Rob turned and smiled politely at the family, then picked up a brochure so he wouldn't have to talk. Pier View was newly refurbished, it said. He looked around at the entrance hall painted lime green and at the wilting flowers. Behind the reception was a small lounge with leather sofas,

211

a chandelier and too many framed prints on the wall. Beyond, the stairs and hallway were unpromising, with faded carpets and grubby walls. When Rob glanced up from the brochure, the other guest was muttering. Behind him stood his wife and two boys, blond and waif-like. The man caught Rob's eye: raised his eyebrows – *another mistake*, he seemed to say, *first marrying that one, then having these*.

Up in his room, Rob made tea in a chipped, lime green mug. There was no spoon so he fished the tea bag out with his pen. If he'd got the wrong week, he might as well stay a night – then find a better place. Perhaps he'd wander around, pretending it was he, not his aunt, moving to Brighton: he'd become the sort of invention his mother might be proud of. He opened the door of the ugly wardrobe and saw himself staring back. In the harsh light the mirror showed a drawn, but good-looking man: brown eyes, hooked nose, hair with only a bit of grey. His features had been pulled into a sceptical expression, as if, even when he surprised himself, the mask was ready. The new trousers he'd bought were tight around the waist. He'd stopped swimming now that he avoided the health club: so easy to give the wrong impression when your brain was foggy, when you found yourself staring, long after people's expressions suggested it inappropriate. He shut the door on himself, not bothering to hang up his coat. When he flicked on the ludicrous rococo lamps, he saw that they emitted a lascivious, red glow.

The one consolation was that if Rob craned his neck he could just make out the Solent. This was the sea he'd once swum in. The first time must have been when his mother took him away mid-term, when he'd barely settled into the new boarding school. He would have been seven then. His father later said this had been an abduction; his mother had stated – *no, salvation*. She'd arrived on a bright day, wearing a black woollen suit and large hat, a pile of empty cases slung in the car; she'd told the masters there'd been a family death in Wales and calmly packed the teddies, clothes and most of the things he'd brought from home. The school exercise books she put in the dorm bin. He never thought to ask who had died, as they moved from Lyme Regis to Weymouth to Bournemouth; perhaps to Sidmouth. He remembered thinking, *I'm glad that people die.*

After they were found, his father sent Rob back to school and his mother stopped sending letters. The family decided he should spend holidays with his grandparents or aunt Mimi, because his father, a Squadron Leader, was too busy. For two years or so, this was exactly what happened. But then, once his father was posted abroad, life metamorphosed. One day at Mimi's, his mother arrived, this time wearing a white lace dress and a small scarf tied over her head and back behind her hair. And so they set off, once more whisking away for adventures. He knew that later he'd write nothing of this to his father, but would tell him how bored he'd been, how Mimi's house was dull and that, this time, he'd done his homework.

They travelled south by train – to cream, pink and pale yellow guest houses. The buildings reminded him of the confections they went out to eat – all unnecessary icing and prettiness: such a surfeit of sugar, you could die of it. He remembered his mother mocking the prim old women, stubbing out cigarettes in plants or saucers, even in the bathroom sink; he has a recollection of her pushing butts down the cracks in floorboards. They went bathing in the sea, to the cinema in the afternoon and took meals out. Sometimes they ate chips on their laps, sitting on benches as the sun sank and the world grew cold.

Staring out of the hotel window, Rob fixed on the waves cresting in, on that white, drenching line, just beyond the stony shore. There was the pier, water sloshing against its iron legs, as if it were a beast striding out for an evening constitutional – strapped to its belly were metal arches, pirouettes of machinery, games, rides and gambling. And along this pier he and mother might have gone, drifting past rides because money was scarce, past the fortune-teller, the guns that made him wince, past the doughnuts that smelled like heaven. Sometimes, his mother would stop and buy, watching as he ate one after another, disappointed when he didn't finish the bag. Rob put his tea on the bedside table, took off the tight shoes and stretched himself out.

The dream swelled into a steam train, thundering down narrow-gauge tracks, through steep ravines and across tidal, muddy rivers. Somehow, he was the train, and then he was face down on the sharp gravel, trying to remember the name of the pungent weed that brushed his face. A cat on the verge scrutinised him and set about grooming its black fur. *If I were you, I'd run*, it said. Rob rested there, the weed caressing his open mouth, the cat purring. Only then did he realize that the urgent vibration was not the cat, but an oncoming engine, stinging its way along, hot and metallic: he knew because the cat laughed. High in the muddied sky, seagulls screeched and the weed with its milky stem, a bitter plant he'd once sucked on, caressed him as the dark train bore down.

With a spasm, he was awake.

'Ah! In the land of the living.'

Mimi sat in the bay window, a glass of wine in her hand. She must have been waiting some time because a magazine was spread across her lap, olives were set on the table and a letter lay half written. Outside, it had grown dark, and Rob was conscious of sweat: the smell of his fear. From the bedroom next door came the drone of a vacuum cleaner and people disagreeing. Children's voices came darting along the corridor. He could see the glow of soft lights spreading from houses and hotels on the other side of the regency square. He groaned.

'You gave me a fright. How on earth did you break in?'

'Carlos let me in, gave me a bottle of wine, too.'

'You could have been anyone – a thief or a murderer.'

'I'm both, Rob, so don't get on my wrong side.'

Mimi went into his bathroom and came back with a smeared glass, into which she poured a liberal amount of wine. He might have preferred tea, and a ginger biscuit.

'Rise and shine; it's nearly seven. We need to talk – and eat, and drink.'

It was disconcerting, the way she made him stuffy and old, as if she were forty-three and he sixty-five. But that was perhaps why he adored her. Today, she was wearing a purple outfit and dangling earrings, and, with her curly hair pinned back and her heavily made-up eyes, she seemed like an old fashioned gypsy.

In Kemp Town, the shops were open, spilling clothes rails, vegetables and café tables onto the narrow pavements. The streets were thick with students, women wearing garish clothes and men holding hands with men. The exhibitionism felt like a different sort of drunkenness, as if, while he had been sleeping, Mimi had been topping up the town's glass. His aunt linked arms with him as they walked, gesturing out at this new world as if it were a present. Last month when she'd phoned, she'd told him that an offer had been made on the Norwich house, that her friends had begged her not to leave, but she was adamant. Even if Emile regretted moving out, well, by the time he changed his mind, she'd be gone. She was telling Rob this again, as if the split had only just happened and she hadn't told him already. It gave him a chance to look around as he murmured vague things in response.

'It's for good this time. Six years of back and forth is too wearing.'

'But you said you were glad he'd gone – were tired of

his affairs.'

'He went because of mine.' That was new; he let it sink in.

They walked on in silence and then Mimi stopped and steered him into a flower shop. There were mirrors everywhere and greenery climbing, trailing and twisting. Out of a side door they glimpsed a huge palm tree filling a lit and cobbled courtyard. On a white table were two cups, wine glasses and a fat bottle that may have contained brandy or whisky. In the shop it was warm and the perfume of flowers was overwhelming. A man came in from the cobbled yard and nodded at them. He slid behind the counter where a book lay upturned.

'I want to know,' announced Mimi, going across, 'if I can grow olive trees back in Norwich. Will they survive?' She placed her hand, with its jangly Indian bracelets, over the top of the man's. 'It's a special present for a friend who's no longer special.' Rob sensed a conspiracy, tacit information being delivered, some sort of pact between mutually devious people.

The man shook his head. 'No good, I'm afraid. There's a microclimate here – although it's never predictable. But the frostiness would probably kill plants – and people, too – that far north.' And he raised an eyebrow.

'Well, that's why I'm here – to transplant. So I don't die. The olive would be a farewell present.' She stared for a moment, perhaps imagining her grand gesture, or visualising the scene that might come after. 'My nephew,' and she turned to Rob as if only just taking on board his presence, 'He knows it's sink or swim. He'll ensure I buy the right sort of place.'

The shop owner appraised the pair and Rob wondered what he saw. A crazy woman? A man who wore nice clothes and was successful, who'd cleverly changed jobs and moved up the career ladder – or someone who didn't like difficult choices, who was good at hiding? Mimi poked around in the shop's recesses, first picking up one pot then another, peering at labels, and standing plants down in the wrong places. Rob knew that without her glasses she wouldn't be able to decipher anything, but also that she'd be too vain to put them on. In one corner, two gilt framed mirrors suggested that the green and exotic world they'd stepped into was infinite; he could see himself spiralling back and back. There was a pungent smell that reminded him of weed; the associations were pleasant and drunken. After the man had looked Rob up and down, he wandered over to Mimi, who was efficiently messing up his shop.

'One of these might do.' He had picked up a prickly rose, potted up with winter jasmine. 'Easier to carry, too.'

Mimi clapped her hands together. 'Perfection. I'll pop in on my way to the train.'

And Rob knew she undoubtedly wouldn't. The shopkeeper probably guessed so, too.

'Well, anyway, come back when you move in; I'll help make your new place a palace.'

And when they left, the man smiled and blew a casual kiss, and Mimi extravagantly returned it.

They walked for an hour, fussing about where and what to eat. Several times they stood outside restaurants, only to decide the place was too commercial, too expensive or too vegetarian. Finally, they turned a corner and came across a cafe tucked down an alley. Inside, it was noisy and narrow, like a packed, careering train. Mimi and Rob found themselves sharing a table with a couple and a lone man. Within minutes, Mimi was spilling news of how she was moving towns: *selling in Norfolk, downsizing, end of a tempestuous affair.* The young man with his book frowned, keeping his finger on the place as he looked up. Rob picked up the menu and shoved it at Mimi.

'I'll choose for you, if you can't ... make up your mind.'

'It's a new start,' Mimi declared, holding the menu as

she talked, her eyes sweeping – but probably not seeing – the lists of vegetables, polenta, couscous, stews.

Later, as they ate, Mimi described the hotel they were staying in, making the man laugh and all the time acting as if his wife weren't there. Eventually, she noticed Rob's silence.

'My nephew will tell me I'm talking too much: he keeps me in check.' Somebody needs to, thought Rob. Mimi, scraping lentils and chorizo onto her plate, turned again to the man, who had placed his arm over his wife's shoulder, as if to communicate some complex message, to indicate that this time, she had nothing to worry about. 'In Norwich, I work in an arts centre. But I shall hand in my notice.'

'And will you work here?' the woman asked.

Mimi paused. 'I shall play.' But, at this she looked glum, as if the thought of unrelenting play might be hard going, what with so many wives about. 'My nephew wouldn't give up a job that easily; he's an accountant – in Bristol.' She patted Rob and he wished that he could give up; he was conscious of his neat clothes, the dark, expensive suit, his polished, Italian shoes.

'Perhaps Brighton's not the best place to boast of being sensible.'

'There's plenty of accountancy here – and calculation,' said the woman, 'but people pretend they're carefree, even when they're counting every penny or they're up to things; Brighton's not what it seems.'

'Are any of us? Anyway, Mimi likes surprises – I'm the boring one who can't deal with change. I'm just the minder.'

'Perhaps you had better come and mind her, then. Keep the wolves at bay.'

Next day they strode up and down streets, across Regency squares, and along the beach. Mimi was dressed less flamboyantly – baggy jeans and a poncho type thing that swirled around as she paced the terraces and the Laines, doubled back to the pretty squares. Rob was tired after an hour, but discussed the merits and drawbacks of flats over houses, the possibility of crime in ground floor flats, the lack of light, but this, of course, offset by the greater value for money. They visited four houses and three flats, and all merged into a composite of white walls and period features. On the way back to the hotel, Mimi halted outside a clothes shop, then went in and bought Rob a blue top, with subtly frayed edges, a red cardigan for herself.

'For our meal out,' she told him. 'And when you wear it again, you can remember the colour of the sea, our escape.'

He mentioned that the sea was dull brown here – green at best.

'Summer,' she murmured. 'When you live here in summer, the sea will be blue.'

'So you're going to make me come too. I thought you had more independence than that. What about your time alone in India, in Canada?'

She pulled a face – pushed bags at him, indicating that he should carry.

'I've never been alone. Let's go to the Royal Pavilion.'

George IV's palace was a surprise: lustres of green and pink, swirls of red and gold, Chinese scenes on the walls, dragons uncurling from the ceiling. In the music room, with its domed ceiling and flaming reds, Rob fantasised; he could imagine the delicate echoes of his cello filtering through the ethereal space. He had played in school, performing in a small group, but now wasn't even sure where his cello was. A palace guide, leading a group of shuffling Americans, told him that concerts still took place, and Rob imagined himself in periwinkle and waistcoat, in a chamber orchestra playing Handel. When Rob found Mimi, she was talking to someone.

'Come back into the music room; why did you rush through?'

'I thought I saw someone I knew – or didn't want to know. So I talked to this man and he's been telling me about kings and queens.'

'Was that an official guide?' Rob asked after they'd moved away.

'How should I know? But he knew a lot. Look he's waving me upstairs.'

'Ignore him. You can imagine the music in here. See the elegance of the players and courtiers, the wooden harpsichord, the oboes and flutes, the violinists bowing, the cello with its orange coloured wood.'

'Hear the courtiers whispering because they're bored. See George with his hand on some woman's knee. That person I was speaking to outside at least dealt in facts.'

'Since when have you trusted facts? Here's a fact; you could come to concerts. They still have them.'

'Forget that. There's better uses for a palace.' She pointed out cars arriving in the drive, a bride in a white billowing dress being ushered into some back rooms. 'It's fate that you like it so much here. George is your middle name – the name I suggested: father's. He was an explorer – of sorts.'

'Well, perhaps the name was one of your less good ideas.'

Rob drifted over to boards detailing the history, how George IV had built the palace as a summer retreat while he waited – ten years – for his mad father to hand over Kingship. He tried to stuff the details into his head so he could regale the friend he baby-sat for, describe to her the place's beguiling campness. He paused at the board that told how, later, the Victorians had been outraged by the luxuriance, the effeminacy.

'Listen Mimi. It says Queen Victoria despised it; she said too many of the wrong sort came to Brighton. That the railway brought them.'

'That's us – we came by train. We've always been the wrong sort – fortunately.'

'It says Victoria stole the fireplaces and the furniture she liked, then abandoned the palace.'

They looked around at the meticulous reconstruction. He felt cheated, as if everything he'd seen so far counted for nothing.

'It's nice to know you can rebuild a shell,' said Mimi enigmatically.

In the upstairs café they claimed a quiet alcove. Grand windows overlooked the park and in each of the interconnecting rooms they glimpsed marble fireplaces, laid tables and high ceilings. Rob stirred his black coffee.

'It's hard to believe that this is all replica, a restoration, a made-up Georgian life.' He considered adding sugar, then decided against it – he needed to get back to the gym. He stared at the visitors crammed in at every table. 'And yet this all seems so real.'

'It is and it isn't. Nothing's really real! We make life up. And that's glorious.'

'That's the fantasy, Mimi, and you know it.'

'Do you need to pin everything down, always be cynical and clever?

'We could trade clichés for hours, but we've spent our lives tightrope walking, always pretending. We were born to it. Nana and Gramps thought they were aristocratic; the house was a ruin, their debts were huge and they had no friends.'

'Perhaps if they hadn't spent so much on your education.'

'Ouch.'

Mimi poured more tea and smiled softly. 'I don't begrudge you; if I'd had a child, they'd have done the same for me.'

They sat for a while, letting the life of the room press in. Sometimes they were more like brother and sister. Rob knew Mimi would take the argument back up. Sometimes he felt sorry for her boyfriends.

'Anyway, if we're talking reality, how *real* was George IV's palace in the first place? An oriental fantasy? Onion domed buildings? Come on!'

'You win, Mimi. It was fake; this is fake, we're both fake.'

'And it's about time you sold your house. You can't leave your ex-wife living there forever.'

'It's on the market; she's moved in with her mother. My builder wants it – he likes the idea of a big study while he does his OU degree. And he trusts the quality of the restoration – it's his own work.'

'Still the same builder, with his leaf tea and bone china tea set?'

'Still the same John Hawke. He intends to retire. Says he'll make that old pit of a swimming pool an indoor one; it's what I meant to do. But the size of the place, and the decay, defeated me.'

Mimi was demolishing cinnamon cake with her fork. She smiled out at a child who had been toddling from table to table, begging crisps, scavenging as expertly as seagulls. The dark skinned mother, crouching behind, gave a tentative smile, probably assessing whether Mimi minded the child grabbing at her bag and clothes.

'Hello again,' she said to Rob. Without a hat pulled over her face, the girl looked different – more beautiful, and younger.

'Ah – on the platform. So you were on your way to Brighton, too. How's the cat?'

'Back with my uncle Max. Biting him instead of me.'

'What's the little boy's name?' asked Mimi. She studied the child who, with the help of a chair, was trying to hop.

'Solomon – so I've probably condemned him to

stupidity. That's the way with names. My mother wanted him to be David – a nice Welsh name.' The girl took a morsel of cake from Mimi and offered it to the child. Solomon bit off the icing and dropped the rest. Then held his hand out for more. Rob saw how the child might become a fat, sated Solomon, pleasure filling him up. Was that so bad a thing? It did not hurt to eat too much, to let life go slack. The girl shook her head as Mimi offered extra icing.

'I think Solomon's a splendid name – a regal name,' said his aunt.

'Perhaps – only Mum thought being ordinary would help him fit in. I wasn't so sure he'd want that. I didn't want it for myself.'

The child, with his tawny skin and black curls launched out and toddled off, the girl a step behind. Mimi sighed and watched them go.

'I thought you and Susannah might have had children. But your parents' marriage didn't last. None of mine did, either. And what sort of a role model was your grandfather? Your mother and I spent our childhood delivering messages. If your granny ever spoke, it was just to win a point.'

Mimi shrugged, as if infidelity and non-communication were occupational hazards. Rob stared down at his delicate hands and then at his aunt. No one was within hearing distance.

'To have had a child would have made things complicated. Once I'd decided not to stay.' He almost added something else, but as Solomon came past again, he stopped himself. 'You never had children, Mi. Did I ever tell you how the men frightened me when I stayed.'

'I knew that. I was too selfish to be much of a mother, even to you – or perhaps too scared.' She stood up and touched him on the head. Signalled for him to follow with the bags as she made for the royal bedrooms.

'See!' she said when he joined her. 'Even the Georgians had to turn off sometimes. Downstairs is all public display and over the top. If we don't count this gaudy yellow, it's mostly delicate blue and green here – take your wig off and chill-out time.'

Over the next three days, the only 'chill-out time' Rob got was in the dreary hotel bedroom. He'd suggested moving to a better place, but the town was utterly booked because of a crime writers' convention. Mimi complained about each of the flats they viewed: too ugly, too pokey, too smelly, too large. There seemed little point in continuing: why didn't she view at home over the Internet, dash down when she'd narrowed her choice? Even he knew the town's topography, had picked the terraced house he wanted, had imagined his aunt's furniture transported – some of which he'd one day inherit. 'You could get a place leading down to the sea.'

'Not enough sun,' Mimi replied, petulantly.

Next day, they trudged once more towards Hove, the area that Mimi said reminded her of Norwich. She came to a halt, as if her thoughts were clogged with full stops and her body had to replicate the hesitations, the turnarounds. It was spitting rain and clouds scudded across the rooftops; white bulbous sails, detached from unseen moorings. Soon there was a regatta, clouds dashing inland, fearful of the sea. Mimi tugged at Rob's sleeve and muttered something, but the traffic rushing up and down made it hard to hear. He wished they had taken the beach route and were not trailing down a street full of cars, buses, rough looking houses and dingy shops.

'I said that I needed to sleep.'

She looked terrible and Rob wondered if she might lie down there and then, while he, like some courtier, would have to wait, standing on the dirty pavement, holding the shopping bags until she once more deigned to move. There were broken bottles, spilled litter, seagulls fighting to pull chicken carcasses from black bags. Mimi cast the birds a look, as if their plaintive cries meant something, as if they recalled some memory. She wheeled around, aiming back in the direction they had come.

'You go and look for me.' She did not even address him directly. She stared out at the grubby sea, taking in the boarded-up houses, the shards of glass in the gutter, a broken wardrobe and chairs piled in someone's garden. 'You can choose as well as me. Find me paradise.' Then she turned, with a snort of laughter and fixed on him. 'Do you want this? This charade?'

'What charade?' He, too, was tired. If she was going to indulge in word games, he'd rather it were somewhere warmer. There was a pub just down the road, with the glow of a fire through a bow window. Even fake flames, with their illusion of warmth and a couch to sit on, would be enough.

They sat by the window, secluded from everyone else and Mimi kept her hat, scarf and gloves on, as if the pause were provisional. She looked odd, cupping her green woollen hands around a half of bitter, her shoulders hunched and defeated. At various tables, men sat drinking and chatting; near the fire were grouped young people playing monopoly. Occasionally someone glanced at Mimi, with her black woollen hat and grey hair cascading out. She had not pinned it up with the silver clasp, and the wind tugging around her face had made her look unkempt and viciously tangled.

'If this is a charade, why are we here? Why are you pretending to buy a house.'

'I'm not pretending.'

'Then what charade are you talking about?'

'Life.' It was not offered ironically. Mimi stared out of the window as if, with an act of momentous concentration, she could keep things at a distance.

And he then said, ineptly, with his talent for avoiding emotion and the problematic, knowing his words would suppress any further revelation – as they so often had with his wife, 'Is there anything new that's wrong, or is it just the usual grievance – money?'

Later that evening, feeling guilty, he knocked on Mimi's door. After his mother had died, it was Mimi he'd stayed with during school and then university holidays; Mimi who listened to his problems; who swept him off to parties and private views. Outside Mimi's door, on the draughty upstairs landing, with the sound of Bob Dylan coming from room 22, he knocked and waited. It was three storeys up, and the hotel narrowed here. He could see out over back gardens to washing on lines, children's climbing frames planted on scrubby lawns. Normal lives, he presumed, those people who had worked out where happiness might lie. He could hear, behind his aunt's door, shufflings and the noise of drawers being opened and shut. Eventually, when she opened the door, it looked as if she had been crying.

'Give me an hour. I'm a bit off colour. How about the Thai place? Last supper?' She did not look him in the eye, but handed him a book. 'You ought to read this. You don't read enough.' It was a book about sexuality and painters. On the front was a picture of a naked man on a bed, his genitals sprawling. 'I'll take you to Freud's next exhibition.' He was used, now, to these sudden launchings – into other cultures, other countries, other mind-sets. He depended on her to turn things upside down, but he was used to her doing it cheerfully. '*He* wasn't running away.' she said. He was not sure if he was meant to reply or even what his response might be; she looked too serious for him to offer back – *Well, I wish I could.* He stood, instead, like an awkward schoolboy, waiting to escape.

Mimi sighed and shut the door with a decisive click; he

looked down then at the extraordinary painting. The man was curled into a foetal position, his body white and his bottom thrust up; the face seemed calm and, although the person slept, there was a hint of a smile, as if, in his coded and covert dreams, he had discovered what wakefulness hid. Rob wondered who had given Mimi the book. There had always been lovers – mostly male, sometimes female. Was the person who had given it to her the cause of her present misery? The door of the other occupied room opened abruptly; the smell of weed, rank and over-sweet, spilled into the corridor.

'Is Carlos around?' Rob was surprised at being addressed. 'The man at the desk. Has he sent you up here?' It was a skinny lad, wearing tight jeans. He leaned against the doorframe looking him up and down. It would not have surprised Rob to see Carlos appear between them in a flash of smoke. 'Tell him it's no good,' the boy said, pouting and stagey. He noticed the book that Rob held, the graphic cover, and he looked at Rob's dark hair, sallow skin and electric blue shirt. 'If you see him, tell him it doesn't matter anymore.' And he smiled directly, turning into his room and leaving the door open.

The bed was unmade, shelves on the wall held books toppling on their side, the desk showed a computer that flashed apocalyptic images. On the floor was spread a beautiful red rug and on it was an open bottle of wine, two glasses, empty and waiting.

In the Thai restaurant a female waiter bowed then led Rob and Mimi to a table overlooking the street. A girl lit the candles and Mimi stared into the yellow light and declared she was so tired, more tired than she had ever expected. She said she was looking forward to Norwich, especially to her garden; she had seen no decent gardens in Brighton. He felt he should keep the pretence going; in any case, he genuinely liked the place, wanted to stay longer. Today he had surprised himself, or been surprised: he wasn't sure which.

'That large flat looking out to sea was stunning – it even had a balcony for your plants.' He wanted to jolly her along, as he might have his secretary.

'Who wants to look out at grey sky and muddy sea?'

'Ah, but in the summer…'

And she laughed as he had cornered her, as she might have him. She called across a boy who had been hovering, small hands clasped before him, as if in obeisance. She quizzed the lad about the food, wanting to know which recipes were authentic. Later, as she poured wine, she said, almost absentmindedly. 'I shouldn't be having this. It gives me mood swings.' She went ahead and took a deep draught, then ordered food for them both. Almost immediately, she called the boy back and cancelled dishes, then added others – she seemed unable to decide. 'It's not a failure to change your mind,' she asserted as Rob frowned, concerned that the boy had become utterly confused. 'Perhaps it's braver to stay put, to face your demons at home.' But she altered the subject when Rob asked – tactfully – what she meant, what demons she had in mind.

They lingered over the main meal and pudding. Later a man came and sat at the adjacent table, ordered a coffee and pulled out a newspaper. Every now and again he looked up and out of the window. Eventually he took off his glasses.

'Ah! The flat hunter. The one who wants an olive grove.'

'Maybe not,' said Mimi. And she did not even flirt as Rob detailed the flats they had seen, the ones he had liked.

'Well perhaps your nephew will take up cultivating olives.'

'I'm a lazy gardener: I usually pay for my services,' said Rob fixing on the man's eyes, not dropping his own as the man stared back.

There was a tap on the window and they all jumped. The plant man, rising, placed a card on the table, between the emptied silver dishes and bottle of wine.

'Look me up if you're here again.'

On the pavement opposite, a police car had stopped. There was some business going on, with kids being frisked, voices raised. The man and his friend walked away together, shoulders touching, ignoring something one of the kids shouted.

'I'm not sure I could take this pace every day.' Mimi was emptying the last of the wine into Rob's glass. 'Perhaps I need more chill-out than I realised. Too many red dragons would see me off. I need doses of pale blue – Norwich, in fact.'

'I find Brighton restful.' But Rob had only just thought this. 'It feels more honest. You can choose what to pretend to be.'

'That may be naïve. There's probably a whole set of other conventions you'll discover when you live here.'

She was probably right, and he challenged neither that, nor the assumption that he would move. He took a last swig of wine, then filled his lungs with air so he could swim the deep, muddied water closing in. He breathed out, slowly.

'I'm gay, Mimi.' She did not respond, merely watched, staring at the curly hair, he knew to be receding. He felt he should say something more. 'That's why things went wrong with Suzy and me.'

She nodded in agreement. 'But I don't think Susannah realised.' Mimi looked as if she thought him deluded or naïve.

'She wanted me to stay, was happy for us to be friends. But she wanted a child.'

'She was nearly forty,' countered Mimi. 'The clock ticks.' He took another breath and came up for air. He thought of the boy on the landing – the taste of dope, cheap wine, lips, and cigarettes. In the boy's room, there had been a Turkish rug with intricate patterns of red and muted pink; the design was exotic and yet casual, making you want to sprawl, finger the strange and smooth weave.

Mimi raised her glass. 'To you! To us both!'

She called across the waiter, demanded a bottle of champagne and extra glasses; they were passed to a woman dining alone, to the last couple in the corner, and to the young waiter. Rob felt hot and wondered how drunk Mimi was and what she would say. He stared at the debris, the pudding plates on the table, the delicately shaped lemon slices that decorated them. This gesture of beauty and elegance, like the radishes carved as flowers in the middle of the table, seemed significant. Life was about art, he thought, just as Mimi had said; you could choose to be merely functional, or you could reach for something else. But he was too drunk, at that moment, to know what he should search for.

Mimi rose to offer the toast. 'To my nephew! Who has given me a wonderful life.'

And the other people smiled cautiously, taking a quiet sip of the bubbles and fizz, before placing their glasses back on the table. Over coffee, Mimi was thoughtful. 'I rather hoped you'd have the child before you left; I fancied being a great-aunt. And poor Susannah, she'll have to move fast, now.'

It was the first time Rob considered that begetting a child, and then leaving, might not have been a burden. As if reading his thoughts, Mimi reached over and smoothed his hand.

'You're so sweet, so proper. I've always thought you were gay – even if you didn't.' She seemed calmed, as if this trip had not been a failure after all. 'A toast! A new life, for an old!' They clinked glasses, even though the champagne tasted acid, and they had both already drunk too much.

As they talked, he did not know if it was the wine or the confession making him so happy. He did not want use the stupid cliché – coming out – but it was something of that sort. Being honest, anyway. Facing the demons that were perhaps not so demonic. While the staff cleared around them, wiping tables, setting chairs upside down, sweeping the floor, he confided about school and crushes – the boy Chris, for instance, who had been his best friend and who he'd lost touch with, then found again living in Spain, bringing up a daughter, definitely not gay.

'My life's been a waiting room,' Rob told Mimi.

Holding his hand, she offered back the abortions, the miscarriages (one at seven months), the women who'd been so close, the violent men.

'So you're gay and I'm depressed.' She laughed at her own joke. 'I always have been, you know. But I try to make the best of things, to just get on with it all. It's hard at the moment; I'm coming off the tablets that keep me bright – so I can finally stop pretending and sort out my health. Only I'm not doing a very good job.' She did not tell him about the two overdoses.

Next day he delivered his aunt to the railway station. Sheltering out of the cold in the waiting room, he kissed her on the cheek and hugged her, while his head thumped.

'I wish you'd been properly gay before,' she said, 'if this is how it takes you. Come and see me soon – in Norwich. And let me know how asking for a job transfer goes.'

Later, in the echoing station, standing by the rows of carriages, like a mother and son, they exchanged inconsequential chat, filling up time, waiting for the delayed train, wanting each moment of parting to be momentous.

Although he could have caught Mimi's train, he pretended he needed to buy a present – and she agreed that Brighton was a good place to shop. As soon as he had left the precinct, he called work and said he had food poisoning, smiling to himself at how easy it was to deceive. Once he had clicked the phone off, he looked around with fresh eyes at the shops, taxis, buses and estate agents. This would be his city, he thought, and felt proprietorial. He dawdled, staring into shop windows, enjoying being a part of the crowd, then stopped outside a delicatessen and peered in, attempting to read the cheese labels; as good as anything he'd get in Bristol.

'Is she going to buy the dream flat, looking out to sea, the one with the balcony for plants?'

He turned to see a man in a tailored suit, dark glasses covering his eyes. He did not initially recognise him, despite the Irish accent.

'I've been at a funeral. An old friend. I've just discovered I've been left a Siamese cat.'

Beside him stood another man, also in black, staring into a clothes shop. He flicked his eyes dismissively over Rob and then signalled that he was going inside.

'Mimi didn't like the city as much as she pretended. She says Brighton is too noisy and cloudy; she's gone back to Norwich. Told me to buy the flat, and then she'd come and stay when the sun shines.'

'But your aunt told me that Brighton was wonderful…' The man pulled cigarettes from his pocket and offered one to Rob, who took it, though he'd given up the day before. When the man struck a match and leaned in, cupping the flickering light in his hands, his lit face became momentarily distorted, and Rob thought of the paintings, of how honest Freud was about bodies. When Rob inhaled, he swam into his past and was pressed close in the school bike-shed, trading secrets with Chris, shivering in the dark. He blew out smoke and concentrated on the present.

'Mimi keeps a lot of things to herself; you never know where the truth lies.'

'Actually, when I think about it, your aunt's words shouldn't surprise. She said I was utterly wonderful, just like

Brighton.'

Rob thought how words had become a strangely approximate tool. Sometimes people were transparent, but for the most part they remained opaque. He sighed.

'Mimi can only take small doses of wonderful. The air's too bracing, even for her.'

'It can be bracing.'

They stared as a pair of cross-dressers, holding hands, sashayed past in heels. Rob realised how things kept slipping, even as you thought you'd pinned them down. Naïve to think that Brighton might cure or bring happiness. The man seemed to intuit this.

'But I don't know where else I'd rather live. When I go home to Ireland, the stuffiness…'

'Bristol's not so great…' And Rob remembered the coracle that he and Chris had set off in, thinking they could escape. It had spun around and around, and in the end they had just sat there, waiting to be saved, and then beaten. He looked straight at the Irish man and smiled. 'Do you fancy a coffee or something? Perhaps you could tell me good areas to buy in.'

Rob kept his eyes averted from the clothes shop, hoping the other man would not come out. As he inhaled on the cigarette, he remembered the weeds he'd sucked as a child, pretending to smoke as his mother did. He remembered the bitter sap and how, when he wasn't smoking, he was climbing trees or paddling along reedy riverbanks. Where had that other self gone? Rob seemed to have slipped from one dream to another, temporary rooms that he'd not so much lived in, as waited in.

People were pushing past, rushing with their shopping back to work, some probably going home. A part of him wanted to run away, catch the next train to Bristol.

'You know what, Rob? I could do with lunch. A liquid one, anyway. Josh and I were just on our way – drowning our sorrows or celebrating that we're not dead yet.' The

Irish man smiled and took the sunglasses off, squinting into the spring sunshine. The seagulls screeched overhead: *take your chances, don't run, gobble up life.*

In the distance Rob saw how blue the sea was, and he imagined Mimi on her train, hurtling back to Norwich, chatting to whoever sat next to her, telling the story of how she had gone to Brighton to help her nephew buy a flat. He smiled, and let himself be led down the narrow street. They paused outside a pub where people sat and smoked at tables. As they went in and he stepped from the brightness of day into the darkness of the pub, he remembered.

He had been at a dinner-party and for some reason had come into the hall. Standing alone, he had heard a cry; upstairs he discovered a woman giving birth on the bathroom floor, and another guest, who was a midwife, helping. He remembered too, as all the other people pressed around, the calmness of the midwife – there by chance - and the scrawny baby with its crumpled face and blue eyes. And then he thought of kind and patient Susannah. Would it matter, he found himself wondering, if, in their protracted break-up, a child was conceived? How could he be any worse than his own father?

The pub was noisy – music playing, people drinking, eating, talking and laughing. He imagined a complex configuration, the space that comes from not even trying to fit in. First there would the waiting, the nine, amniotic months – and then there would be a child: beautiful eyes, a crumpled face and smooth olive skin. Seagulls lined up outside on a small lean-to roof were shrieking: *Have we taught you nothing? Just go at it.* Rob blocked them out, for like George III, he was temporarily mad, making up life, and changing the rules.

The room was warm and jolly; a woman breast-fed a baby near to the wood-burner, its glass door open. The barman shoved in more fuel, shushing a group of noisy

234

students who read one another's palms and shouted as they sat on stools at the bar. The Irish man scanned the blackboard of cocktails and food and turned to Rob: *what do you want?* his quizzical expression asked. What did he want? To manage – not to claw at one thing after another. To sail through the choppy bits, and learn how to take chances. To invent himself and then sprawl naked, not always covering what he was. Would that do for a beginning?

Also by Shelagh Weeks:
Up Close:

When Owen and Jan take their three children on
holiday in North Wales their untidy family life is
already unravelling. As relationships are fractured
and made, a carefully pieced patchwork of events
unfolds; seen from the different perspectives of
parents and children. Years pass and on holiday in
South Wales family secrets are confronted, but there
are resolutions still to be negotiated.

Shelagh Weeks story of marriage as it is really lived
resonates with authenticity. Written in lyrical prose,
the characters are vibrant; the story emotionally
compelling and the final denouement subtle and
satisfying.

"The spirit of the book is a resilient dark comedy
rather than tragedy – and when from time to time
real things get said, and get heard, the effect is
convincing and moving. The writing is careful, alert
and subtle. ...Ambitious and sophisticated."

Tessa Hadley

You will find *Up Close* at www.cinnamonpress.com/
up-close/ and on Kindle at Amazon.co.uk

Shelagh Weeks has worked in many jobs, including as a market stall seller in Cambridge and in community education. She currently lives in Cardiff with her partner and children and works as a lecturer in creative writing at Cardiff University. Her award winning story 'Mint Sauce' won the Cinnamon Pres short story prize in 2007 and was published as the title piece in an anthology. Her novel Up Close is also published by Cinnamon Press.